PRAISE FOR

Dinner with the Schnabels

'Sharply observed characters and comic set-pieces to make you laugh out loud' *Sydney Morning Herald*

'A charmer of a book' *Daily Telegraph*

'Toni Jordan at her finest – brilliantly observed and highly entertaining' JOANNA NELL

'Hilarious' *The Bookshelf* (ABC Radio)

'A modern Melbourne Oscar Wilde comedy of family conundrums, perfect for David Nicholls and Beth O'Leary fans' DANIELLE BINKS

'Pokes affectionate fun at contemporary Australia – all with Toni's trademark warmth, sensitivity and tenderness' KATE FORSYTH

'Smart, tender, wise and hilarious' KATHRYN HEYMAN

'Toni Jordan is at her best here, rivalling Liane Moriarty' *InDaily*

'Once again proving why Jordan is one of this country's most exceptional writers' Better Reading

'This will be Jordan's most-loved novel yet' Readings

'Terrific . . . Warm and quintessentially Australian . . . Extensively engaging' Sydney Arts Guide

ALSO BY TONI JORDAN

Addition
Fall Girl
Nine Days
Our Tiny, Useless Hearts
The Fragments
Dinner with the Schnabels

TONI JORDAN

Prettier if She Smiled More

hachette AUSTRALIA

Published in Australia and New Zealand in 2023
by Hachette Australia
(an imprint of Hachette Australia Pty Limited)
Gadigal Country, Level 17, 207 Kent Street, Sydney, NSW 2000
www.hachette.com.au

Hachette Australia acknowledges and pays our respects to the past, present and future Traditional Owners and Custodians of Country throughout Australia and recognises the continuation of cultural, spiritual and educational practices of Aboriginal and Torres Strait Islander peoples. Our head office is located on the lands of the Gadigal people of the Eora Nation.

A catalogue record for this book is available from the National Library of Australia

ISBN: 978 0 7336 4514 3 (paperback)

Cover design by Debra Billson
Cover and dinkus illustration concept 'Donut Girl' by Beck Feiner, beckfeinercreations.com
'Donut Girl' body courtesy of Ellegant/Shutterstock
Author photograph by Tania Jovanovic
Typeset in 10.75/15.8 pt Sabon LT Pro by Bookhouse, Sydney
Printed and bound in Great Britain by Clays Ltd, Elcograf S.p.A.

For the Kylie in every family

MONDAY

Chapter 1

You know how it feels to hit the snooze button and pull up the covers and nestle back into the pillow and snuggle down for ten more minutes?

Kylie Schnabel didn't.

Look at her now – awake before the alarm, straight and stiff under the doona in her sensible pyjamas with her hands folded on her chest like a dead Egyptian queen. She didn't need to check the app on her phone, connected by invisible waves to the Fitbit on her wrist, to know last night's sleep score. She felt rested. Relatively speaking. Yet no matter how poorly she slept – and some nights she tossed and turned doggedly, repeatedly, as though training for the World Nocturnal Tossing and Turning Championships – she always dragged her creaking limbs upright on time. She never succumbed to the snooze button.

This was because she was practised at the art of not sleeping. Her bed hadn't been a place of comfort since she was twelve, so what difference would ten more minutes make? Oh, some nights were fine. For a long while, her sleep seemed to be getting better.

Over the last year though, sleep had become harder and harder for Kylie to reach, a floating balloon bobbing overhead with a dangling string. And what had she done about it? Absolutely nothing. As a pharmacist, Kylie had any number of effective and safe over-the-counter insomnia remedies at her disposal that she recommended to customers suffering from her exact problem, but she refused to resort to pills herself. They were fine for other people, but for her they seemed like a crutch, like a moral failing.

Kylie was a woman of science with no time for either superstition or folk wisdom. She did not avoid ladders or black cats, she did not knock on wood. Picking up a coin in the street was lucky in itself but would not change the trajectory of her day.

She certainly did not believe that bad things come in threes.

If Kylie had known what was coming that week, she might have broken the habit of a lifetime and stayed in bed. Instead she swung her feet to the floor. She showered, ate her porridge, made her bed, packed her lunch and dressed in her usual work clothes of business-appropriate blouse (white) and pants (navy) and jacket (navy) and flight-attendant block heels (black).

Unfortunately for Kylie, today would enter into Schnabel family folklore as The Monday of the Week of the Three Disasters. (Or as Nick sometimes called it, The Week of the Two Disasters and One Mild Annoyance.)

On the subject of bad things and their frequency, Kylie was about to be proved wrong.

Chapter 2

As Kylie drove to work that Monday morning, she had no inkling of the three disasters that were already in train, unstoppable, racing towards her. So she behaved normally and phoned her sister, Tansy, from the car.

Kylie spoke to her family – Tansy, their brother, Nick, and mother, Gloria, and half-sister, Monica – often. They spoke on the phone and over dinner and over coffee and while going for a walk individually or together, as though they were trapped in an Austen novel and walking was a social event. What the Schnabels found so much to talk about all the time was mysterious to non-Schnabels like Kylie's boyfriend, Colin, and Tansy's husband, Simon. Kylie didn't always know herself.

This week was school holidays so Kylie spoke briefly to her niece and nephew, then Tansy talked about her news, then they touched on random current affairs and neighbourhood happenings and reviewed their weekends before ringing off when Kylie arrived at work. She parked in the side street around the corner from the pharmacy, which was roughly in the middle of an old-style suburban shopping strip surrounded by houses in a leafy suburb.

When Kylie first started work at the pharmacy straight out of university, neighbourhood strips like these were dying. The shops were either empty, with sad, sun-faded *For Lease* signs permanently in the window, or open, but run-down and neglected. Not so long ago, the wide footpath was dotted with potholes marked with witches hats as warnings to the non-existent pedestrians or, more likely, to provide the council with some defence in case it was sued for a broken ankle. Shoppers didn't come to places like these, not if they could avoid it. Instead they drove to huge booming mega malls, hulking with gleaming intensity like alien cities.

Over the last few years though, things had begun to change – because of the pandemic perhaps, when fresher air and fewer crowds were preferable, or merely due to a cyclical rediscovery of the pleasures of shopping where everyone knew your name and you didn't have to park half a mile away from a coffee. Street beautification schemes saw the shoddy footpath paved and trees and park benches installed. The coin laundry on the far end of the strip had been transformed into a specialty pie boutique run by a team of woman with geometric tattoos, and at the other end, the tax accountants with the front window almost blocked by lever-arch files had blossomed into a florist that specialised in banksia. The pizzeria with the fly-blown tables and the kind of unappetising menu and improbable hours that made Kylie suspect that their customers ordered their pizza with an additional, off-menu extra – meth – was now a sparkling Indian restaurant.

It was unnerving.

The sole remaining hold-out from the earlier era, other than the pharmacy itself, was the drycleaners directly next door. Its faded lino and heavy chemical air had been unchanged for decades. Kylie found it reassuring that even in these most uncertain of times, some things were as solid as stone.

This morning, as Kylie passed the drycleaners, she stopped. The door was closed and there was a butcher's paper sign stuck to the inside of the window with blue electrical tape. *Dear Valued Customers*, it read in black sharpie. *Thank you for supporting our business over the last eighteen years.* Et cetera, et cetera. On the floor inside, a dusty array of clear-windowed envelopes and flyers were splayed across the checked lino and sad, forgotten clothes, still in their plastic shrouds, hung like ghosts behind the counter.

The drycleaners – that beacon of stability, that anchor in a world adrift – had closed down.

It had been a tough few years for drycleaners, Kylie knew. No one needed spotless suits to eat Pizza Shapes out of the box balanced on your stomach while lying on the couch streaming cash-strapped Koreans playing children's games to the death. You could do that in your underpants. This particular drycleaners was double-fronted with extra space in the back to house equipment, storage and an automated rail that whizzed around like a miniature chairlift at a theme park for the decapitated. Once emptied and renovated and de-toxified, it would make a fantastic retail space.

When did the drycleaners close down? She'd parked in the other side street for most of last week – the sign in the window might have been there for days. Did Tim know? Why had he not mentioned it to her? And where would she take her dry-cleaning from now on?

'They take away every useful thing,' said a voice beside her.

It was Mrs Lee on her way to the supermarket, pulling her floral trolley, her toothpick arms dotted with bandaids.

Kylie shook her head at the sign. 'Why can't people just leave things alone?'

'It's *young* people, changing everything. Always texting, doing their tweets.' Mrs Lee grasped Kylie's arm with her papery hand. 'Not you, Kylie, love. You're a very steady, sensible girl. We might get something good, who knows. Maybe a fried chicken shop.'

'Fried chicken is bad for your cholesterol,' Kylie said. 'We discussed this, remember?'

Mrs Lee's gaze darted sideways. 'We did?'

'Fried foods are only for special occasions. Cakes, too.'

Mrs Lee laughed and pulled her knobbly fingers through her hair. The veins on the back of her hand stuck out like blue worms. 'When you're my age, darling,' she said, 'every day is a special occasion.'

Kylie often organised medications in blister packs so her older customers wouldn't miss any doses, as well as hanging onto repeat prescriptions so they didn't lose them, but motivating eighty-year-olds to follow dietary advice wasn't always successful. Today, Mrs Lee's hair was matted on one side and a new purple bruise bloomed above her elbow. How long had it been since Kylie reviewed her medication? Before Mrs Lee continued to the supermarket, Kylie made her promise to come in later in the week for a chat, and to have her blood pressure checked.

'You take such good care of me, Kylie,' Mrs Lee said. 'Don't you ever go anywhere!'

Not likely. There were people, Kylie knew, who thrived on the fresh and the new – as good as a holiday, that's what they said. But these people were wrong. This is what change is: it's when you've finally steadied yourself in the surf with your feet buried in the sand on what you think are two strong legs and you feel secure at last and out of nowhere, an enormous wave appears and dumps you headfirst and salt water goes up your nose. Change is going off to school secure in the knowledge that your family has a particular shape, then coming home to find it's now completely different.

That's why Kylie was still working here after all these years, and why she'd been saving instead of squandering money on frivolous trips and pointless consumer goods and wasteful nights out. She intended to buy the pharmacy from Tim when he finally retired – then her life could be like this forever. Okay, she would make *some* changes when it was hers. Carpet from this century and new chairs for waiting customers, but Kylie had already organised everything exactly as she liked it. The only real difference when she was the owner would be the knowledge that the pharmacy was hers: her own queendom, in which she was officially the boss.

But all that was years away. Mrs Lee was right. Kylie was only forty-three, which was practically a girl. She had lots of time.

The closing down of the drycleaners was not Disaster Number One. Kylie was rigid, but not that rigid.

She pushed open the door to the pharmacy. The bell jingled. Inside the air was still and quiet and smelled foreign and artificial.

'Tim?' she called out. 'Do you know about the drycleaners?'

There was no reply. She came around one of the tall shelving units to see Tim, Sandy and another person at the back of the store, gathered around the dispensing counter. As Kylie came closer, she saw an array of cosmetics on the counter in front of them: glossy boxes and gleaming trays of lipsticks and eyeshadows, glass perfume bottles in a range of colours and shapes, and white paper testing strips splayed like fans. Kylie knew almost nothing about the beauty shelves but even she could see that these weren't the brands they currently stocked, which Tim had chosen back in the 1980s and which stood mostly untouched in their fading, warping wall units. They were brands from another time. They had a blue-eyeshadow-for-a-maiden-aunt-who-loves-murder-mysteries-set-in-a-quaint-English-village vibe about them.

The person in front of Tim and Sandy was a middle-aged woman with a halo of curly red hair and red glasses perched on her head. She was standing in a position of some authority, facing them as though she were mid-lecture.

At the sight of Kylie, Sandy coughed. Tim ran his fingers around the inside of his collar, then opened a plastic palette of eyeshadow and closed it with a click. He held it in his hands as if he couldn't bring himself to set it down.

Kylie didn't wear make-up at all, because anything more than a tinted lip gloss was a slippery slope to consumerist frippery and budgetary blowouts, but even she understood the appeal, theoretically. The samples, she noticed, were from European brands, or at least brands pretending to be European, and there was something addictively compelling about those shimmery, clicking cases and weighty tubes and pots in black and burnished gold, filled with the promise of mythical transformation. *If only you could find the perfect shade of red lipstick*, the products seemed to say, *you would become a better woman. Someone similar to you, but thinner, and French.*

'Kylie. You're here,' Tim said.

'Tim,' Kylie said. 'What's going on?'

There was an uncomfortable pause. Tim took off his glasses and cleaned them on his shirt. Sandy – who, as pharmacy assistant, was primarily responsible for all the beauty products – ran her hands over the perfume bottles, which in the dim light looked like mystical treasures recovered from a tomb. The air was heavy with florals and orientals and floral orientals, but there was an even more pervasive essence that Kylie could detect.

That essence was guilt.

It radiated from Tim, like he'd stepped in something nasty that was stuck to the bottom of his shoe.

The red-haired woman cleared her throat.

'This is Gail Osborne, from Pharmacy King,' Tim said weakly.

Pharmacy King, the nationwide behemoth. Monarch of medicines, or so the jingle went. Sovereign of savings. Whatever you needed, night or day, Pharmacy King sold it. They were the Bunnings of the high street, except for drugs instead of hardware. Pharmacy King had a beauty club, photo printing, Covid shots, makeovers, you name it. You could pop in for a bandaid and came out with a dozen rolls of toilet paper, a box of chocolate weight-loss shakes and a tube of plumping lip gloss, chilli-flavoured.

'I wasn't expecting Gail so early,' Tim said. 'I thought I'd have a chance to talk to you first.'

'I was up early!' Gail chuckled. 'My youngest just moved out! I'm an empty-nester! I don't know what to do with myself!'

Gail's face was round and smooth and her expression was amused and warm and welcoming – she might have been a preschool teacher delighted by a toddler tying her own shoes. She seemed to Kylie like the kind of woman who said *Bless!* at the end of her sentences.

Tim, on the other hand, looked like a man nursing a hangover.

'I was planning to tell you, Kylie, but it never seemed the right time,' he said. 'You know how you can get.'

Seconds passed. The pharmacy didn't have a grandfather clock but if it did, it would have been atmospherically ticking.

'How can I get, exactly, Tim?' Kylie said.

Sandy coughed.

'Hear me out,' Tim said. 'Nothing stays the same forever.'

'Why not? Why can't it?' said Kylie.

Gail beamed at her. 'What Tim means is that, going forward, every ending brings with it a new beginning.'

Kylie narrowed her eyes. 'A new beginning? As opposed to an old beginning?'

'They've been after me for months,' said Tim. 'Pharmacy King. With a very generous offer on the table.'

'And now at last he's said yes!' Gail's teeth were a kind of white that did not occur in nature. 'Hallelujah! At the end of the day, to take it to the next level, we need to expand, obviously. That's why we snapped up the drycleaners next door.'

'Right,' said Kylie.

'Kylie,' said Tim.

'Tim certainly made us wait for it! He's quite the wily negotiator. Bless!' continued Gail Osborne from Pharmacy King. 'But that's all behind us now. It's a win-win because Tim and Chris can finally relax and enjoy their retirement without a care in the world. The sale will be finalised in a matter of weeks.'

Sale? Kylie knew what the word meant, of course. But sales were things that occurred in the pharmacy. The word sale didn't apply in this context. Not when they were talking about the pharmacy itself, which would eventually be sold to her, as she'd always planned.

Gail kept talking, as if everything was making sense. 'At Pharmacy King, we look at sales per square metre, yes, but EBIT as well. A gross profit of, say, close to forty per cent, makes everything easier for everyone. Once we take out that wall' – she gestured towards the drycleaners – 'this will be our flagship store in the northern suburbs. The location is perfect! We're putting in new floors, fuller shelves organised by SKU sales frequency, new products. A revamped waiting area. Consulting rooms at the back. A drop-off window, so we're not taken by surprise by another pandemic! A herbal dispensary manned by a qualified naturopath. We're sparing no expense.'

'Right.' Kylie's face was becoming hot and tingly. She pressed her tongue between her teeth.

'He didn't tell me either,' said Sandy, flicking her pink, emerald-tipped hair. Today she wore jeans and a silver jumper dotted with sequins and her nose ring was a gold snake with diamanté eyes. She picked up one of the perfume testers, a squat, purple glass bottle, and squirted it into the air.

Kylie was hit by a wave of what smelled to her like vanilla fridge cleaner mixed with blue cheese. She blinked involuntarily.

'Believe me, Kylie, when I say this,' Gail said, 'Tim has spoken very highly of you, and we definitely want to keep you. There are procedures that must be followed!' She giggled. 'Otherwise, anarchy! So we're advertising your position. But your application will be favourably considered, I promise you that!'

'You want me to . . . apply for my own job?' Kylie said.

'It's a formality, really,' said Tim.

Gail slapped the counter. 'Exactly! A formality. Anyway, that's your actionable. Sandy will reapply also.'

Sandy raised one eyebrow at Kylie and wiped the orange shimmer from the corner of her lips. 'Or not.'

'And should you be successful . . .' Gail continued.

'At applying for my own job, which I've been doing for twenty years?'

'You got it! Once you're one of us, I mean, no promises, but you could work your way up to deputy assistant pharmacist-in-charge. I'll give you a tip – volunteer for a regional posting, that really zooms you up the ladder. And after that, who knows? Deputy assistant territory retail manager wouldn't be out of the question, if all goes well. Or – and I'm not promising anything – but how does supply chain logistics assistant manager sound?'

'Unbelievable,' said Kylie. The perfume that Sandy had sprayed seemed cloying now and the air felt thick and soupy. Kylie breathed faster. Her armpits were damp and her underwire was itchy. Dark patches were likely blooming on her blouse.

'What else can I tell you? Oh, we have a yearly conference that everyone loves. Things can get pretty crazy! In a HR-approved manner, of course! We even have company-wide games, which are so much fun. And also compulsory.'

Kylie looked at Tim. Tim looked at the floor.

'And we're not as' – Gail scanned Kylie and her navy suit from top to toe – 'corporate as you might expect. Uniforms' – she pinched her own pastel blue polo shirt with *Pharmacy King* embroidered in cursive on the upper left breast – 'are less intimidating for customers and give us a feeling of solidarity. And we have a generous staff discount program for make-up, which has been a godsend since my divorce, believe me! The dating world isn't what it used to be! You have to know how to contour.' Gail squinted at Kylie's face. 'I'm sure one of our makeover specialists would be happy to give you a little . . . zhuzh.'

'Oh boy,' said Tim.

Kylie realised her arms were stiff against her body, elbows locked. She massaged the one bicep with her other hand, then swapped. 'I don't need zhuzhing and I'd rather watch cats than wear a uniform,' she said.

'Everyone would rather watch cats,' said Sandy. 'I'd rather watch cats all day than do anything else.'

'Not actual cats. *Cats*, the movie,' said Kylie.

'Oh,' said Sandy.

'At Pharmacy King, we pride ourselves on being approachable. We're very equal-opportunity and diverse, if that matters,' she said. 'Very diverse. Not saying it would matter. Just so you know. We put a rainbow flag on our Facebook page at least once a year.'

'Kylie's not gay,' said Sandy.

'But if she were, it'd be fine with us,' said Gail. 'We're one big happy family. Also if she were, it'd look great on our annual diversity spreadsheet.'

Kylie opened her mouth.

'Kylie,' said Tim.

She closed it again.

'We're deciding on the new make-up brands collaboratively right now,' said Gail Osborne. 'Because that's the way we do things at Pharmacy King. Just because we have hundreds of pharmacies nationwide and return substantial earnings to our shareholders doesn't mean we don't care about the little people. We love little people.'

'Gail is really interested in your opinions,' said Tim.

'I really am!' Gail chuckled. 'My door is always open. I want to hear what you think.'

'You really don't, trust me,' said Kylie.

'But I do! It's in our mission statement,' said Gail 'Whenever one of our staff volunteers their thoughts, we're obligated to listen.'

'I don't have any thoughts about make-up,' said Kylie.

'But you can get some, right?' said Gail. 'Because maybe "volunteers" isn't exactly the right word. We expect you to bring your whole self to work.'

'Kylie, I can't keep going forever,' said Tim. 'I'm seventy. Chris has already retired. He wants to drive up the coast of Western Australia and swim with whale sharks. Please understand. Nothing stays the same forever.'

'Why not? Why can't it?' Kylie said.

'I've told Gail and her team how wonderful you are,' said Tim. 'Indispensable. You're the manager, if we were big enough to have one. You do the ordering, keep the records, deal with the local medical centres, look after the staff. You wrote all the SOPs, half of which I can't even follow! I'm not sure why you're still here, to be honest. I feel like I've been holding you back.'

Who would guess that Kylie worked at a community pharmacy if they saw her in the street or in a bar after work? No one, that's who. She was a little too sleek and pressed, a little too corporate. Tim's pharmacy was neither sleek nor corporate. It was cluttered with dump bins that were battered and faded and at the front, a set of glass shelves held last-minute gifts: cosmetic bags and soap sets for overlooked birthdays and cheering up the ill, if the ill had very low expectations. Too much floor space was devoted to orthopaedic sandals and podiatrist-approved inserts to suit every type of misshapen foot. Standing in the pharmacy without her white coat, Kylie might have been mistaken for a drug rep taking up Tim's valuable time or a customer picking up a prescription between corporate takeovers.

But she loved the peace of it here, the dagginess. It wasn't challenging, that was true. Some days were boring, there was no other way to describe it. But Kylie knew that the more you stretched, the more you strived, the greater the chance of failure. Here, nothing could go wrong. Here, wedged between a drycleaner and an Indian restaurant in the job she'd had for twenty years, Kylie had manageable responsibilities that she could control, make perfect, without the risk of letting anyone down.

'Here are some documents explaining the process of moving your employment across. The small print, as it were. I'm here for the whole week so we'll have plenty of time to get to know each other. Could you have your application on my desk by, say, next Monday morning?' said Gail. 'We'd hate to lose you, Kylie.'

The sale of the pharmacy out from under her – that was Disaster Number One.

The pharmacy was the still, calm centre of Kylie's world. She had never considered working anywhere else. Her plan of owning it was ruined, but of course she would reapply for her job. Of course she would.

Kylie hesitated for only a moment. Yes, she would apply, she told Gail. She would hate to be lost.

Chapter 3

'I think you need to re-evaluate the meaning of the word disaster,' said Tansy.

Kylie was sitting in her car on her morning break, keep cup of coffee (triple-shot, from the pie shop) in the holder in the console, sandwich that should have been lunch balanced on her lap. Even her body knew she was in the midst of a disaster, hence her queasiness and unusual midmorning hunger. Unsurprisingly, she'd called Tansy again, the second she was out the door. Later, she'd call Nick to tell him of her disaster. And tonight she'd probably call Monica to tell her.

There were two people, however, she wouldn't call. One of these was her mother, Gloria. Kylie didn't present Gloria with problems. She waited until she had a solution.

'I know the meaning of the word *disaster*, thank you,' Kylie said. 'Look it up in the dictionary, it says, *Plan for my future in the bin.*'

'I can't believe that Tim didn't offer you the pharmacy, if he wanted to sell,' Tansy said. 'You've been working towards it for so long – doing all those courses, organising your finances so you're ready to go. Did he say why?'

Kylie paused. She inched the top off her coffee, angling it so any drips of condensation would fall inside the cup instead of the car seat. 'It didn't come up.'

'Kylie,' Tansy said. 'Did Tim even know you wanted to buy the pharmacy?'

Kylie looked out the window at a small girl in an Elsa costume tearing down the footpath on a scooter in front of a pale young woman in a spaghetti-strapped hippy sundress with a baby in a carrier on her chest. The woman's blonde hair was braided close to her head, and even from Kylie's spot in the car it was obvious the skin on her shoulders and the top of her back was flushed pink. She wore no hat or even sunglasses, which was a bad example to be setting the child. Someone should definitely tell her.

'I've been meaning to ask, have you had a mole check lately?' Kylie said to Tansy. 'Has Nick or Mum?'

'What? Just . . . answer the question. Did you tell Tim you wanted to buy the pharmacy?'

'That's immaterial,' Kylie said. 'We've worked together for decades. He should have told me what he was planning.' It was galling, the injustice of it. Now, not only would the pharmacy never be Kylie's, but she had to spend the week writing a stupid job application. Which was just a formality, but still.

'Kylie! People can't read minds!'

'I had a plan, which is what responsible people have. I needed an accounting course, that was the last thing on my list. Besides, no one could have predicted that Tim would retire. He's only a little older than Mum.'

'It's not the only pharmacy in the world, you know. You can buy another one. Or maybe you should see what other jobs are out there. This could be your chance to try something new.'

Kylie snorted. 'Hard. Pass.'

'What did Colin say?'

Kylie's boyfriend, Colin, was the second person that Kylie did not plan to call about her disaster – but that was because of logistics.

'He's at a conference at Darling Harbour. He's home tonight.' She took a tiny bite of her sandwich.

'What kind of conference?'

'Something to do with computers?'

'That narrows it down.'

Kylie sipped her coffee and frowned. Colin had been looking forward to his conference for weeks. There was a whole stream about the Cloud! and AI! and Blockchain! Whatever they were. She remembered her own industry events in the glory days of yore when supplier company reps with fat expense accounts shouted the bar and pharmacists lined up for shots of flaming sambuca – which was always Kylie's cue to retire. Even at Colin's conference, which would surely reach new heights of tedium, shenanigans would ensue. *If it's okay*, Colin had said, *I probably won't phone you? I'll be concentrating. Networking. I'll have my phone switched off. You know how these things are, okay, babe?*

'Are you sleeping?' Tansy said. 'I was reading an article that said no screens within two hours of bedtime. And not too much caffeine.'

'Of course I'm sleeping.' She checked the Fitbit on her wrist absentmindedly. Her heart rate was seventy-five, which was reasonable considering the shock she'd had. 'Oh, and Tansy? Don't mention this to Mum.'

'Mum doesn't care what job you have, Kyles, provided you're happy. You clash with her sometimes but that's because you're so alike. She only wants to help.'

After Tansy rang off, Kylie considered her advice. Not about screens at night – Kylie knew that. She was a health professional. It was her job to tell other people these things. Her Fitbit had such a tiny screen it barely counted. She also knew about warm baths and only using the bed for sleep and sex and she knew about avoiding too much caffeine. She lifted the hand that held her coffee; the tremor was only slight.

This could be your chance to try something new. That's what Tansy had said.

It was common for people to underestimate Tansy. Up until the pandemic, she'd done most of the parenting of Mia and Lachie and worked part-time doing admin in Simon's architecture firm. She hadn't been happy, Kylie could tell, and she'd refused to let Kylie help. Which was ridiculous. Kylie was her big sister. It was her job to look after Tansy, and Nick as well. Then, when Simon's firm shut down, Tansy found a full-time job looking after rentals for a real estate agency, and now she seemed calmer in herself, less stressed. Tansy was the middle child, the golden mean, the template from which the other two had been made. The resemblance was obvious but it seemed that Tansy's features had been stretched and sharpened to make Kylie and polished and muscled to make Nick, the baby of the family. Tansy was the kind one. She was the porridge that was neither too cold (Kylie) nor too hot (Nick) nor too sweet (Monica, their much younger half-sister) but that didn't make her naive. Her advice was almost always right.

But not this time. This time she was definitely wrong. Finding another job and starting all over again somewhere new? Knowing nothing, getting things wrong, feeling like an idiot? No, this was definitely a Disaster, capital D. And Tansy was also wrong about Gloria and Kylie being alike. They couldn't be more different! But Tansy was also right. Gloria did only want to help.

Kylie didn't need help, obviously. From anybody. It was bad enough that Pharmacy King was taking over and Kylie would never own the pharmacy. The only thing worse would be losing her job.

She returned her coffee to the holder, leaned back against the headrest and closed her eyes for just a moment. The pharmacy was where she'd first met Colin. Everyone in Melbourne was allergic to rye grass pollen but Colin had come in far too often and bought too many nasal sprays for a man with only two nostrils. How many airborne allergies could one person possibly have? And surely, at his age (mid-forties, a little older than her) he should have some idea of the treatments that suited?

Yet every time he walked in, he ignored the groaning shelves and Sandy hovering at the front and came straight to the prescription area at the back where she was dispensing.

Even if Tim was free, he waited for Kylie. He always singled her out to ask for advice – tablets versus sprays, the benefits and drawbacks of brands. He asked the same questions over and over. *Perhaps*, Kylie thought, *he had a learning disability.*

He also had a nice neck, particularly where the neck met the shoulder area. That whole clavicle and upwards region. She could see this neck/shoulder area because he rarely wore a tie and his collars sat low and wide on his broad, quite-nice chest in a vaguely 1970s way.

Kylie told him that if he required so much nasal spray to manage his hayfever, he should see a doctor.

You're right, I know you're right, Colin had said sheepishly. He then confessed he had enough bottles stored at home to survive the pollen apocalypse. He came in to the pharmacy so often and bought so much because he was building up the courage to talk to her.

To talk? To her? People usually avoided talking to her, if it was at all possible. She wasn't the kind of woman asked out by strangers. She wasn't the kind of person who was asked out by people who knew her either, frankly. She'd always been the one to do the asking.

Colin, however, did ask her for a coffee, then drinks, and then dinner, and that was the beginning of them. It was romantic, Kylie supposed.

She hadn't called him while he was away at his conference. To be honest, he'd barely crossed her mind. It would do him good, a little digital holiday, because he seemed to spend every waking moment glued to his phone. She hoped he wasn't behaving too wildly. He shouldn't drink too much, and he should be making some effort to reach his 10,000 steps a day. If Colin hadn't exercised all weekend it might be better to take a long, sensible walk when he arrived home rather than sit on the couch.

Sitting in her car, drinking her defibrillator-strength coffee and obsessing about her Disaster wasn't achieving anything. Her fingers strayed to the Fitbit on her wrist again and she cycled through the data collected: steps, distance, heart rate and SPO2.

Kylie's Fitbit was pink and rose gold with a big square screen, and with it she could control of every aspect of her body and her life, even those parts that were usually unconscious. It was as if she were a tiny pilot driving her body from a cockpit filled with gauges and levers and easily measurable and attainable goals: if she hadn't managed 10,000 steps she could take a few laps around the block after dinner to achieve a perfect day. She'd even bought Colin a matching one for his birthday, and then she'd synced them. Kylie usually checked both of their Fitbit accounts when she arrived home from work in the quiet few minutes before she made dinner, looking back over each of their days to see the number of steps taken and heart rate and sleep quality, because monitoring was the first step to improving performance.

Considering she had an unexpected spare moment, sitting in her car composing herself after this morning's Disaster, Kylie thought she'd check Colin's activity levels now. That's why she'd synced their accounts, after all. So they could motivate each other.

So she did. As a direct result of the Disaster that had befallen her this morning, she changed her usual routine and opened the app on her phone hours before she normally did.

It took her a while to find the right screen but when she did, she saw that Colin had been exercising, which was a good thing.

Though . . . wait a second? There was something strange about his activity pattern. He was only exercising in short spurts – which was understandable. It was a conference; he was undoubtedly busy. The good news was his heart rate, intensity minutes and calories burned had all peaked during the two days he'd been away.

Actually, they had all peaked alarmingly during both nights he'd been away.

But only for ten minutes.

Kylie felt tension gripping along the line of her jaw, turning the sides of her throat to carved marble. Colin was only exercising, it turned out, between midnight and one o'clock in the morning.

She stared at the screen, unblinking. Possibly there was some error in the settings. Technology was unreliable, she knew. Everyone put their trust in circuits and chips and ones and zeros but were so often let down. Colin fell asleep on the couch at 9.30 pm and rarely exercised enough to raise a sweat.

She checked the previous week, and the week before that. There was the occasional missing day when he'd forgotten to wear it, but the data mostly showed his usual pattern of long, joint-aware walks either at six in the morning or after work. Only the nights of Colin's conference weekend, last night and the night before, showed a sudden spurt of intense physical activity at such an unlikely hour.

One thing Kylie knew: Colin was not jogging at 1 am. He was not on a treadmill or a stationary bike in the hotel's gym.

What could a man with his own hotel room at an interstate work conference possibly be doing at 1 am that would raise his heart rate so markedly?

Her own heart began to race.

Because it was obvious that Colin was having sex.

There was no other explanation. Ten minutes was the exact duration of sex with Colin. After nine months of dating, Kylie could time it down to the minute. How often had he looked at her at 8.15 pm on a Monday night and waggled his eyebrows, which meant: how about a quickie before *Four Corners*?

As if there was any other option. Sex with Colin could never be called a 'longee'.

She swallowed the remnants of her sandwich, turned to Clag in her mouth, and rested her forehead on the steering wheel. She felt humiliation rising from her toes and a vague nausea filled her mouth with saliva.

Kylie fought down the bile taste in her throat. It was twenty minutes before she felt calm enough to go back to work.

Chapter 4

Some days there was mystery and magic in Kylie's work. She often felt like a WWII codebreaker crouched over her Enigma machine, analysing prescriptions that afforded her secret glimpses into the lives of others. There was an intimacy in these pharmacy walls. She felt honoured and humbled by the vulnerability of her customers, by the knowledge of what was going wrong for them or, rarely, what was going right. These clues to their stories.

This afternoon though, contained no magic. Kylie's mind was elsewhere. How was it possible that the rest of the world was going about its normal business? Neither Tim nor Sandy nor Gail had felt the ground quake beneath their feet, and customers proceeded to ask Kylie questions without any understanding that Colin was sleeping with someone else. She didn't want to talk to anyone. She didn't want any other person to see her face and ask if everything was all right because – what could she say? That nothing was all right, that everything was wrong, that she felt hollowed, scraped, skinned, boneless? The pharmacy wasn't busy, so she left the prescriptions to Tim and stayed in the storeroom, ordering stock and checking invoices until it was time to go home. Hidden behind the locker door, collecting her handbag, she overheard Gail talking to Tim.

'She doesn't spend much time interacting with customers, does she?' Gail said.

Kylie couldn't hear Tim's reply.

Once she was parked out the front of her house – a two-bedroom semi she'd bought years ago and rented out until she could afford to move in by herself – she sat behind the wheel. She loved her house. It was a little dark but solid, as though she were living in an air-raid shelter. She liked the absence of anything faddy or fashionable; she liked the shared wall that ran the length of the house because there were no windows in it and she never felt exposed. Thick walls meant it was usually cool inside, even in the glaring summer. She liked the arch that led to the dark orange Laminex kitchen that caught the morning sun. Glass doors at the back looked out on the small brick courtyard and garden. The house was small, and she liked that too. The second bedroom couldn't hold a double bed so she felt no compulsion to find a housemate or ask anyone to stay over.

Yes, occasionally her rare visitors made comments about her lack of decoration and hard surfaces. The few small knick-knacks were Colin's. There was no art or cushions or throw rugs or photos. No novels post-1960 even. If Marie Kondo had popped over, she would have taken one look around and said, *Steady on, no need to go overboard.*

She and Colin didn't live together, which meant there were no complications. No joint accounts, no pets, no holidays booked and paid for. All small mercies, things she should be grateful for, she told herself.

Right now though, none of those things seemed like mercies at all.

If Kylie stayed here in the driver's seat she wouldn't have deal with any of this, but she struggled out of the car and let herself inside. She put her bag and keys on the hall table and kicked off her shoes. Everything was pressing against her skin; she could feel each individual fibre of her clothing and they were irritating and too heavy. She took off her blouse and stepped out of her skirt and left them where they fell. She poured herself a glass from the opened bottle of tempranillo Colin had left in the fridge, then she took a blanket from the hall cupboard and sat on the couch with all the remotes in front of her. She pressed the channels idly for a while before settling on a Netflix Christmas movie about a young American woman pretending to be someone she wasn't and an easily deceived prince with a poor understanding of best-practice democratic governance who was plainly unqualified to rule an independent principality. Why did she even have Netflix? Because Colin had pressed her, that's why. *You live in the world, at this present moment, Kylie*, he'd said. *You should have some awareness of popular culture.*

Ah, no, she shouldn't. She would cancel it, straight away, and spend her evenings learning Indonesian or retiling the bathroom.

This, this . . . *introspection* was useless. She forced herself to sit upright through the twinges and creaks from her neck and shoulders. *Snap out of it, Kylie*, she thought. What she needed now was fury. She needed to rid herself of the chest-crushing pain of betrayal. A sliver of self-consciousness was working its way into her mind: the start of worrying about her weight and the cellulite on the back of her thighs, and how the skin at the base of her throat was puckered and loose. *That's how it begins*, Kylie thought. *A woman can so easily think that the poor decision of a man is a judgement on her body.*

Well, Kylie refused to think that way. Instead she considered the question of how she'd ended up in a relationship with Colin in the first place. And why on earth had she agreed to sync their Fitbits? It was asking for trouble. Allowing your boyfriend to monitor your physical activity was a bad idea, philosophically. It was Orwellian. It was Atwoodian. Perhaps it was Orwoodian.

She had by now completely forgotten it was her idea.

It turned out their Fitbits had a better relationship than Kylie and Colin did.

She would follow her usual routine, that's what she'd do. It made no difference to her if Colin was there or not. Should she go for a walk? She didn't feel like it. She felt like staying in, frankly.

But if she skipped her walk today it would be because *not having Colin there* was influencing her behaviour, and she couldn't allow him that kind of power. She refused to be the kind of person who moped on the couch like a heartbroken teenager. She put down the wineglass and heaved herself up.

It was a pretty park, as a person less focused on her breathing and her stride would have noticed. The elms were turning golden, the fern gully was lush and calming. There were plenty of walkers, most of them older than Kylie – couples in matching leisure suits, a few relatives wheeling patients from the hospital across the road – all of them dawdling. *Come on, come on*, she thought. She would never get her heart rate up at this pace. She dodged cranky miniature dachshunds on expanding leads and a conga line of teenagers setting up for a late picnic, carrying chairs and cushions and eskies across the path, all of whom seemed to be deliberately in her way. Near the west entrance, a group of theatre nurses sprawled on the grass, smoking in their scrubs. So many people wasting so much time. She marched on, gaze fixed on the path before her. Only when a volley of runners lapped her did she raise her head. She felt a sudden urge to join them – there was something entrancing about the pounding of their feet, their easy loose-limbed gaits. Instead she thought of the damage they were inflicting on the cartilage of their knees by running on concrete and opened and closed her fists and shook her fingers and watched them as they passed.

When she arrived home, step count improved, she felt more like her old self. She kicked off her shoes and poured a glass of water. She felt a fizzing course through her veins culminating in her head. After everything she'd done for him! After all the energy she'd expended, all the trouble she'd taken. She rang Tansy to tell her about Colin's heart rate, which was Disaster Number Two.

'He's shagging someone else,' Kylie said when Tansy answered.

'What? Colin?' Tansy paused for a moment. 'He's at a conference at Darling Harbour, didn't you say? Where, exactly?'

Kylie didn't know.

'A conference centre? A hotel?'

Kylie had no idea.

'Is it just his company? Or is it an industry thingy?'

'I didn't ask, okay?' said Kylie. 'It was so boring, I tried to avoid the subject.'

Which, she now realised, could well have been part of his plan. Every mention of the conference was so mind-numbingly dull that she'd been discouraged from asking.

When they first started dating, Colin had told her about his job, but in those early few coffees and wines she hadn't imagined she and Colin would become *a thing* so Kylie had allowed the jargon to flow over and around her as though Colin were whispering endearments in some arcane foreign language. Yet somehow they did become *a thing*, but by then the time to ask questions about his work had passed. Oh, she knew all about his boss and his co-workers and the office politics – she'd been instrumental in motivating him to apply for a promotion just months ago – but her ignorance of Colin's actual tasks would have betrayed her initial disinterest and now she had no idea what he was talking about.

'He's sleeping with someone else, I'm positive,' Kylie said. She explained about the Fitbit, the heart rate, the consistent ten-minute duration.

'I think you dropped out for a minute there,' Tansy said. 'I thought you said ten minutes.'

Silence.

'Tans? Are you still there?'

'Ten minutes?' Tansy said. 'Ten? One zero?'

'You're missing the point. His heart rate was off the chart. Colin is having sex in Darling Harbour. I am not in Darling Harbour, Tans.'

'Sure, but ten? Perhaps Colin stayed up and watched some porn that really got him going. Or there was a fire alarm and he jogged down eight flights of stairs carrying a little old lady from the room next door.'

'Two nights in a row? No.'

'What I'm trying to say is this – I find it unlikely because he's lucky to have you. Really. He's reasonably attractive, yes, but you are amazing. He's punching above his weight. I can't imagine Colin wakes up in the morning to a queue of women outside his door.'

'So, he would if he could? But he can't, so he's not? Is that what you're saying?'

'That's not what I'm saying.'

'Because single men in their forties are terrifyingly scarce, and there are millions of awesome women in their forties. A forty-something man can be on parole and have a neck tattoo of Princess Di and literal fangs and women will still queue up. Is that what you're saying?'

Tansy exhaled. 'I'm saying that you can't be sure what Colin was doing in the middle of the night unless you ask him. Or, why don't you have a chat with Nick? He'll cheer you up. That's what brothers are for.'

'What do you mean, Nick will cheer me up? God, he doesn't like Colin, does he? That's what you're saying. You're saying that Nick doesn't like Colin and he'd be happy if we broke up.'

'Not happy . . . exactly. But Nick would probably categorise this as a mild inconvenience rather than a full-blown disaster.' Tansy sighed down the phone. 'I'm so sorry, Kyles. If you're right, and you're never wrong, you must be heartbroken.'

'Well, I'm not,' Kylie said. 'Absolutely not. That's the last thing I am. If he is so stupid as to not realise how lucky he is, then I am better off without him because I do not need someone that stupid in my life.' She felt a sudden rush of nausea and her breath caught in her throat as she inhaled, both of which were normal feelings that happened to non-heartbroken women every day. 'Listen, don't tell Nick and don't tell Monica. And especially don't tell Mum. You know she likes intricate revenge scenarios.'

'She is great at revenge. Maybe I should tell Mum,' said Tansy. 'Kyles? Do you want me to come over?'

Kylie didn't, but they both decided that drinks tomorrow night were a self-care necessity so plans were made. Tansy would organise Simon to feed the children and Kylie would call her friend Alice and ask her to join them. Monica studied graphic design on Tuesday nights so she wouldn't be able to come anyway.

'Why don't you buy a new dress, or something?' Tansy said. 'To cheer yourself up?'

It was a good thing that eye rolls were silent. Kylie was going out on a weeknight at short notice; that was out of character enough.

Over the course of the afternoon, Colin had rung three times. Kylie hadn't answered. The first two calls, she guessed, were just before he boarded the plane and when his flight landed. He was the kind of person who phoned to check in with her at departure and arrival as though it was the nineteenth century and he was sallying forth on a clipper to Antarctica and might never be heard from again.

He called for the third time just after she hung up from Tansy. She guessed it was just before he left home to drive to her place.

He was on his way. What was she going to do?

She was not entirely without defences. She fluffed her hair and sprayed it with something she found at the back of the bathroom cabinet, bought in an uncharacteristic moment, that promised thickness, and she added two coats of a crusty, dried-out mascara sample, pressed upon her by a sales rep, that also promised thickness. She wriggled into her skinny dark blue jeans that guaranteed thinness, which were apparently out of fashion now but she didn't care – there was no way she was wearing high-waisted flares, not ever. They could cut her skinny jeans off her cold, dead corpse, which would be the only way they could be removed should she die in her skinny jeans.

Tansy was right. There was no definitive evidence that Colin was cheating on her. Yes, he'd been glued to his phone lately. Yes, he seemed moody – at times vague and distant, then at other times, weirdly attentive. Again, evidence of nothing.

Was she one of those insecure, jealous girlfriends who imagined infidelity as soon as her boyfriend was out of sight?

No. No, she wasn't.

She found a spare cardboard box and walked around the house room by room, seeing her home with fresh eyes, collecting his bits and pieces and putting them in the box. The pink scalp massager, its plastic teeth shiny with oil advertised to stimulate follicles to within an inch of their hairy little lives. His salt and pepper shakers shaped like pineapples that he'd found at the Camberwell market and couldn't be without. His toothpaste for sensitive teeth. A tiny cactus in a pot of duck-egg blue that he'd bought for the coffee table. And from the kitchen: a plastic tub of psyllium husk powder, excellent for regularity; three unopened jars of apricot jam he'd made while recovering from the flu, and half a dozen little oval tins of aniseed sweets he bought compulsively but never ate. The vase was his, and the candle holders. The photo of the two of them on a beach holiday in a silver frame.

Her house looked even plainer without his stuff. Cleaner. Sparser. Scandinavian almost. She liked it better this way.

The Fitbit on her wrist was sullied by association. She undid the clasp, removed it. Put in the box. At once, her skin began to itch. She felt naked, adrift, exposed, so she fished it out of the box again and returned it to her wrist.

Kylie leaned against the brick wall and felt the integrity of it, the impregnability against her back. It shouldn't have surprised her that their relationship had an undignified end because it had had an undignified beginning. How could she possibly have envisaged a relationship with a man whose idea of chatting her up involved the best way to clear mucous from his cavities? How nice of a neck/shoulder/chest region did a man need to have in order to erase such an awkward meet-snoot? One of Hemsworthian proportions, which Colin assuredly did not possess.

Then she waited.

Chapter 5

Kylie heard Colin's Subaru pull up out the front.

She tucked the cardboard box under her arm and headed for the door. Outside, the day was calm and fine. The air was still in that way that meant tomorrow would be windy enough to knock a tattoo artist off his skateboard. She unlocked the security door, stood on the front step and watched him park. Her street was empty of people in both directions. All she could see were houses in which no one was dumping anyone and no one had been cheated upon.

Colin waved at her as he got out of the car. He was wearing his designer sunglasses, of which he was very proud, sneakers, checked tailored shorts and a coarse brown jumper knitted by his mother, as though each half of his body lived in a different hemisphere.

'Hi,' he said, smiling at her from the footpath, jangling his keys. 'How was your weekend? I'm exhausted. You have no idea how boring that conference was. Boring and exhausting. Let's stay in. Get a pizza and watch a movie.'

Was he speaking too quickly? Was his face a little redder than usual? She walked down the steps to the front gate but didn't open it. Her arms were quivering and she felt jittery all over. Low blood sugar, obviously, from eating lunch too early.

For a moment, he froze. His expression was blank. *Studiously blank*, Kylie thought.

From the other side of the gate, he gazed down to the contents of the box. 'What's all this?'

Her heart was thudding in her chest like a single sneaker in a tumble dryer. 'This is your stuff. If you'll just give me back my key, we can both put this sorry interval behind us.'

Kylie had last seen Colin only days ago so he ought to have been unchanged. And he was still a tall man with red cheeks, very pale skin, a cute, upturned nose and tiny dark eyes. His limbs were still thin and his fingers were as elegant as before. She could never mistake his hair for anyone else's: it was shiny, black and lush, the result of his scalp vigilance. He looked like a grown-up Astro Boy.

Yet it seemed that something had shifted in her vision. His thin limbs and elegant fingers somehow appeared creepy and skeletal, and his hair, affected. His ears had never made an impression before, yet now they seemed the most unpleasant ears she could recall seeing. There was a meadow of fine pale hairs protruding from them. Had those hairs always been there? There were crumbs sprinkled over his jumper, remnants of his lunch. Had she spent nine months in a relationship with a prawn-eyed man who had a field of teeny swaying cornstalks growing vertically out of his brain and half a piece of toast crumbled down his front and never noticed it until now?

'What do you mean?' He pushed the sunglasses atop his head. His forehead showed the obligatory quizzical furrows of a blindsided innocent man.

Another woman might have felt her confidence shaken by the speed of his denial, but that wasn't in Kylie's nature. Besides, Colin's prawn eyes did not inspire trust, and the 'confused' lines on his forehead seemed deliberately drawn as though with a biro. The sound of his voice made Kylie feel like taking a Beyoncé-esque baseball bat to his car windows.

'Think, Colin.' Her legs felt weak and she wanted more than anything to sit down on her front step, but that would mean looking up at him, which was out of the question. She spoke through gritted teeth. 'If a woman meets you at the door with a box of your belongings and asks for her key back, what do you reckon she means?'

He blinked. 'You're breaking up with me? Why?'

Even the way he said it annoyed her. *Breaking up* made them sound like they were children, as though she'd need to ask her mum to buy her a new pencil case because hers had *I ♥ Colin* etched across it in liquid paper.

Kylie leaned the box against the gate and lifted her wrist and pointed to her Fitbit, by way of illustration. She swung her forearm backwards and forward before him. 'I know you slept with someone else.'

She watched emotions sweep across his face in calculated waves: the widened shrimpy eyes of disbelief and the crinkled nose of shock, then the tilted head of confusion.

'Are you saying . . . my Fitbit data was weird? Because it's not. Take another look.'

'I don't need to take another look.'

'Seriously, look again. I didn't even wear it over the weekend. Those days are blank, I swear! I'm one hundred per cent confident.'

He was afraid, that was plain. Kylie knew what she saw. Colin's *confidence* could only mean one thing. 'If they're blank, it's because you've erased them.'

'Babe, you always do this. You're an overthinker. It's your trademark.'

Moments like these were why women in their forties were so angry all the time. A weird tic began to throb near her right eyelid but there was no expression whatsoever on her face, as though she'd been dead for three days.

'And, wow. My things, all packed up in a box.' He blinked fast. He was building up to something now. He'd made a decision to dial down the laid-back bewilderment and double-up on indignation – a poker player gripping his rubbish hand with all his strength and hoping no one noticed the beads of sweat on his forehead. He sniffed. 'I must say, I'm feeling pretty hurt at this point.'

'You're feeling hurt, is that what you said?' Kylie dug her nails into the cardboard of the box. 'You are hurt?'

Colin tilted his head back and opened his mouth, then swivelled his face from side to side. *Here it comes*, she thought. He was weighing his chances of success. Would he continue denying? Or was it time to fold? One, two . . .

He couldn't hold her gaze. He moved his sunglasses down again to cover his eyes and decided on the slumped shoulders and bowed head of contrition, digging his hands deep in the pockets of his shorts.

'I wanted to tell you. I tried to, several times. You were never meant to find out this way. You never look at my Fitbit data on the weekend or during the day, only ever when you get home from work!'

All at once, Kylie felt more disappointment than anger. Who had disappointed her the most, though? Was it Colin? She really couldn't say. From where Kylie stood, she could see the curtain in the front window of the house next door twitch, then the yappy terrier that lived there and was always sticking his nose through Kylie's fence appeared, his toffee-coloured feet flat on the glass. He saw Kylie and yapped, playfully, scraping his nails against the window. He was adorably, blissfully ignorant and Kylie was not. It's all right for dogs. All they need to be happy is food, belly rubs and the occasional walk. Add a Schmacko and something revolting to roll in, and it's Christmas every day. She forced her attention back to Colin.

'I was planning to break it to you gradually,' he said. 'So you didn't, you know, freak out.'

Typically, Colin would spend a couple of nights midweek with her, and they'd be together over the weekend. She avoided his place, a cluttered two-bedroom apartment that he shared with a pair of married nurses from Kerala who worked impossible shifts at a busy residential addiction clinic and so slept fitfully and at odd hours. Kylie found them enthralling. Colin's blah-blah tales about the drama of his office in which he did something with computers couldn't compete.

Colin barely listened to the nurses. For him, they were part of the furnishings, like twin bleary-eyed fridges. He didn't understand their motivation. How could intelligent people work so hard, in such difficult circumstances, for so little reward? *Do you have any idea what you could earn in the private sector?* he often said to them, shaking his head. When Kylie paid them too much attention, he became snippy. It was much easier if they hung out at Kylie's place.

Yet in all these months neither she nor Colin had raised the idea of officially moving in together. Why was that? It would have saved Colin all that driving, and splitting the bills would have helped pay down her mortgage. Besides, that was how relationships worked, wasn't it? People date for a while and if things go well, they move in together, and then they buy a houseplant, and if they don't kill that, they progress to sharing a Netflix account, and if they don't kill each other deciding what to watch next, they go halves in an Italian coffee machine. That was the normal way of doing things. Why had the thought of logical couple progression with Colin never popped into her mind?

'I hope we can still be friends,' he said.

'Um . . . let me think about it.' She blinked furiously. 'No.'

He set his mouth in a tight line and straightened his spine. 'You see? This is exactly the problem. You're so bloody rigid, Kylie.'

She felt a red film descend over her brain. 'The problem is your penis. And your brain, but primarily your penis. Your blood is at the wrong end of your spine, that's the problem.'

'Go ahead, keep deflecting. That's super mature.' He ran one hand through his lush hair and paused for lame dramatic effect. 'A normal woman would be in tears right now. Look in the mirror. No red eyes, no sniffling nose. You don't have the smallest amount of feminine feeling. Look at your bumper sticker.' He waved at her Honda in the driveway.

She looked. *My other car is a broom*, the sticker on the back said. She'd bought it from a market stall last year while shopping with Monica, Tansy and the kids; she'd thought it funny. She hadn't considered it a personal mission statement.

She'd like to show him feminine feeling. The feeling of the palm of her feminine hand connecting, hard, with his cheek. Why had she wasted so much time on him?

She took a step towards him. He lurched back, dramatically, almost tripping, then he reached into the cardboard box and pulled out the cactus, holding it by its tiny ceramic pot. The cactus was a sage green colour and it branched into three fleshy lobes and was covered with thin, sharp needles. 'Did you ever wonder why I bought this?' He brandished the cactus at her. 'Because it reminded me of you.'

'Are you on glue?' she said. 'In case you weren't paying attention, I'm not a plant person.'

'I know that about you, Kylie.' He held the cactus awkwardly in one hand while using the other to count on his fingers. 'You're one of those empty fruit bowl women, Kylie. There's no evidence of hobbies or interests, no chess sets, no musical instruments. You've never had a pet, not in your whole life, because you're not an animal person.' Then, with his final finger, a triumphant, 'You're not a *people* person, Kylie.'

'You couldn't be more wrong. I'm a healthcare professional. Healthcare. I love people.' She shifted her weight on to one leg and crossed her arms.

'It's impossible to talk to you, you're being deliberately obtuse. Look in the mirror, Kylie. Just look at your face.'

'What about my face?'

He held the cactus up again and shook his head. 'See the spikes, Kylie? Those sharp little prickles all over that plant? See how all those pointed bits make it impossible to get close?' And then he said, 'It's like you're not even trying to be attractive.'

It's all fun and games, her mother would say when Tansy and Nick were little and running around the backyard like maniacs, *until somebody loses an eye*. Until that point in her conversation with Colin, Kylie was focused and determined. She was righteous. Like most other woman of her age, Kylie always had a glowing ember of fury deep inside, fanned by all those small indignities from decades of being female – catcalls from passing cars when she was young enough to be startled; having to walk home from the tram with her key knife-like between her fingers.

But she didn't feel angry now. Instead, Kylie felt the air being sucked out of her. The street looked the same as it had before – the same neighbouring houses, the same leaves on the same trees, unstirring in the still air – but that was an illusion. In reality, nothing was the same. She could taste metal, maybe iron or steel, something that blades are made from. She was frozen to the spot, elbows bent and hands forming into claws as though she still held the cardboard box.

After that first dinner she'd had with Colin, he'd taken her arm on the footpath outside the restaurant and kissed her right there and she'd thought, *This is what's been missing in my life, being kissed like this.* Colin was a good kisser, there was no denying that, and she was a sucker for someone who knew how to kiss.

So she had let him into her life. He'd met her whole family; he'd been included in birthdays and celebrations and their usual Schnabel family dinners at Tansy's place. He knew them all, because she'd let him.

All the things she had wasted on him – her attention, her energy, her time.

No matter how safe you try to be, no matter how you try to protect your heart, if you're a human, you're always exposed. You can make all the rational choices, like a career caring for people from the other side of a counter. You can buy a house when you're too young, saving every penny when all your friends are focused on nights out and music festivals and taking extended overseas gap years. A house, not a flat, which would be so much more affordable and sensible for a single woman, everyone said. Flats have common doors and walls and body corporates. You wanted a house, which you chose for its potential for protection, as though you're a retired ASIO operative who never sits with her back to the door.

You can even choose a relationship with someone who should be 'lucky to have you', because that makes you feel secure. That you're the one holding all the cards.

But then that someone will go to a conference and their heart rate will spike in the middle of the night and you'll be sitting in your car looking at the screen and all at once you're right back where you started.

Now, as Kylie watched Colin drive away with his analogous cactus and his pathetic box of possessions, she felt her shoulders sitting under her earlobes. She unconsciously fingered the Fitbit strap around her wrist, thankful for it and also cursing it. How long would it be until someone kissed her again? Would anyone ever? Despite the safe job and the safe house and the safe boyfriend, in the end you're just a woman standing at the front of your house with your chest cut open and your heart exposed to the wind and the rain and the casual judgements of others.

TUESDAY

Chapter 6

That night Kylie lay in her bed and saw one o'clock then two o'clock glow on the square screen of her Fitbit. Despite her afternoon walk, Monday's activity level showed only 6000 steps for the day, which wasn't enough to promote sleepiness and which made her even angrier when she remembered that at least 1000 of that was from stomping around the house collecting Colin's crap.

Perhaps she couldn't sleep because her feet were cold. There was data from one study – was it Korean? She was pretty sure it was a Korean study – that showed that cold feet caused insomnia. So she found a pair of fluffy hiking socks in a drawer and put them on. She swapped pillows then she turned the new pillow over for the cool other side, which, she realised as soon as it touched her head, was the wrong side. So she turned it over again, then she took a blanket to the couch where she lay with her head up one end, which was obviously the wrong end, so she kicked the blanket off then lay with her head at the other end. Still she wasn't sleeping. The problem was the socks – the socks were too tight and irritating. What a stupid idea. What did those Koreans think they were playing at?

She took the socks off. She went back to bed and lay still and folded her hands across her chest and tried to count backwards from 300, but only got to 298 before Colin popped into her head, and she refused to think about Colin because Colin had occupied quite enough of her life. The fact was, he'd been perfect for her in so many ways. She hadn't wanted children and neither had he. He'd even had a vasectomy at the beginning of the year so she hadn't needed to worry about contraception. Now that she was single, she'd have to go back on the pill because she likely still had eggs dozing in her ovaries waiting their turn. You can't be too careful. Plenty of women had babies in their early forties. Plenty. She met them at the pharmacy, advised them on nappy rash and cradle cap and teething. Many of these mothers were coupled, but quite a few were single. They were tired of waiting. They'd realised that men were not necessary. She wondered what the perception of time was like for men. Time as a dimension, time as a way to measure physical change. The inner world of men was unfathomable, lacking as it did both the built-in monthly structure that divides forty years of your life by menstruation and the overarching, constant awareness of the finite nature of ovulations as you approach your fertile cliff. Men aren't normal. They can't be. Everything in their reality must feel loose and adrift without this chronological/mental scaffolding holding both the short- and long-term balance of their days.

Go to sleep, Kylie. Don't think about men and their weird brains, just don't. Relax. Breathe. Not like that. Slower. If she could just learn to let go, drift off. She should start boxing classes, or some kind of martial art; after all, she had plenty of free time, far more than Tansy, with the demands of motherhood. When the night was particularly long like this one, and tonight was going on for decades, Kylie thought about how glad she was not to have children of her own. She had her niece, Mia, and her nephew, Lachie, though, both of whom she adored, and both of whom she often dreamed – when she did dream, when she slept – were drowning in a wide blue ocean and she was swimming out to rescue them amid the chopping briny waves. Or sometimes she imagined them needing one of her kidneys or a piece of her liver or a cornea, any of which, or even all three, she would gladly hand over without the smallest hesitation. If this was the amount she tossed and turned in the middle of the night worrying about her niece and nephew, and nieces and nephews in terms of probability share only around twenty-five per cent of an aunt's DNA whereas her own children would be fifty per cent her, and if worry was correlated to genetics – if it was, and it might not be, she couldn't recall any evidence – she would worry at least double and possibly more about her own children than her niece and nephew, which would be untenable to a balanced and productive life and likely result in her never sleeping again.

Chapter 7

Storms, and weather events in general, rarely occur indoors. As a rule, once all the windows and doors of a building are closed, wind gusts don't slam cupboards or jolt tables or rattle shelves. Another thing – it takes a variety of passive cooling features like wide eaves and double-glazing to keep the internal temperature comfortable when the day is warm and fine outside. The operative word here is 'comfortable'. Under normal circumstances, it should not be meteorologically possible for the inside of an average retail space in an average shopping strip in a temperate country – say, an Australian pharmacy – to feel like a freezer, without the installation of industrial-strength refrigeration.

'Is she always like this?' whispered Gail, loud enough for Kylie to hear.

'She's excellent with the customers,' Sandy said. 'It's the rest of us who need to watch out.'

Sandy was right. Kylie, the navy-suited low-pressure system in question, was excellent with customers. Mostly. She didn't mind the long hours, or the continuing education, or the occasional altercations that were an intrinsic part of working with the public. While other health professionals burned out and left their profession entirely following years of being stretched impossibly thin, Kylie believed in the importance of pharmacies more than ever. Medicare benefits kept shrinking and co-payments kept increasing and everywhere she turned, the selfish and the stupid were peddling fake therapies that caused so much harm to so many vulnerable people. What was in the brains of people who took advice from someone who'd failed Year 10 biology instead of someone who'd devoted their lives to understanding the workings of the human body? If the pandemic had taught her anything, it was this – pharmacies were fast becoming the only place to receive free and qualified medical advice.

Tim felt the same. He wasn't focused on sales. They both took the time to chat with people, whether they bought something or not. Sure, there were things about community pharmacy she didn't love. The relationship with the customers could be distant and compartmentalised; clearly 'customers', in Kylie's mind, not 'patients'. Only doctors had patients. She remembered one customer – an elderly woman with mauve hair and poorly managed type 2 diabetes. Kylie filled her scripts but also stressed the importance of changing her diet, gave her pamphlets and offered to help her with a meal plan. The woman huffed out of the pharmacy only to return fifteen minutes later with a glazed pink donut half the size of her head which she proceeded to eat while staring aggressively at Kylie and dusting icing sugar all over the carpet. What was the point of that woman maliciously eating a donut at Kylie? Couldn't she see that the only person she was harming was herself?

By late morning, there was a temporary lull in the forces of nature. Gail was standing at the back of the dispensary, notepad and pen in hand, watching the former Cyclone Kylie calmly discussing antibiotics and the necessity of fluid and rest with a stringy-haired woman in her mid-thirties. On the woman's hip was a red-cheeked toddler, too big to be carried, with his thumb in his mouth and damp hair stuck across his forehead. A snail trail of snot inched its way to his upper lip.

'It's important to finish the whole course.' Kylie, box in her hand, was pointing to the dosage instructions.

The woman's eyes were half-closed. She nodded, perhaps in agreement or perhaps because she was falling asleep where she stood. She hitched the boy higher, stuck her hip out further. 'And how do I check his temperature again?'

Kylie took a digital thermometer and held it like a television remote. 'Push this button for two seconds, then point it at his forehead and wait for the beep.'

The toddler coughed, rattly and wet, and the woman twisted to move him to her other hip. She squinted at the device. 'Push where?'

'Kylie,' said Sandy, behind them. She raised her eyebrows and gestured to the woman.

Kylie turned to look at her. 'What?'

Sandy gestured again, pointedly staring at Kylie and moving her hands from Kylie to the woman, as though suggesting they dance.

'I have no idea what you're saying,' Kylie said.

'Oh, for heaven's sake.' Sandy stepped towards the woman and reached for the feverish toddler. 'The poor woman can't do two things at once. Give him to me for a sec.'

Whether due to his misery or Sandy's confidence, the toddler went to her without crying or fussing, with his thumb in his mouth and his eyes closed. She walked him a few paces away, within sight of his mother but giving her enough room to concentrate on Kylie.

'There,' Sandy said, swaying him from side to side. 'What a good boy you are.'

The relief in the woman was palpable. It was obvious in the way her spine released. She stretched, then sagged into one of the chrome chairs and passed the back of her hand over her forehead.

She looked up at Kylie. 'I'm on my own. He's a handful,' she said. 'How old are yours?'

It was a fraught question for so many women who'd suffered miscarriages and loss, infertile women and sterile ones. Still, if Kylie had a dollar for everyone who asked her how many children she had, or the ages of her children, or her plans for children, she would have had enough money by now for a tattoo on her forehead that said *I have no children*. And the tattoo could be in gold dust and studded with little diamonds.

'I don't have any,' Kylie said. Questions about children had never been fraught for her. 'But I have years of aunt experience.'

After the woman left, Gail made another note in her little book. 'That was excellent customer service, but inappropriate infection control,' she said.

Gail was probably right about infection control, Kylie knew – although that wasn't the reason she hadn't taken the child herself. Kylie wasn't squeamish about germs or bodily fluids. Even as a child, the interior of bodies had always captivated her: the pipes and tubing and bones, the mechanics of tendons and the squishiness of organs. Everyday things had seemed like bodies writ large. She imagined joints as hinges on cupboards and lungs as the lozenge-shaped yellow sponges she used to clean her father's car. Her kidneys were like her mother's Brita water jug and her liver was a swimming pool testing kit regulating a river of blood.

Kylie hadn't taken the toddler because she wasn't keen on small children, that was all. She didn't dislike them – rather, she had no feelings towards them at all. Mothers of her acquaintance offered Kylie their precious infants to cuddle, with an air of pity for her childless condition; she always declined. She didn't understand the fuss and felt no inclination to goo or gah. Babies were basically interchangeable, after all. They were unformed blobs with no real personalities who couldn't interact much. Even Mia and Lachie had failed to interest her until they reached school age.

Was this a character flaw? Very possibly. If everyone felt the same as her, intentional procreation would end and human life would cease. Even if it were a flaw, it was the way Kylie was. Some things, she knew, could not be fixed by taking a course or reading a book, or by any amount of willpower.

For the rest of the afternoon, Kylie had trouble concentrating. Every time the bell above the door rang, she had the unreasonable thought that it might be Colin coming to apologise, to beg her forgiveness. But it was never Colin. She was kept busy because Tim had the day off, but every so often she caught herself thinking about things she wanted to tell Colin, then remembering she would never tell Colin anything again and feeling freshly furious and, at the same time, hollow. She spoke with an elderly gentleman with a stooped back confused about his medications, then a spotty teenager having trouble using his inhaler, then a woman in a multicoloured kaftan with bloodshot, itchy eyes. She looked at someone's unidentified back rash (bad news: shingles) and someone else's ghastly toenails (good news: athlete's foot). She listened to complaints about persistent dandruff and helped someone choose the right reading glasses, and not one of these people knew what Colin had done. Kylie felt herself torn between two opposing forces: telling everyone she saw, everyone in the whole world, that Colin was sleeping with someone else and they had broken up, and never, ever mentioning it to anyone, ever. All the while Sandy was there, warm and chatty, ringing up purchases, labelling cosmetics with an old-fashioned pricing gun, saying, *What a shocker, poor you,* to customers with just the right amount of frowning sincerity even when the problem was self-inflicted.

Midafternoon, Sandy came up beside Kylie. 'Are you okay?' she said.

Kylie folded her arms. 'Of course I'm okay. Why wouldn't I be okay?'

Sandy held up her phone. The screen showed the Pharmacy King website.

'The advert for your job's already up,' Sandy said. 'It sounds amazing.'

Kylie expanded the text with pincer fingers. *Senior Community Pharmacist*, it read, promising *flexible working hours, bonuses for innovation, opportunity for advancement within the company, study leave and a genuine commitment to work/life balance.*

'I'm not worried,' said Kylie. 'A formality, Gail said.'

'I bet Pharmacy King has lanyards.'

A lanyard! As much as Kylie liked working for a small business, there was something deeply sexy about a lanyard.

'Gail told me she's had a dozen applications already,' Sandy continued. 'Really impressive ones.

Kylie sniffed. 'Irrelevant.'

'The ad also says you need to have a "welcoming demeanour" and a genuine smile for every patient.'

Kylie grabbed the phone and peered closer. Sandy was right. What a ludicrous requirement! How could a recruiter possibly know whether someone's demeanour was welcoming or if their smile was genuine? It was impossible to determine in an interview – an artificial and formal interaction – and subjective traits do not belong in a résumé. What would Pharmacy King do? Spy on every applicant all day and count the number of smiles per customer and their degree of genuineness and plot them on a graph? Also, it was inherently sexist! Are men ever told to smile? No. A woman is expected to look as though fetching tinea cream is the highlight of her day; a man merely has to not look like he's going to jump the counter and strangle someone. And what about equal-opportunity laws? There are people with facial differences who are unable to smile in a pleasing fashion – does that mean they shouldn't work with the public? The whole thing was ableist and discriminatory and infuriating.

Sandy whistled. 'And look at the salary range. It's more money than Tim was paying.'

Kylie swallowed and ran her fingers under the Fitbit band, tight on her wrist. 'I can smile,' she said. 'I just haven't had sufficient motivation until now.'

Perhaps this application would not be a formality. Perhaps she was in real danger of losing her job, of the pharmacy no longer being part of her life. Just in case, she would write the perfect job application. She started to compile a mental list of what she'd need: fresh paper for her printer – 120 gsm would be ideal; the perfect résumé template. She'd completed dozens of professional development courses and recently a graduate diploma, and all the certificates were filed by date order in her cabinet at home – she'd list them all so Gail could see her level of commitment. She would include her performance reviews, which admittedly Kylie conducted on herself. Tim's idea of timely and specific managerial feedback was telling her she was excellent, brilliant, of course, then taking her to the pub to chat about the overblown emphasis on clamping dovetail joints and other woodworking controversies over a schnitzel. Kylie was tougher on herself than Tim would ever be.

She could count on Tim and Sandy to say good things but – this was vital – for the application to be successful, she needed an outstanding reference from someone whose opinion mattered. Pharmacy King would then realise that she was irreplaceable. She needed someone high-profile, beyond reproach. Someone with wow factor.

She asked Sandy if she had any suggestions.

'You should get Costa the gardener,' she said. 'Or the guy from the Lego show.'

'I don't know Costa the gardener or the guy from the Lego show,' said Kylie.

'You didn't say you had to know them,' Sandy said.

Kylie blinked. 'I thought that was implied. It should be a pharmacist, or someone in the industry.'

'If you're worried about the smiling thing, how about trying some make-up?' Sandy said. 'It might make your face a bit more . . . pleasing.'

Kylie curled her lip. 'I refuse to cover myself with paint to suit someone else's aesthetic ideal.'

Sandy's lipstick was a shimmery orange. Her eyeshadow was the colour of toast, and it shimmered also. Her cheekbones shimmered and her crystal nose stud sparkled. She glared at Kylie. 'You do you, Kyles,' she said.

Chapter 8

'What a prick,' said Alice. 'You need to get on Tinder, like, yesterday.'

It was just past 7 pm. Kylie and Tansy and Alice were perched on velvet-covered stools in a Fitzroy bar, the kind with deliberately tarnished mirrors, banquette seating and cocktails that cost more than the food. Huge ornate chandeliers and tiny red-tasselled lamps gave the space a Fitzgeraldian hue. The wall behind the bar was covered in dozens of bottles of spirits and liquors, more than anyone could ever identify or drink, and the sound of ironic 70s hits wafted through the open windows and out into the softening dusk.

Alice had chosen it. It spoke to Kylie's vulnerable state that she'd agreed.

None of them had driven – they were expecting a big night. Tansy, in her satin maxi-dress, was sliding forward on her stool, resting her feet on the rail and leveraging herself upright again.

Silky girls-night outfits, slippery leather, tipsy clientele – the stools were an insurance payout waiting to happen.

'No new dress, then?' said Tansy.

Kylie, in her standard drinks outfit of black skinny jeans with a navy knit and black boots, raised one eyebrow. 'What am I, a Kardashian?'

'I love any excuse for a new dress,' said Alice. 'Look at those girls over there in Gorman. It cheers me up just looking at them.'

She pointed her chin at three women standing together in a row against one of the windows. They looked to Kylie like a magic eye picture: if she crossed her eyes and walked backwards from them, they would turn into a galloping horse.

Kylie picked up the drinks menu and peered at it. 'It's so upsetting,' she said.

'If you want to cry, just go ahead,' said Alice. 'Better out than in.'

'Cry? Kylie? As if.' Tansy was flicking through her phone with one hand. 'She's talking about the price of the cocktails, aren't you, Kyles.'

Kylie slapped the menu on the bar. 'For twenty-four dollars, I could buy a third of a bottle of vodka and a whole pack of those little umbrellas and make half of these at home from a YouTube tutorial.'

'You know how little girls want to be princesses? Not her. Queen Kylie, we used to call her.'

'Princesses have no practical power. They're subordinate,' Kylie said. 'Only the monarch has royal prerogative recognised in common law.'

'You must have been a fascinating child,' said Alice.

'She was always trying to rule the world. Oh my god, let me tell you about something that happened when we were little,' Tansy said to Alice.

'If you tell the bath story again, so help me god,' said Kylie. 'Alice doesn't need to hear this.'

'Yes Alice does.' Alice leaned forward on her stool to better hear over the sound of 'Dancing Queen'.

'Once when we were little,' said Tansy, in a burst of enthusiasm, 'Nick and I were in the bath together. Mum had gone to do something.'

'You're not supposed to leave children unattended in the bath,' said Alice.

'It was a simpler time,' said Kylie.

'Anyway,' Tansy said, 'we were messing around, splashing each other, and Nick was whining as usual and Kylie was trying to separate us and she slipped against the side of the tub and fell on her arm.'

'You're supposed to be supportive of me,' Kylie said. 'That's what this whole girls' night is for.'

'It started to swell up and turn hot and red. Right here.' Tansy leaned over and wrapped her hand around Kylie's forearm an inch above her Fitbit.

'You and Nick broke her arm?' said Alice to Tansy. 'You must have been in so much trouble with Gloria.'

'It was an accident! And no, we weren't in trouble, because Kylie didn't make a sound.'

'What?'

'You're not telling it right,' said Kylie. 'Dad was away on some business trip somewhere. Or so he said. They'd had a fight, it's obvious now. He told me to look after Mum and the little kids. I was in charge, he said. I didn't want to cause her any trouble.'

'So Queen Kylie *breaks her actual arm* and doesn't say anything for the rest of the day!' Tansy continued. 'The whole day! Not a peep! I can't imagine how painful it must have been. By tea time, she could barely move her fingers – using a fork would have been impossible. She was about to be discovered, so she knocked over the chair in her bedroom and told Mum she tripped over it.'

'And Gloria never found out how it really happened?'

'Snitches wind up in ditches,' said Kylie.

'Mum did find out, because when she came home from the hospital in a cast, Nick cracked,' said Tansy.

'What a baby.' Kylie shook her head.

'Intense,' said Alice.

'You don't understand what it's like to be the eldest,' Kylie said. 'It's like having children of your own that you never wanted.' She felt a rush of memory: as a child, before the influence of tea parties and miniature ovens, she had played at imagining herself a great and mighty warrior queen protecting little Tansy and toddler Nick at her feet.

They'd been chatting since they first arrived and now the bartender was lurking expectantly. He was cute in that bartender way – beard and hair impeccably styled to look scruffy and sharp collared shirt with the sleeves rolled up, silk waistcoat and tie. It was the incongruity between the messy and the prissy that was hot – that, and the forearms. Alice leaned over the menu and tucked a curl of hair behind her ear. Kylie already knew that Alice would tip him outrageously.

'Are we ordering?' said Alice, smiling at him. 'Shall we get a bottle? I'm ready for a big night! How about bubbles? Tansy?'

'Sorry, what?' Tansy looked up from her phone.

'Stop looking at that thing,' said Kylie. 'Whatever it is, Simon can handle it now that he's over his early Unabomber period.'

'It's not that,' said Tansy. 'It's—'

'There you are,' said a voice. 'I wasn't sure I had the right place. It smells of pee in that alley.'

Kylie felt a sinking in her stomach, in her very bones. She didn't want to turn around, but she did. Behind her was Gloria, in three-inch heels and a sequin swing coat.

'Mum? What are you doing here?'

Gloria raised one eyebrow. 'I can't imagine,' she said. 'I just thought I'd catch a taxi all this way for a drink at this random bar that almost seems deliberately hard to find. Honestly, it's a wonder they have any customers at all. Someone should have a word with the management.'

Kylie loved her mother. Of course she did. She adored her. Most of the time. Gloria cast a very big shadow, that was all. Sometimes they clashed, yes, but on any other night she would have been happy for Gloria to join them. But Kylie and Tansy and Alice were here for a specific purpose, and that purpose would likely involve certain disclosures. And while Gloria would certainly not object to hearing these disclosures, Kylie would prefer not to share these disclosures, which would almost certainly be of an intimate nature, in front of her mother.

Gloria couldn't keep a secret, for a start, and she had no filter between her brain and her mouth.

Because these were no ordinary drinks. This was a relationship post-mortem.

'But don't you have something on tonight?' said Kylie. 'You always have something on.'

'Of course, but I cancelled it.' Gloria cupped her hand around Kylie's cheek. 'Tonight is for cheering up my beautiful girl, post-Colin.'

'That's so nice,' said Alice.

'I didn't want to go to the other thing anyway. I'm beginning to think those tennis club people are too old for me. Hello?' This, Gloria said to the waiting bartender. 'Can you manage a gin martini, very cold and extremely dry? In fact, just have the vermouth nod brusquely at the gin from across the room, that'd be fine.'

'Shaken not stirred, right?' said Alice.

Gloria looked at Alice as though she had a dead rat on her head. 'Another example of the mediocrity of middle-aged white men. Shaking ruins a martini by watering it down with ice chips. If James Bond really can't handle his liquor, he should order a Diet Coke and skip the entire macho charade. In fact,' this, to the bartender, 'because we are *women*, make it four martinis. *Stirred*.'

'I might just have a lemon, lime and bitters?' said Alice. 'I've just remembered – early start in the morning.'

Gloria gave her a withering glance.

'I didn't realise Mum was coming,' said Kylie, who was staring at Tansy. 'In fact, I distinctly remember not telling Mum about Colin.'

'I might have vaguely mentioned that we were catching up. She was worried about you,' said Tansy, avoiding Kylie's gaze and moving another stool closer for Gloria. 'Weren't you, Mum?'

'Hmmm.' Gloria clambered up onto the stool with grim determination, using the bar as leverage. 'Colin was never worthy of you, Kylie. After everything you did for him! Your emancipation deserves a celebration.'

'Anyway,' said Alice. 'It's lovely to see you again, Gloria.'

'Which one are you?' said Gloria. She wasn't wearing glasses, but if she were, she'd have been looking at Alice over them.

'Mum, you've met Alice before. Kylie's friend from uni. She's a vet, with a little brother Nick's age,' said Tansy.

'Of course, the vet,' said Gloria. 'You mustn't dwell on it. Not everyone can get into med school. They make it hard for a reason. Look at Kylie. She loves being a pharmacist. And she's so good at it! Practically runs the place. I don't know what Tim would do without her.'

Kylie swallowed. 'Anyway. Work is boring. We're not here to talk about work.'

What was happening now was an integral part of the relationship post-mortem – the time-honoured tradition of running down the ex. For all these women knew, Kylie and Colin could reconcile tomorrow and they themselves would either be dumped or forever be the 'friend' who'd said cruel things about her boyfriend's prawn eyes. There was generosity and courage in the way they were slagging him off; they were each taking a risk to make Kylie feel better.

'I never liked him,' said Gloria. 'I kept waiting for hidden depths but all I kept seeing was obvious shallows. And the way he always looked at you before he spoke. Honestly, what was he scared of?'

'But he had nice shoulders, didn't he?' said Kylie. 'I'm going to miss those shoulders.'

'My daughter is a pharmacist who owns her own home.' Gloria indicated Kylie with a nod as the bartender delivered the martinis. 'She's single.'

'Unbelievable,' he said, then he winked before turning to serve a date-night couple at the other end of the bar.

'Mum,' said Kylie. 'He's, like, thirty.'

'Also, ugh,' said Tansy.

'I think he's lovely.' Alice rested her cheek on her palm, gazing at the bartender. 'Do you think he has any pets?'

'The man should be younger than the woman in every couple. Women outlive men by six to eight years and outnumber men in aged care by fifty per cent,' Gloria said. 'Unless you want to be one of those widows who gallop up and down the halls on their Zimmer frames chasing anything with a functioning prostate, you need to take that into account.'

'There are lots of old people on Tinder,' said Alice. 'Lots and lots.'

'You don't need to be on Tinder. Aren't there any hot Russian singles in your area?' said Tansy.

'I've been single for six minutes,' Kylie said. 'I'm not thinking about aged care, Tinder or hot Russian singles.'

The martinis were as cold and dry as Gloria had requested, with a twist. Alice took one after all, though it wasn't obvious if the four martinis were ordered for each of them or if they were all for Gloria. Regardless, Kylie thought they tasted like heaven. They tasted like having her own house back, like free weekends and sleeping in her comfy pyjamas instead of the sexy ones. They tasted of no toothpaste residue or fingernail clippings around the sink and of no one kicking the covers off in the middle of the night. What on earth did men dream about to get the covers in that state? Karate tournaments? Swing dancing? Why can't they sleep like they're paralysed, like a normal person?

Really. Having a boyfriend meant putting up with so much inconvenience, and for what? Nice shoulders/neck; nice, regular if unimaginative and abbreviated sex, and allergies. It was much better to be here with her friends (and her mother). The background music changed to Sherbet's 'You've Got the Gun'. The martini flowed through Kylie's veins and she swayed on her stool in time with Daryl. Who cared about boyfriends? The most important relationships in life were the ones with other women. Kylie and Alice and Tansy and Gloria talked about books they'd read and movies they'd seen; they talked about celebrities and their dating history.

'I'll have another,' said Gloria to the bartender.

If Kylie was still with Colin she wouldn't be here on a weeknight. She'd either be alone at home in her jammies by now or with him, watching something mindless with superheroes in it, made for fourteen-year-old boys. This was much better. This was exciting and engaging, this was a taste of the real world outside of coupledom. Gloria ordered hibachi Padrón peppers and salt and pepper tofu *raciones* from the Asian Tapas menu, with only a fractional side-eye and without comment, although Kylie could tell she was thinking, *You may want to reconsider the insensitive and unnecessary mixing of your cultural references.*

'I've been single for more than thirty years,' Gloria announced with the moral superiority of an electric-bike-riding vegan.

'You're not lonely?' said Alice. 'I'd be lonely.'

'It's idyllic. Imagine training a new man. Breaking one in.' Gloria shuddered.

Alice didn't look convinced. 'Any advice for us reluctant singles?'

'Mum's not big on advice,' Kylie said. 'Although she's always available if you need pointless sarcasm.'

Gloria turned to her. 'Excuse me. My sarcasm is extremely pointed.'

Alice seemed to take that as an invitation. She wriggled closer to Gloria. 'I'm on Tinder all day. If I have even five minutes between appointments I'm there, swiping away. Check a weird rash on a dog, swipe. Palpate a vomiting cat, swipe. If I quit Tinder, I'd save enough time to learn Spanish and finally finish that Donna Tartt.'

'I do have advice for singles, as a matter of fact,' said Gloria.

'Would you ladies like another round of martinis?' said the cute bartender as he leaned across towards them.

'A German vibrator,' said Gloria, in a voice that reverberated through the crowd at the exact moment the song ended.

The bartender's eyes bulged. All around, heads spun in their direction.

'You can't be stingy if you want quality,' Gloria said, oblivious to the draining of oxygen in the room. She finished her martini and reached for another piece of tempura manchego. 'Germans make the BMWs of vibrators. Consider it an investment.'

Around them, a sea of wide eyes and open mouths.

'Mum . . .' Tansy said. 'Use your inside voice.'

'German vibrators are more expensive of course, and quite limited in their functionality, but that needn't be your only one. If you want to have seasonal, fun vibrators, pink glitter PVC with ridges, multi-speed, strobe lights—'

'They have strobe lights?' said Kylie. 'Why, for god's sake? It's not a disco down there.'

'—or whatnot, you certainly can. Rabbits and the whole rabbit family.'

'The rabbit family is Leporidae,' said Alice.

'But beware. They won't last. Gimmicky. Shoddy manufacturing. Buy a classic investment piece first. Being single again, at your age, could well last a long time. A *looong* time.' She leaned across and placed one hand on Kylie's knee. 'Splurge. Treat yourself.'

'Jesus, Mum,' said Kylie. 'Thanks for coming to my TED talk.'

'On that note,' said Alice.

'I should probably get home to the kids,' said Tansy.

'You're quite right,' said Gloria. 'I've got my under-eight's tomorrow. Half the time they can't tell left from right. Small children are actually terrible at tennis and extremely slow at following simple instructions. I tell the parents exactly this and they laugh, if you can believe it! It's as though they think I'm joking.'

She slid from the stool, preparing to drain the last of her martini. Now that she was standing, Gloria seemed more lopsided than Kylie expected. And substantially shorter.

'Mum,' said Kylie.

They all looked down. Gloria's right shoe was firmly on the floor, but on her left, she was standing on her ankle.

'I don't think ankles are supposed to bend like that,' said Tansy.

Chapter 9

For Kylie, the next hour passed in a blur. Once Gloria's attention was drawn to her ankle, she stumbled. Kylie instinctively threw out her arms but Gloria was caught by a large, bearded bear in a group of fellow large bearded bears, all in plaid shirts and braces, perfectly positioned behind them to break Gloria's fall. Kylie ordered the crowd to move back and they did, gasping and peering. She hooked one of Gloria's arms over her shoulder and the bear did the same on Gloria's other side. Together they hopped her to a leather couch which was hastily vacated. A woman abandoned her date to grab some cushions from the window seat for propping and the Gorman girls moved the small table out of the way. In an instant, Gloria's ankle had become the focus of the whole bar. Tansy thanked the Gorman girls, the woman on the date and the bear graciously.

Alice kneeled beside Gloria, eased off her stiletto and lifted her ankle onto one of the cushions.

'Don't fuss,' Gloria said.

'You're going to need an X-ray, I'm afraid,' said Alice. 'Did you hear anything when you went over?'

'Only a cracking sound.' Gloria, reclining like Cleopatra on a bank of cushions, somehow hadn't spilled a drop of her martini.

Alice looked up at Kylie and Tansy. 'I think it might be broken.'

'Are you sure you're qualified to make that kind of a diagnosis?' said Gloria to Alice. 'I'm not a schnauzer.'

'Broken? No way. No, no, no. She'll be fine,' said Kylie. 'You'll be fine, won't you, Mum?'

'Of course,' said Gloria. 'I'm far too busy for a broken ankle. It's just a little strain. Another drink, that's what I need. Excuse me?' she called to the bartender and when she caught his eye, waved her glass. He nodded.

Alice shook her head. 'Nothing else by mouth,' she said. 'In case they need to operate.'

Kylie curled her lip and wrested Gloria's glass from her iron grip while Tansy rang for an ambulance. With no blood or screaming to entertain them, the crowd's attention soon drifted away and people resumed their conversations. The buzz returned, along with the music.

Meanwhile, Gloria was still talking about how ridiculous all this fuss was, and how unfair they were, and how she wished Nick were here instead of Tansy and Kylie because he'd let her have as many martinis as she wanted.

'Fascists,' Gloria said under her breath.

This, right here, was the reason Kylie and Gloria clashed. Why couldn't she just do as she was told? Why did she insist on having things her own way all the time?

'Shut. It,' said Kylie.

'Don't speak to me that way. I gave birth to you,' said Gloria.

Kylie groaned. 'That was one time.'

Gloria glared at her. Kylie glared back.

The paramedics arrived in less than twenty minutes. They were two jocular, short-haired young people with a can-do attitude and the calm flippancy that comes from seeing people at their most vulnerable every day. They joked about only being here to pick up takeaway cocktails, then one of them went back out to fetch the carry-chair.

'I'm not getting in that thing,' said Gloria when she saw it.

'Sorry, love,' one said to her. 'It's policy. On account of your age.'

'My fucking *what*?' said Gloria.

'Do. As you. Are told,' said Kylie.

'Mind. Your own. Business,' said Gloria.

Tansy kneeled beside her, and took Gloria's hand in hers. 'Mum,' she said, 'think what a great story this will make! You hurt your ankle drinking martinis in a hipster bar and had to be carried out. Nick will be so proud. He'll probably tell all his friends about how cool you are.'

'Well, if it's policy, I suppose so,' said Gloria. 'Far be it from me to be difficult.' She gave the ambos a faux-reluctant nod and they lifted her into the carry-chair and began to manoeuvre her down the stairs.

'Atta girl,' one of them said.

'This is very inconvenient,' Gloria said, as if it was their fault. 'I'm a tennis coach. Saturday is my open day, for first-timers.

It's my biggest event of the year. I pay for a face painter. The Rotarians run a sausage sizzle.'

'You might need some time off, love,' said one of the ambos. 'Or you could coach wheelchair tennis for a while. I saw that Dylan Alcott at the Open once. He's awesome, hey.'

Outside on the footpath, Kylie, Tansy and Alice huddled in a small circle while a group of girls in sequinned outfits, who'd given them right of way on the stairs, giggled past. Compared with the snug bar, it was quiet and cold. The dark was lit by the flashing blue and red lights on top of the ambulance. The few cars driving past slowed with the hope of seeing an accident then sped up again, disappointed.

'I'll get in the back with you, shall I?' said Kylie, as Gloria was being loaded.

'I'm not five,' said Gloria.

'Goodo,' said Kylie cheerfully. 'See you at the hospital then.' They all waved her off as the ambo closed the doors.

The wind had picked up again. An empty slushy cup and a blue disposable mask whipped down the footpath beside them. Kylie pulled her coat tighter and turned up her collar.

'You poor love. I can drop you at the hospital if you like?' Alice hugged her while pressing buttons on her phone to call her ride. 'What a crappy end to the night. I'd hoped we'd be doing something much more cheering, like vomiting in the gutter.'

'She'll be fine. She's a tough old bird,' said Kylie.

'There's no reason you have to do everything,' said Tansy. 'Why don't I go to the hospital instead?'

'I've got it,' said Kylie. 'Go home to your kids.'

'Are you sure?' Tansy said. 'Simon is more than capable of looking after things these days, and you've got your work disaster and your Colin disaster. I'm worried.'

Kylie replied without a pause, without a moment's thought, because she was the big sister, and also there was no one waiting up for her and no one she needed to call, and her nights were empty and Tansy's were full. 'Seriously. I'll text you and Nick from the hospital. Mum's indestructible, you know that.'

'Oh Kyles, I know Mum's indestructible.' Tansy hugged her, then rubbed her upper arm as though she were consoling a small child. 'She's not the one I'm worried about.'

Alice's Uber dropped Kylie at the emergency department. Inside, she approached the reception desk.

'I'm looking for my mother. Her name's Schnabel, S C H—' she began.

'Oh, we know Gloria,' the emergency nurse said cryptically. 'She's in X-ray now. We've given her some pain relief. Take a seat.'

The waiting area was full of people having a bad night. Some were having the worst night of their lives. They were all here because they trusted that the smart and caring people who worked here would help them. This trust was part of the social contract that binds us together. Helping people at the pharmacy was important, Kylie knew, but here, professionals worked to make strangers' worst nights a little less terrible. Here, in the Emergency Department, a difference was being made. Lives were saved. The work the staff here did made every other job in the world seem unimportant by comparison.

In front of Kylie, a row of bored and distraught people sat in moulded orange chairs. She found a spare seat next to a pale-faced woman in a gold puffer jacket with a toddler on her lap. Kylie flicked through the screens on her Fitbit: heart rate acceptable, step count again pathetically low. She really should do a few laps of the hospital but instead she flicked through a sixteen-year-old *New Idea*. She inadvertently made eye contact with the toddler, who buried his face in his mother's chest. The woman took this as an invitation.

'It's my dad, hey.' She spoke quickly, relieving some kind of psychic pressure. The skin of her face was tight, pulled up severely by her dark, high ponytail. 'He had a heart attack. My dad! I dunno how. All he does is watch the football on TV. He gets worked up though, hey.'

'If it helps, the survival rate after a cardiac event is improving all the time,' Kylie said. 'I just read a paper in *Circulation Research*.'

'A heart attack, though! My dad. You think they're bulletproof, that they'll be around forever.' Her head bobbled on her neck.

'My mum fell off a bar stool after three martinis because she was wearing stilettos and lecturing half the bar about the finer points of choosing a vibrator,' said Kylie.

'Good one,' the woman said. 'As if.'

The room hummed with a constant, high-frequency vibration, from either the vending machines in the hall or the range of medical machinery on the other side of the flimsy walls and curtains. High up in a corner of a room was a TV with the sound off, where Maggie Beer was making something with parsnips. The people waiting around her were mostly in pairs, Kylie noticed. Kylie was the only one on her own. If Gloria had broken her ankle last week, Colin would be here. It was all so monstrously unfair.

Sitting was suddenly impossible, so Kylie paced to the vending machines and stared through the glass where snacks of dubious nutritional value were queued and waiting. Even the muesli bars, huddled together with the dehydrated apple slices and popcorn in a faux-health food ghetto in the farthest machine, were unacceptably loaded with sugar and kilojoules. This was a hospital! Kylie had a good mind to write a letter. Yet for some reason, she bought a packet of Cheezels and wandered back to her seat where she crunched them with her eyes half-closed and her fingers turning orange under the resentful gaze of the neighbouring toddler. He stuck out his tongue at her. Kylie stuck hers out back at him. He then buried his finger in his nose up to the first knuckle.

Charming, Kylie thought.

Her phone pinged: a text from Tansy, checking in and offering again to swap with Kylie at the hospital.

I'm fine. No news yet, Kylie texted back.

Then her phone rang. It was Nick.

'Tansy just called,' he said. 'Mum, hey? What a classic.'

'She's one in a million, all right.' She told Nick they were still at the hospital.

'Do you want me to come in? Because I don't want you to, you know, reorganise the casualty department so that it functions more to your liking. Kidding. But also not really.'

'No thanks.'

'It's no drama. Or if not me, what about Monica? Or one of the Battle Axes?'

Yes, Monica or one of Gloria's axe-throwing team would have come had Kylie called them. An ember of fury was sparking inside Kylie's chest. She'd had a bad day already. She really didn't need this. She should be home now, working on her résumé, and Nick should be sitting on this plastic chair eating Cheezels in front of a resentful toddler. And she knew that Gloria would prefer Nick be here, or one of her friends. *Yes*, Kylie wanted to say. *Come in and take over*.

Instead, she said, 'I'll manage.'

'You always do this,' Nick said. 'We're here to help. We *want* to help.'

'I'll manage, I said.'

Nick groaned down the phone line. 'It's your funeral.'

After another hour or so, Gloria appeared in a wheelchair, her left foot outstretched and bandaged, her sequin coat draped over her shoulders and her handbag on her lap, a single platform heel poking out the top. She was accompanied by a doctor with dark hair in a plait who looked about twelve, if twelve-year-olds had enormous blueish circles under their eyes and an air of general exhaustion.

Kylie jumped up when she saw them. 'Well? How are you feeling now, Mum?'

'Excellent.' Gloria gazed into the middle distance. 'I haven't had this many drugs since Whitlam was in power.'

The doctor handed Kylie a huge X-ray envelope. 'Her ankle's broken.'

'Fuck!' said Gloria, as though she were hearing this for the first time.

'Indeed.' The doctor went on to explain that it was a left lateral malleolus fracture and Gloria was lucky in two ways: because she had come straight in, they could control the swelling (Kylie gave a silent prayer of thanks to Alice) and also because it was the best kind of broken ankle to have (at which point Gloria rolled her eyes). The X-rays showed good alignment so she didn't need surgery. They'd already made an appointment for her at an orthotics clinic to have a moon boot fitted first thing tomorrow.

'Tomorrow?' said Kylie.

'My daughter has an extremely important job and many people relying on her,' Gloria slurred. 'She can't be expected to drop everything. I'll manage on my own.'

'You must be Kylie,' said the doctor. 'Gloria tells me you really have your life together.'

'Kylie has always been exceptional.' Gloria blinked slowly and nodded her head a little. 'She has very high standards. Completely and utterly on top of everything.'

'Gloria says you have a great job where you're appreciated, that you have fabulous prospects.' The doctor dragged one hand across her head and gave her plait a sharp tug. 'I don't have the time to *find* a boyfriend, much less dump one. I haven't slept in two days.'

'Kylie's always been like that, since she was a little girl. Perfect at school, perfect at home. Never gave me a moment's worry.'

Kylie swallowed and buried her fists in the pockets of her jeans. 'Ah, yes, I'm both perfect and completely on top of everything. I'm sure the doctor doesn't want to talk about me. Back to your ankle?'

'I'm fine. Right as rain to head off.' She rested her head back against the back of the wheelchair.

'She'll need a lot of help at home for the next few weeks. And keep that ankle iced tonight.'

Kylie swallowed. 'How many weeks is a few? And how much help is a lot?'

'Six to eight, or thereabouts. It's probably best that she's not left alone, at least in the beginning. She can move around on crutches but any pressure on it will be pretty painful. And it's important to keep it elevated. Keep the weight off it as much as possible. Cooking, showering, going to the loo – she'll need assistance for all that.' The doctor dropped her chin to her chest. 'What I wouldn't give for a broken ankle. I'd sleep for a month.'

Gloria, her eyes glazed, looked up at Kylie. 'Do you know how long the shifts are for junior doctors? It's practically slave labour. No wonder doctors burn out.' Gloria was contorting her mouth as though she'd lost feeling in her face – but not enough to stop her talking. 'Suhala hasn't had a weekend off in three months. They need a better union. It's unconscionable.'

'Understaffing, that's part of the problem,' the doctor said. 'Not enough doctors, too many patients. We need more hands, it's as simple as that.'

'Suhala loves it, though. Don't you, Suhala?'

The doctor raised her eyebrows. 'Most days.'

Gloria's ankle looked . . . well, non-existent. Although it was strapped and had an icepack on either side, Kylie could tell it was the same shape exactly as an elephant's ankle, which was similarly non-existent.

'You'll need painkillers and muscle relaxants.' the doctor said. 'Here's a script, but do you have anything at home to get you through until morning?'

Gloria narrowed her eyes. 'Maybe. One or two. Nothing to worry about, Suhala, all completely above board.'

'That sounds very . . . legal, when you put it like that. And don't give your daughter any trouble.'

Gloria turned in the chair to look at her. 'Who, me?'

It was almost one in the morning. By now, Kylie had realised that this, Disaster Number Three, would take up more of her life than one night.

'Let's get you home,' Kylie said to Gloria.

Chapter 10

Gloria was quiet on the ride back to her house, but that was because she was pleasantly drugged. Kylie wasn't so lucky. She had a lot to think about.

For example, Gloria's bedroom was upstairs so Kylie would need to set her up on the old sofa bed in the spare room downstairs, currently used as a study of sorts, though Kylie remained unconvinced that any actual study took place in there. Would Gloria agree to the downgrade? Or would she be difficult about wanting to sleep in her own bed? And how could Kylie possibly be at work in the pharmacy tomorrow morning to make a good impression on Gail, while at the same time take Gloria to have her moon boot fitted and look after her during the day?

The end result of all this strategising was that while Kylie appeared to be in the front seat of an Uber travelling down Canterbury Road with her mother asleep in the back, in reality, she was in a time machine careering into her past.

Even when they arrived at Gloria's house and negotiated her inside and Gloria agreed to sleep downstairs, Kylie still didn't register the psychological effects of this return to the house of her childhood. She was too busy. First, she parked Gloria on the couch while she checked the medicine cabinet. Inside was a vast assortment of painkillers: paracetamol with and without codeine; ibuprofen of every brand; aspirin of every type; along with some prescription opioids and some iffy unlabelled tablets in random containers.

'I couldn't find your pyjamas,' Kylie said, when she returned downstairs, arms laden with reading glasses, tissues, ibuprofen, a fat Hilary Mantel and hand cream.

'That's because I sleep naked.' Gloria's eyes were closed.

'Yeah, not while I'm here you don't.'

Gloria wrinkled up her face. 'You must take after your father, the prude.'

After some hunting, Kylie found an old cotton nightie in the back of a dresser drawer and helped Gloria change. Kylie held her up at the sink so she could brush her teeth, then she made up the ancient sofa bed and arranged Gloria with her icepacks and pillows under her foot.

More icepacks would be ideal, Kylie realised. On a whim, she checked the freezer. Inside were ice cubes of different shapes (expected), a bottle of vodka (definitely expected) and half a dozen bags of frozen peas (unexpected). Gloria was queen of the cheese platter, of the pâté on toast. The most she ever cooked was an omelette so why she had so many peas, Kylie couldn't imagine. She strapped two bags to Gloria's ankle with tape.

Neither Gloria nor Kylie talked much through all these exertions. Gloria was dozing and Kylie knew better than to speak because if she spoke, she'd vent, and if she vented she'd have to be angry at the person who was responsible for putting her in this position.

And who was that thoughtless, selfish, responsible person? Gloria, mostly, because she wore those ridiculous shoes. Tansy was partly to blame because, despite offering to help, she was already stretched too thin. It was Nick's fault as well because although he had offered, he was altogether too cavalier about everything and Kylie couldn't trust him to do things right. Monica also bore some responsibility. If she hadn't been already committed on Tuesday nights, she would have been in the bar with them and probably been here instead of Kylie.

So instead of thinking or talking, Kylie grabbed some sheets and a pillow from the linen cupboard and made up her mother's couch, the same brown leather one she'd sat on when she was five years old.

'Goodnight, Mum,' Kylie said. But Gloria was already asleep.

From the couch, Kylie could see the teal wall-to-wall shag carpet and the twisted metal wall sculpture, all unchanged. When she turned her head, she saw the palm-frond wallpaper in the kitchen and, if she leaned forward and looked down the hall, the amber glass bricks on either side of the front door. There was a misshapen pottery ashtray on the glass and chrome coffee table that was bought at the school art show back when people used to smoke, and each of the three ornately framed paintings featured gumtrees and a horse, and one had a swaggie. Every room had heavy curtains, and none of those curtains matched – one set was floor to ceiling gold damask with a plastic liner. It was as though the nineties had never happened, as though the 2000s and the 2010s and these early years of the 2020s were still to come.

Upstairs would be even worse, she knew. Why had all evidence of Kylie's bedroom disappeared? What had become of all her old childhood toys – her Barbies, and the hospital bunk beds made from shoeboxes where she'd splinted their broken limbs with Paddle Pop sticks and ribbon; the plastic skeleton named Yorick that hung in one corner. Was it because Kylie had been the first to move out, shortly after she'd started uni? Or, as she half-suspected, would Nick and Tansy's rooms be kept as shrines regardless of the moving-out order? Seeing their rooms exactly as they were reminded her of Tansy and Nick as small children, and she remembered that old desperate clawing worry, as though her heart was physically outside of her chest. Gloria had kept Tansy's and Nick's rooms unchanged for a reason. She had removed all trace of Kylie for the same reason.

She shut her eyes and tried to sleep on her side. Then on her other side. She sat up and rested her head against the back of the couch. Soon her Fitbit would need charging and she hadn't brought the charger and Gloria wouldn't have one – that kind of sensible monitoring of her health parameters was in direct opposition to Gloria's laissez-faire approach to everything. Take this house, for example.

The feeling that other people reported when returning to their childhood home was that the building had somehow shrunk over the decades while you, the returnee, remained the same size. You felt like a giant moving through a house for dolls, people said, ducking so your head didn't bump on the ceiling, keeping your arms close to your body for fear of knocking over a lamp.

Kylie did not feel that way. This house's effect on Kylie was way creepier.

She felt that she, Kylie, was still here – but twelve-year-old Kylie. And if she sat up and turned her head, she could see twelve-year-old Kylie in the kitchen. She felt that she was here, still. That she'd always been here, she'd never left.

Tansy and Nick had been too young to remember life before their father went away, and Gloria had deliberately expunged all evidence from her brain. Kylie alone remembered.

When you're a kid, your own family is all that you know so your own family becomes your definition of normal. It was only when Kylie went to her friends' homes after school that she realised other families were different from her own. One thing young Kylie noticed was that other kids' mums were kind, mostly. They scowled sometimes, and grumbled when hordes of kids descended on their houses after school, but they still delivered plates of Iced VoVos and orange cordial to the bedroom where half the kids in the street were gathered around a canasta tournament, or to the backyard, where some complicated game was in progress involving sharpened sticks being thrown at small children.

So often though, there would be a scattering of kids the moment a father's car pulled up in the drive. The energy of the whole house would change. Fathers brought a grizzling, cranky aura of unwelcome. Fathers worked hard. They didn't know their kids' friends and they didn't want random kids at their home.

Her own father was never like that. When David was at home – in this very home, where nothing had changed – everything seemed calmer somehow. He travelled a lot for business but Kylie remembered playing Monopoly on rainy weekends and, through her bedroom wall, the soft sounds of him and Gloria talking in bed at night. His car was in the garage and his suits were in the wardrobe and every little thing betrayed his presence: the business magazines lying on the floor on his side of her parent's bed; his 10CC albums stacked beside the record player. He was steady. She remembered the clang and tinkle of him emptying coins from his pockets to the crystal bowl on the dresser when he got home from work at night. You could set your watch by him falling asleep on the couch at 9.30 pm. The reliability of your father being as surprised as you when you opened birthday and Christmas presents accompanied by a card that said, *With love from Mum and Dad.*

One moment they had lived with David in their family house, in a family suburb, the five of them. Then all at once, as though a witch had cast a spell, he vanished. His clothes were gone, and his car. The house no longer smelled of him. The space David had filled now seemed to envelope the house, as if his very absence was something concrete and tactile. Every day from then on was tinged with a kind of anticipation, as though their father was just about to walk in the door. But he never did.

And now he never would again. David had moved away, and remarried, and had Monica. He died in 2020 but his memorial service had been postponed until last year so that more people could attend. It was a beautiful ceremony, in Tansy's friend Naveen's backyard – although Gloria had, as usual, orchestrated something else behind the scenes so that almost nothing about the day seemed to be about David. Kylie had been the only person thinking of David at all.

Now that she thought back, it was the day of her father's memorial last year that things had started to go wrong for Kylie. Her insomnia had begun to get worse, as had her need to tighten her grip on all the loose things in the world. That's when the ad for the Fitbit had popped up in her feed and at once she knew how much better her life would be if she owned one. The very act of strapping it on her wrist made her feel that everything was in its place.

It wasn't the Fitbit's fault, but look at her now – out-of-control job situation, out-of-control romantic life, out-of-control injured mother. Clearly Kylie needed to work harder, strategise better. Tighten her grip, re-order her life – otherwise everything would spin off its orbit. Her fingers went to the band on her wrist. If only a device could measure more parameters than merely the physical: current emotional commitment level perhaps, or job satisfaction, or parental patience quota.

This house was snap-frozen in the 1990s, and so was she.

The house was dark and still. Kylie found herself breathing faster. Colin was her father, she was Gloria; patterns of infidelity were repeating themselves before her eyes like wallpaper. She sat up, leaned forward and put her head between her knees.

WEDNESDAY

Chapter 11

Kylie woke to a distant ringing. She'd slept, if you could call it that, covered by a still-folded sheet in her underpants and a fitted yoga tee belonging to her mother. The lamp beside her was on and her eyes felt like the rim of a margarita glass and that ringing, that bloody ringing would not stop. Instinctively her fingers went to her Fitbit but the ringing wasn't an alarm. It wasn't in her head either. It was coming from her phone, wedged down the arm of the couch. She fumbled until she found it. It was Gloria.

'Finally,' Gloria said when she answered.

Kylie sat up, blinking.

'I've been dying for a cup of tea,' Gloria said, still talking into the phone.

'That is . . .' Kylie began, before ending the call and dragging herself upright. Her sleep patterns had not been helped by being roused twice during the night to change the peas, nor by the slats of Gloria's couch, like railway tracks under her spine. Her feet throbbed as she staggered to the spare room door. 'It's disconcerting, waking up with someone staring at you like that. It's an invasion of my personal space.'

Gloria laughed. '*Your* personal space? You spent nine months *in* my personal space. Literally inside it.'

Kylie threw her head back and crossed her eyes. 'Not my idea.' She yawned.

'It's not uncommon for women your age to sleep badly, Kylie. Your hormones are surging like nobody's business. *And* you're newly single. Sleeping alone takes practice.'

'It's not that,' Kylie said. 'It's this top, it's like a straitjacket. Don't you own anything loose?'

Gloria didn't. Anything baggy or old went straight to the op shop, or else she repurposed it into racquet grips or sweat bands on the Janome in Kylie's old room.

Kylie blinked again, and focused. 'You can't possibly wake up looking like that.'

Gloria's face was flawless, like she was a woman in a soap opera set in a mythical small town – ostensibly in Northern California but actually filmed in Canada for the tax advantages – who woke with fresh make-up, as though forest elves had broken into her cabin and painted her face during the night. Her lips were a fresh and shimmery rose, her eyelids the colour of warm cognac.

'A little mascara, a touch of eyeshadow, a smidge of lip gloss. Brushed my hair. Don't give me that face – I didn't get up. I used the make-up and mirror in my handbag.'

Honestly, how frivolous! How anti-feminist! It's a miracle Kylie turned out to be so pragmatic with Gloria setting this kind of antiquated, patriarchal example. Kylie was a serious person and serious people did not smear shimmery pink goo on their faces.

'Mum. You have a broken ankle. There's no one here but us. You don't have to look perfect every minute.'

Gloria rubbed along her cheekbones, blending something that Kylie couldn't detect. 'Oh my darling, make-up is *not* about being perfect. Throughout history humans have responded to art and art is not merely something that hangs on a wall. We can *each* be a work of art by expressing our authentic selves. There's much joy to be found in colour and design.'

Joy? What would *joy* achieve? What was the point of it? Absolutely nothing. Kylie opened the camera on her phone and examined herself, then looked back at Gloria. It was Kylie who looked like the patient, and not merely of a broken ankle. She felt bloated and crampy and she looked like the victim of a hit-and-run who'd landed in a tree.

'What does that say about me, Mum?'

'It says you're naturally beautiful, my beautiful girl,' said Gloria. 'But if you wanted to borrow some lippy that would be fine too.'

Kylie made her not-amused face, which was just her usual face. Honestly! She was in her forties – it was far too late to become the kind of person who wears *lippy*. By the time a woman is Kylie's age, every aspect of her appearance is frozen in carbonite, like Han Solo. The hairstyle you have at forty, for example, is the hairstyle you'll have until you die. (Your movie references also stagnate after thirty-five.)

She threw on her jeans, top and boots from last night – which, with her hit-and-run hair and margarita-glass eyes, gave her a Courtney-Love-at-a-bail-hearing vibe – gathered herself and set about repeating last night in reverse: helping Gloria with her toilette, brushing her teeth then dressing her. She sent a quick text to Tim to let him know she wouldn't be in. Taking a day off was no problem – she occasionally did, because Tim disapproved of her working six days a week. This kind of short notice, however, made his life difficult. She hoped he could organise a locum to cover for her.

She turned her attention to breakfast. At home, Kylie made overnight oats with chia seeds and yoghurt in glass jars for her and Colin, weighing each ingredient on her digital scales the night before. (At the thought, a chia seed of resentment sprouted within her, towards ungrateful men who took home-made, nutritionally balanced breakfasts for granted.) In Gloria's cupboards, there were no oats or chia seeds, no fibre-enriched cereal or wholemeal bread, and there was nothing in fridge except seventeen different half-opened chutneys, an equal number of jars of assorted pickles, various jars of green olives (for martinis, Kylie guessed, not for eating) and one of maraschino cherries (similarly, but for whiskey sours). How long had it been since Gloria's fridge had been properly cleaned? Kylie hated to think.

While at the fridge, Kylie swapped last night's packets of peas for fresh ones and held a packet up to Gloria. 'Cornering the market?'

'I like peas, don't make a federal case about it,' said Gloria.

'There is nothing else to eat in here. What do you usually have for breakfast?' Kylie asked. 'Toast? Coffee?'

'Who does carbs before midday? No one, that's who.'

What kind of rock was her mother living under? A *magic* rock under which Gloria was *not* a woman in her mid-sixties whose blood sugar would most certainly benefit from the stabilising effect of complex carbohydrates and gut-friendly fibre being broken down by the body to make long-lasting energy?

'What if I make you a diet plan, with some easy breakfast ideas?' Kylie said.

'What if you make me . . . a tea?'

So Kylie made her a tea. Black, two sugars.

'What do you call that?' Gloria said, when she saw it. 'You know how I take my tea.'

Kylie did know. For some reason beyond her comprehension, she had made tea for Colin, which was absolutely infuriating. She vowed never to make black tea with two sugars for anyone, ever again. She stomped back to the kitchen and made another for Gloria: milk, no sugar.

The second cup fared no better.

'That tea is so pale it could be in the cast of *Neighbours*,' said Gloria. Please don't tell me you put the milk in first. Could things get any worse? First, I break my ankle, then you put the milk in first.'

Kylie breathed, which was supposed to relax her but did nothing but supply more oxygen to her smouldering brain. This was the kind of nonsense that would be banned on pain of death when Kylie was crowned Emperor of the Universe. She refrained from telling Gloria that whether you put the milk in first or not, it all winds up in the same cup and then in your stomach. That's science. Instead she took the tea back into the kitchen and made another cup. This time the colour was right but, according to Gloria, the water had been too hot when added to the cup.

'Boil it, then cool it down?' Kylie said. 'That's ludicrous.'

Gloria rolled her eyes. 'Despite what you may think, you don't know everything, Kylie.' She drank the tea anyway, grimacing for effect.

'Close the roof,' Gloria said. She was settled on the back seat with her foot extended. Gloria rarely drove the convertible – her third grandchild, she often called it – with the roof closed.

Kylie turned from where she sat behind the wheel. Gloria was wearing a paisley silk scarf covering her hair, tied under her chin, and large Jackie O sunglasses. She looked amazing, frankly. If Kylie were to attempt the same, she would looked like an elderly Greek peasant recovering from a corneal graft.

'Hiding from the paparazzi?' said Kylie.

'I don't want any of my friends to see me incapacitated,' Gloria said. 'They'll think I'm old.'

'Mum, you can't care about things like that,' said Kylie. 'Also, who would see you?'

'The Battle Axes, the girls from my U3A Medieval Poisons class, everyone from the tennis club. I have lots of friends,' Gloria said.

Fine, yes. Gloria had lots of friends, including her axe-throwing team. Definitely more than Kylie, who only had Alice. She and

Colin – back when there was a *Kylie and Colin* – had *couple friends*, yes, but couple friends weren't *actual* friends. They'd hosted their couple friends for barbecues and movie nights and visited their places. She liked most of them – and those she hadn't liked, Colin no longer saw (after Kylie had explained in detail what was wrong with them). She'd connected with the female halves of these approved couple friends (and with Oliver, who was married to Trent). She'd seen a matinee at the Nova with one of them.

After you split up with someone though, it soon becomes obvious that couple friends are like library books. You can hang on to them for a while but at some point they always go back to where they belong. And all of Kylie's couple friends belonged with Colin. They were his work friend plus partner, his cricket friend plus partner, his uni friend plus partner. They were all a part of Kylie's former couple life, the life with Colin in it. The hole in Kylie's new life was larger than just a boyfriend. Kylie didn't expect to ever see his friends again.

It took her a few moments to get the feel for the car because Gloria was one of the few people in the western world who still drove a manual. When they were at last on their way, Kylie called Tim. She put him on speakerphone – proof that lack of sleep was a direct cause of stupidity.

'Did the locum arrive?' Kylie said.

'Yes and no. Is your mother okay? She did it *how*?' said Tim.

Kylie explained.

'Poor Gloria.' Tim's voice crackled through the car. 'She's at that age where one break can throw her off for good.

Some people never recover. And she has such an active job. She'll be retiring now, I guess.'

'I can hear you,' yelled Gloria from the back seat. 'You must be seventy if you're a day, you old trout.'

'Mum!' said Kylie.

'I missed that, Kylie,' said Tim. 'Can you speak up?'

'You deaf old trout!' yelled Gloria.

'Mum says hello, and that you're an inspiration to everyone your age,' Kylie said.

'Gloria said that? How sweet. Give her my best. What can I do to help? Do you need the whole week off?'

'Absolutely not! I mean, no, thanks for asking. I'll work Saturday to make up the time. I'm calling a nursing agency next, so I'll be back tomorrow.'

Gloria turned towards Kylie, her head spinning like Linda Blair. 'A nursing agency! You most certainly will not. I do not want a stranger in my home. I'm quite capable of looking after myself.'

'Did you not hear what the doctor said? You're going to need assistance.'

'I am a grown woman who will not be babysat like a child. I can make my own decisions.'

'Clearly you can't, because this would be a bad one.'

On the phone, Tim chuckled. 'I'll leave you both to it, shall I? And don't worry about taking the day off. I've stressed to Gail that you're extremely reliable. Usually. It's just bad luck! A weird coincidence that only makes you *seem* unreliable! Honestly, Pharmacy King needs to calm down about one day off! And Emily is fantastic. Fits in perfectly.'

'Emily?'

'Gail arranged for her to come in. I don't know how she arrived so quickly – it was almost as if she was waiting in her car in case someone called! She's one of their casuals – young, keen, very smart. Looking for a full-time position. Anyway, you should focus on Gloria! I'm almost positive this will play no part in your job application.'

Kylie swallowed. 'Almost positive?'

'Very positive,' said Tim. 'Extremely, completely positive. Ninety-eight per cent. Roughly.'

After Tim rang off, Gloria stretched out again on the back seat. 'I don't know how you can work for that man. Some people have no tact whatsoever,' Gloria said, laying her head back and shutting her eyes. 'What was he saying about Pharmacy King? And what job application?'

'He wasn't saying anything,' said Kylie as she crunched the gears. 'There is absolutely nothing for you to worry about.'

There was nothing for Kylie to worry about either. This *Emily* person couldn't have as much experience as Kylie. She wouldn't know their systems, their customers. She was no threat whatsoever.

Gloria sat bolt upright. 'As soon as someone tells me not to worry, that's when I worry. Tell me.'

The more Kylie tried to distract Gloria from asking about Pharmacy King, the more insistent she became. Gloria lay in the back seat of the convertible, not behaving incapacitated in the slightest, bombarding Kylie with questions.

'You can tell me, or I can ask Tansy. And if Tansy won't tell me, she'll have told Simon and I can *definitely* get it out of

Simon.' She cracked her knuckles like a mafiosa. 'Simon will fold straight away.'

That was true. Simon was defenceless against Gloria. He was terrified of her. When she spoke to him, he sometimes shut his eyes as though he were a toddler trying to be invisible.

So while Kylie drove, she gave Gloria the most whitewashed, sterilised, rose-coloured-glasses version of Disaster Number One. She used phrases like *a bigger fish in a bigger pond* and *once-in-a-lifetime opportunity* and *climbing the corporate ladder*. She even mentioned the possibility of a lanyard.

Her mother had no experience with Kylie's profession, or of having a boss at all. She would surely be impressed.

Gloria was not impressed.

'How *dare* they ask you to apply for your own job!' she spluttered. 'Don't they know you were *junior pharmacist* of the *year*!'

That's right – Kylie had been Junior Pharmacist of the Year (Melbourne East Division) not long after she'd started working for Tim. How could she have forgotten? There was an engraved silver tray and a framed certificate on her wall at home to prove it. Kylie had aimed for that award. Focused on it. She'd studied previous winners and made a strategy to work smarter, and harder, and attract the attention of the right people. It had been one of her five-year goals.

She hadn't been expecting such a fast result but at the very next conference, Kylie's was the name called and for one shining moment, she was successful. She went from being a normal woman sitting at a professional association dinner to someone up on stage, acknowledged as Junior Pharmacist of the Year (Melbourne East Division).

The shock and thrill of achieving what she'd wanted for so long had lasted only seconds. By the time she'd phoned Gloria to tell her, Kylie wondered why on earth she'd cared so much for a lame certificate in a frame and a dinky silver tray that she could have picked up in an op shop for five bucks.

It had been the same with every goal Kylie had ever aimed for, she realised. She'd spent her whole life setting herself challenges that were motivating and alluring, floating just out of reach – a distant mountain top that spurred her to work harder, do more. If only she could finish the next course, reorganise another process, master one more skill, everything would be different. Yet everything Kylie wanted so desperately became intensely anticlimactic once she'd achieved it.

That's why it was such a crushing disappointment that her plans to buy Tim's pharmacy had been dashed. That was the goal to end all goals, the achievement that would have made everything in her life better. Finally, Kylie would have had the accomplishment she'd been searching for.

'This is just a temporary setback,' Kylie told Gloria, with as much confidence as she could muster. 'I'll be back where I belong before you know it. I promise.'

Gloria frowned. 'I'm not convinced, but there's nothing we can do at the moment. Now, as to this silly question of a nurse – I'm not having one. I'm not ill and I refuse to be infantilised by my own child. Do I make myself clear?'

Kylie nodded, because it *was* clear. *Of course* she understood that her mother didn't want to be told what to do. People rarely did. They *should*, of course. If people could just knuckle down and do what they were told, everything would be easier for everyone. Kylie had seen it her entire life: kids at school who hadn't wanted to do their homework despite good grades being vital for their future; her friends at uni drinking too much despite how ill they would feel in the morning. Humans didn't eat right, exercise right, organise their homes right, choose the right spouses, read the right books, stick to their budgets. They ate too much and slept too little and wasted too much time on social media. It was maddening, of course, this refusal to act in their own best interests.

Just as well Kylie was here to help.

Could this attitude of hers have made it difficult for her to maintain relationships? Could her recent split with Colin have anything to do with Kylie knowing with all certainty that she knew best for everyone?

Absolutely not. She liked doing things properly, that was all. She had an eye for detail, a keen sense of organisation. In nine short months, she'd revolutionised Colin's life! When they'd met, he'd spent hours playing video games and he'd lived on halal snack packs. She used to find McDonald's bags tucked under the front seat of his car! He didn't eat breakfast! None at all! It was Kylie who'd encouraged him to grow up, to take better care of himself. She'd helped him put in for a promotion and taught him how to stack the dishwasher properly. And what had he done for her? Absolutely nothing.

'Kylie?' said Gloria. 'There is a difference between being *in charge of myself*, which I am, and being *controlling*. I don't want a nurse. Are we clear?'

Wow. Kylie was not *controlling*, that was the first thing. If everyone around her wanted to make terrible, terrible mistakes, that was on their heads. And secondly, Gloria's position was clear – but that didn't mean anything in practical terms. Kylie was a hundred per cent right about this nurse business and her mother was wrong. It was as simple as that.

Kylie opened her mouth to tell Gloria exactly what she thought – but just then they arrived at the foot clinic and Gloria was hustled into a room.

Oh, sure, she could have continued to argue about it, but there was no logic whatsoever behind Gloria's position. Kylie *had* to return to work. Tansy and Nick also had jobs. The doctor had made it clear that Gloria shouldn't be left alone. Gloria could afford to pay for a nurse. She wasn't rolling in it, but she had some money tucked away for emergencies.

So while Kylie sat in the waiting room beneath a television playing advertisements for dinky-looking jewellery, she googled 'nursing agency', and then she rang one, and then she booked a nurse with physical therapy experience to come to the house first thing in the morning, in direct contravention of Gloria's wishes.

Chapter 12

The boot was a heavy black monstrosity and at first, Gloria seemed to loathe it.

'Does it come in any other colours?' she asked the poor technician.

He looked at Kylie, as if to check if Gloria was joking. 'Only black.'

'Black is very minimising,' Gloria said.

Kylie nodded. Of course black was minimising, that was the whole point. It was slimming, elegant, subtle. Kylie wore black, mostly. She wore a navy suit to work so she looked cheerful for her customers.

'I loathe minimising,' said Gloria. 'Be seen! Be heard! Refuse to fade away!'

Then, after a few practice laps of the clinic with her new crutches, admiring herself in the window of the cafe next door, she became wistful.

'I wish it didn't hurt so much when I touch anything,' she said, gazing at her boot with almost admiration. 'I could do some real damage if I kicked someone with that thing.'

Gloria stayed in the car while Kylie shopped for groceries then, at home, she settled Gloria on the couch with her foot elevated.

'Can I get you a book?' Kylie said.

'Maybe later.'

'How about some TV?'

'Christ, no,' said Gloria. 'Daytime television has too many ugly people.'

'Wow, judgey.'

'I didn't mean ugly in appearance, I meant in spirit,' said Gloria. 'Interesting that you immediately assumed I meant physically. Who's the judgey one, actually?'

Kylie opened and closed her hands into fists and creaked her neck from side to side. If she'd had hackles, they would be rising. She had expected an elderly woman with a broken ankle to be like a koala or a cruise ship passenger – happy to eat and nap for eighteen hours a day. She breathed. She forced herself to recall all the horrific stories Gloria had ever told about Kylie's birth – every stretch mark, every moment of screaming agony, every peritoneal stitch – tried to conjure the original, lifelong, red-ink guilt in the ledger of daughters that sprang from having a pristine, pre-childbirth replica of their mother's body.

'Didn't you tell me your tax is late? I could put a few chairs together and set you up at the dining table and we could do it together?'

Gloria looked at Kylie as though she were a kitten in sunglasses behind the wheel of a tiny car. 'My tax? I'd love to help with that, except I don't want to. But I know you worry about things being late so please, be my guest.'

Kylie worry about being late? Gloria was completely wrong. Kylie did not waste her time worrying about Gloria being late for everything, almost all the time – late for her tax, her utility bills, her health checks and her wilful disregard for being comfortably seated in time for the ads before the movie starts. Kylie also did not worry about being late *herself*, because she was never late.

In fact . . . Kylie had a sudden thought. What with everything that had happened in the last few days – her job, Colin, her mother's ankle – she had forgotten her period. Her always-regular, perfectly predictable period, as disciplined and organised as Kylie herself, had been due on Sunday. It still hadn't arrived. See how relaxed she was, about being late? So relaxed that she hadn't even noticed until now. Obviously Kylie's Three Disasters had thrown off her bodily equilibrium. Her period would arrive soon, in a matter of hours probably. In contrast, there would be consequences for Gloria's late tax but Kylie would not look after it. No way.

Only another twenty-four hours until the nurse comes tomorrow, Kylie told herself. Then Gloria would be someone else's responsibility and everything would be back to normal.

All this standing around was exhausting. Kylie was practised at coping after a night of insomnia – she lived most of her life in a state of focused, determined animation – but the trick was to keep on your feet, keep moving. Once you stopped, the tiredness crept into your bones and you felt you'd never stand again.

Besides, there were lots of things around this museum of a house to keep Kylie busy. How could anyone live in this chaos! Gloria's front yard needed raking, the dishwasher was making a funny noise, and who knows how long it had been since Gloria had cleaned the filter on the washing machine? Kylie was here for the rest of the day – she might as well make the best of things.

While Gloria flicked idly through fashion magazines, Kylie began ferrying the dozens of random jars from the fridge to the kitchen bench and wiping down their sticky sides and crusty rims with hot soapy water. Who on earth ate pumpkin and cumquat relish? And banana chilli jam sounded like a crime against nature. Could a woman in her mid-sixties be pregnant? Half of the weirdo condiments were past their use-bys – Gloria ignored dates on jars, which she considered part of a giant conspiracy by Big Pickle to encourage food waste and subsequent repurchase. As Kylie scraped sticky residue from a jar of lime gherkins with a best before of 2015, Kylie wondered why jobs like these always fell to her instead of Tansy or Nick.

Gloria might believe pickles last forever but alas, Kylie's patience would not.

Chapter 13

It wasn't until midafternoon that Gloria succumbed to a nap. Taking advantage of the lull in proceedings, Kylie nipped home. She needed more clothes, her reading glasses, extra tampons and her Fitbit charger, among other things. She also wanted to stand in the glorious, sparse stillness of her own home.

She had finished packing and was walking past her study when the framed certificate hanging over her filing cabinet caught her gaze. *Junior Pharmacist of the Year*, it said. She walked over and brushed her fingertips down the glass. She looked closer. She'd forgotten who the sponsor of her award had been, its name embossed on the certificate in letters larger than her own: Pharmacy King. That's right, she remembered now. The CEO, Brian Challis, her soon-to-be boss, had presented it to her himself. He was a tall man in an exquisite suit who'd given a droning speech about employing more women in pharmacy. She'd immediately enrolled in the workshop he was giving the next day: *Initiative and Assertiveness for Women and Other Under-represented Groups.*

Brian was still CEO of Pharmacy King; she'd read a profile of him in a trade magazine just last month.

Kylie had met him for only a few moments, years ago. It was slim, but still, it was a connection. Would Brian remember her? If the CEO of the whole company agreed to be her referee, her application would be impossible to overlook.

Kylie opened her filing cabinet and flicked through the folders of notes from each of the *many* courses and workshops and seminars that had filled her weeknights and weekends for years, on topics from vaccinations and injections to advanced pharmacokinetics to human resources, in anticipation for the day the pharmacy belonged to her. Preparation is key! Her notes from Brian's workshop were extensive but unnecessary because she remembered almost everything: *develop a personal brand and leadership identity*, Brian had said. *Practise stronger handshakes.* Also, women typically soften their communication by using qualifiers and asking permission. And women apologise too much! In business, you should *never apologise* because apologies admit fault, and fault implies liability. The default language of business is male so to succeed in business, women should learn to speak like men.

That workshop was a complete waste of time because Kylie never did any of those things anyway. Now, she realised, the course had benefitted her in two ways. One, she'd met Brian. And two, she knew he appreciated women who showed initiative.

She reached for her phone.

An hour later she was in a posh suburb on the other side of the river, parked out the front of a cafe. It was the kind of suburb without beggars on the street and with nature strips manicured like putting greens. People dressed better over here. They had better hair and were fitter, or at least owned more activewear.

The house across the road was a gorgeous two-storey terrace painted deep charcoal grey, with black iron railings and clumps of agapanthus along the fence line. It was definitely the kind of place a CEO would live.

I'll show him initiative and assertiveness as a woman or other under-represented group, Kylie thought.

The phone call to the Pharmacy King head office had been . . . weird. She'd explained who she was and what she wanted to Brian's assistant who, by some miracle, had put her through. After a short wait, she'd explained it all again to Brian himself – she'd met him years ago at the award ceremony, she'd done his course, she was applying for a job at Pharmacy King, yada yada. Could she include his name in her referees?

It was an incredible overreach. She half-expected Brian to hang up on her. Instead, he invited her to his house for what he called an 'informal screening'. But, he'd said, she needed to come *immediately*.

To his *house*? Immediately? That had been an unexpected development.

Now, Kylie crossed the road and knocked on the glossy yellow door. After a few moments, Brian opened it, still tall and distinguished but looking like the father of the man she remembered. Behind him, a long hall of pale wood extended deep into the house, leading to a glass wall at the back, beyond which was a shock of green and an azure pool. Both sides of the hall were dotted with paintings in heavy frames. The whole place smelled of fabric softener.

'Kylie Schnabel,' he said. 'It's been a long time.'

'I wasn't sure you'd remember me,' she said.

'Junior Pharmacist of the Year. How could I forget? And your . . . contributions in my workshop were extremely . . . memorable,' said Brian. 'I was surprised that you enrolled, to be frank. I wouldn't have picked you as someone who needed assertiveness training.'

He remembered her! Excellent. Kylie repeated what she wanted – for him to be her referee for her job application. 'I think I have a future at Pharmacy King,' she said. 'I think I could excel there.'

Brian didn't seem to be listening. He looked distracted, as though he was thinking of something else. Perhaps she should have brought the certificate with her.

'Is that the Uber?' a woman's voice called out from somewhere in the house.

Brian stood in his art-strewn house, with its glass walls and sparkling pool, and considered Kylie, the supplicant before him. 'Regarding whether or not I would act as a referee for someone I barely know and have never worked with,' Brian said, 'that's an excellent question. Upon reflection, I guess I would . . . if I was satisfied they were the kind of person prepared to go the extra mile. A real team player. Someone who has my back at all times.'

'That's me,' said Kylie. 'I always go the extra mile. I'm here, aren't I?' She noticed two matching gold suitcases lined up in the hall behind him, and Brian himself, in blue chinos and a floral shirt. 'You're going somewhere.'

'Tiffany's nephew's wedding,' Brian said, running his finger down the page. 'Palm Cove, four nights. We should be leaving now, but we've had a small problem with Caesar.' He called towards the back of the house. 'Darling, could you come here a moment?'

'Caesar?' said Kylie.

'Our baby. By baby, I mean our dog.' The problem, Brian went on to explain, was that just before Kylie's call, they'd received a text from their pet sitter, cancelling.

Kylie made sympathising noises.

'I gave her a piece of my mind, obviously. It's a sad part of life, Kylie, but unreliable people are everywhere,' Brian said. 'I see it every day, even in an organisation as well run as Pharmacy King. Our pet sitter is a prime example. No gumption. One little car accident and she deserts us.'

An approaching clatter down the hall announced a woman, dressed all in white linen, coming towards them. She wore sandals that slapped against the floor with each step, a jangle of bangles on each wrist and oversized sunglasses on top of her head. But neither the bangles nor the sunglasses were the first things Kylie noticed. In the woman's arms was a tiny Pomeranian, luxuriously furred, the colour of rich butterscotch. It was wearing a freshly ironed blue-striped shirt and it looked like a stockbroker on the cover of *Canine Money Magazine.*

It was an alert, smiling dog. It radiated good-hearted beneficence towards Kylie.

'This is Caesar,' Brian said. 'A magnificent animal, yes?'

'And I'm Tiffany.' She shook her head. 'It's devastating. It's called a minor concussion because it's *minor*? That means almost nothing at all. Wait until she sees my Google review.'

Caesar wriggled in Tiffany's arms. Its small pink tongue panted towards Kylie. She looked closer. She realised, to her horror, that she had that exact same blue and white striped cotton shirt but the dog looked better in it.

'I'm sure you can google a kennel,' said Kylie.

'A kennel!' Tiffany said. 'I couldn't possibly enjoy Palm Cove while poor Caesar was in dog Gitmo. I'm going, Brian is staying behind to look after him.'

'Unless we find a mature, responsible person who could take Caesar for a few days.' Brian stared at Kylie, meaningfully. 'Someone prepared to go the extra mile.'

'*Her*?' said Tiffany.

'It'll be too depressing for you to stay in that beachfront suite by yourself, darling,' said Brian. 'Besides, we'd forfeit the cost of my flight. Business class.'

'Are you sure she's . . . suitable?' said Tiffany.

'Kylie is diligent, has an exemplary record, first-aid training and a methodical mind.' Brian raised one eyebrow at Kylie. 'I'd consider your request for a reference favourably. Very favourably.'

Kylie knew nothing about dogs. She'd never had one, not even as a child. She wasn't an animal person.

'How can you possibly know I'm capable of looking after your dog?'

'I know you're a perfectionist. I called your pharmacy just now and the former owner there – Tom something-or-other – well, he told me you were the perfect employee. You never let anyone down, he said. Absolutely reliable.'

Tim was right. Kylie had never let anyone down, and she also knew an opportunity when she saw it. A fluffy, orange, squirming opportunity that would ensure Kylie kept her job, and remain where she belonged.

How hard could it be?

Kylie swallowed. 'I'd be delighted,' she said.

Caesar's honey-tipped ears pivoted to Kylie like miniature satellite dishes.

Chapter 14

Later that afternoon, Kylie was sitting at the dining room table in front of piles of papers and shoeboxes of crinkled receipts, deep in the eccentricities of Gloria's taxes, without Gloria's help. How could anyone live with their financial records in this state? It gave Kylie abdominal cramps just thinking about it. Then she heard the front door open.

It was obviously Nick. Kylie and Tansy had kept their keys to Gloria's house for emergencies but knocked when they visited out of respect for Gloria's privacy, while Nick let himself in as though he still lived here. Since retiring from his brief but glamorous football career, Nick had been a primary school teacher. It seemed an odd choice if you didn't know him well, but he'd always been an entertainer rather than an athlete and happiest when unequivocally the centre of attention. It was only his wardrobe that revealed he hadn't always survived on a teacher's salary.

'Kyles?' he called out.

Caesar, reclining on his fluffy day bed beside Kylie, leaped to his feet and barked.

Kylie leaned down to speak to Caesar. 'This is exactly what I was talking about,' she said. 'You need to give people a chance.'

'What the hell is *that*?' Nick said. 'And keep it away from me. These pants are Ted Baker.'

Honestly, how many times had Kylie told Nick that he shouldn't be spending his salary on designer clothes? They were a terrible investment. Maybe she could set him up with one of those budgeting apps.

The *that* Nick was panicking about was no more than a tiny orange Pomeranian wearing a diamanté collar – Kylie had taken off the blue and white striped shirt because, firstly, dogs in clothes were creepy, and secondly, dogs in clothes that looked like Kylie's made her feel . . . inadequate. Even unclothed, Caesar looked effortlessly chic, as though he were lead Pomeranian in a K-pop band.

Kylie explained, very slowly, that it was a dog.

'I've seen a dog before,' Nick said. 'That looks like the star of a Pixar movie about furry slippers that come to life. What is it doing in Mum's dining room? And why is it barking at me?'

'He's a house guest, and he's barking because he's a guard dog.' Kyle glared at Caesar until he dropped again, growling. 'He acts pretty tough for someone afraid of a vacuum cleaner.'

'House guest?'

'It's temporary,' Kylie said. 'A work-related emergency.'

Nick waved his hand towards Caesar's pile of gear. 'And all this?'

'The bare essentials, I'm told.'

Caesar's *bare essentials* included a bed and leads and toys that squeaked and toys that didn't and containers of food and snacks. Caesar travelled with pyjamas, a tiny Driza-Bone in case it rained and a woollen hat with a pompom in case it turned cold. He had things to chew and a seatbelt and harness for car trips. *Don't worry*, Tiffany had said, cheerfully, when giving Kylie the recipe for Caesar's favourite meal. *The Thermomix does the hard work for you.*

'What did Mum say?' asked Nick.

Kylie explained that Gloria was *underwhelmed* by her new house guest. They agreed upon the following: dog stays in the dining room, eats dry food only, is not allowed on the furniture or the carpeted areas under any circumstances. Should said dog destroy or any way harm any possession of Gloria's, or pee in any unauthorised spot, Kylie is morally and financially liable. Also, Gloria will not be interacting with it in any way.

'And no barking, Mum said.' Kylie looked down at Caesar. 'That means you.'

Caesar gave a soft whine and looked towards the door.

Then Nick clocked Kylie's face as she sat at the table in front of her laptop, amid piles of forms and stacks of manila folders and wads of receipts held together with, for some reason, tortoiseshell hair slides instead of paperclips.

'Wow, Kyles, you look like shit,' Nick said.

'Thanks so much, you're sweet.' He was right, though. Staring at Gloria's taxes had given Kylie the facial expression of a woman watching a four-hour Swedish film about man's search for meaning in a joyless universe, in mime.

'Seriously, you look like you live under a bridge,' Nick said to Kylie. 'Why are you doing this to yourself? Let someone help you.'

'Are you implying I can't manage? Because I can manage. I'm managing just fine.'

A voice called out from the bedroom, plaintive and deliberately thready, 'Is that my Nicky?'

'Just a sec, Mum,' he called out. Then to Kylie, 'Listen, we need to talk later.'

'While you're in there, tell her jewellery isn't a tax deduction.' Kylie circled a number on a pad, viciously. Why did everything fall upon her? *Colin* wouldn't do his mother's taxes, that was for sure. Wherever he was, whatever he was doing, and whomever he was doing it with, it wouldn't be that. Not that Kylie cared where he was or what he was doing, or with whom. At all.

Nick called out, 'Mum?' as though he'd hiked through a blizzard to find her instead of driven from Brunswick. He made his way through to the bedroom but Kylie could still hear them.

'Is that my baby boy?' Gloria said.

'Mum!' Nick said. 'Kylie has a dog out there.'

'I know! It's unhygienic. She had it in *my car*! With no warning. What is it *for*? What do you *do* with it?'

'You've got a broken ankle and you've read *The Accidental Tourist*,' Kylie yelled towards them. 'Teach it something.'

Nick shrugged. 'Also Kylie says that jewellery isn't a deduction, darling.'

Gloria sniffed. 'Shows how little she knows. It's *literally* called a tennis bracelet. That's *literally* my job. I have a good mind to find someone else to do my tax.'

'Someone who you'll also pay *nothing*?' Kylie leaned back on her chair so she could see them. 'Go right ahead!'

'Possibly she's had some kind of psychotic break and thinks the dog is her baby,' Gloria said in a stage whisper. 'She might have broken into somebody's house and kidnapped it.'

'You've got to look after yourself, Mum,' Nick said. 'I meant to bring you some flowers but the florist was closed. Something about a gas leak.'

'Oh Nicky, it's the thought that counts. So many people have reached out, it's been lovely. Even Monica rang to see if there was anything she could do for me because she wasn't working and a bit bored, but I told her not to worry because Kylie has everything in hand.'

'Give me strength,' muttered Kylie from the dining room table. She turned another page with receipts stapled to it, one of which seemed to be written in hieroglyphics, while keeping one eye on Gloria. 'You are unbelievable.'

'How lovely of you to come to see me. Kylie is running this place like a women's penitentiary. I wish you could look after me instead!'

'So do I, Mum, but you know it's impossible for Kylie to let go.'

'I can let go!' she yelled at them, while checking another receipt against Gloria's credit card statement. 'Just watch me!'

'In the old days I would have had a cast you could sign but they don't do that anymore.'

'In the old days you never would have broken your ankle,' he said. 'As soon as you're better, you're coming to the gym with me. More weight-bearing exercise, that's what you need.'

'I knew you'd understand, Nicky,' Gloria said. 'It's terribly depressing being the same age as old people.'

Kylie put her head in her hands. It was also terribly depressing being the same age as people in their early forties – having one single long hair appear on your chin overnight; all at once needing reading glasses in two separate strengths; and being philosophically opposed to owning a Thermomix but at the same time really wanting one. But you don't hear her complaining.

'It's such a shame you'll have to cancel the open day on Saturday,' said Nick.

The open day? Oh yes, Kylie had a vague memory of Gloria mentioning it when the paramedics were loading her into the ambulance. It was the biggest day of her year, when she signed up students for the term to come.

'What? No, absolutely not, I won't be cancelling,' Gloria said.

Regardless of your age, there was nothing so intriguing as the sound of your parent arguing with your sibling. Kylie wandered over to Gloria's room, crossed her arms and leaned against the doorjamb.

'But you have to cancel. You must.' Nick looked at Kylie, then back at Gloria. 'Kylie agrees.'

Gloria's open day involved children, sport and charm, so it was solidly in Nick's domain. There was no way Kylie would ever become involved in something like that. 'Leave me out of it.'

Gloria, in bed, crossed her arms also.

Nick was not deterred. He launched into an impassioned argument in support of cancelling the open day. He talked about the doctor's instructions: Gloria resting her ankle and not overdoing things, almost as though he'd been the one on hand himself, rather than just reading it in a text message from Kylie. Nothing was more precious than her health, he said. He was transparently motivated by a fear he'd be asked to do something.

'We're going ahead,' Gloria said. 'It's almost upon us, there's no way I'd be able to notify everyone in time.' She'd paid deposits for the face painter and the Rotary club had organised the sausages. She'd hired extra equipment and courts. A notice had gone up and RSVPs had been received. And – crucially – the open day was the source of her new students for the rest of the year. Gloria's income depended on it.

'Tennis is more important than the ankle of any one woman, even mine,' she said. 'We press on.'

Kylie was astonished. For once, Gloria was paying no attention to Nick.

'Kyles?' he said. 'Help?'

This was an excellent opportunity for Kylie to show her family and herself that she was not *rigid* or *controlling*, that she could enforce boundaries and let other people make their own mistakes. That she was a chill person. Relaxed.

'I'm sure you'll manage just fine,' she said in her most relaxed voice. Then she stepped lightly away from the doorway, put a lead on Caesar, grabbed some poo bags and headed off around the block.

Chapter 15

Kylie aimed for 10,000 steps per day but the official recommendations for exercise for adults were clear – at least two and a half hours of brisk walking per week. *Brisk*. Caesar, however, had neglected to read the official recommendations. While Kylie fingered her Fitbit, annoyance growing, Caesar sauntered. He pranced along beside her as though he was Queen of Moomba on a meet-and-greet, stopping to sniff everything, lift his leg with the grace of a ballerina and pee. The satisfaction on his pointy little face every time he squeezed out a few drops, as though he were making charitable donations!

'Come on, come on,' Kylie said to Caesar, leash in hand.

Caesar stopped again and stared right at her, panting, while peeing on a letterbox.

As much as Kylie hated to admit it, she thought Gloria was making the right choice about the open day. It wouldn't be easy for her to let Nick take over, sure, but she needed to earn a living. Anyway, it was nothing to Kylie. She'd do absolutely nothing to help, she promised herself. Always has to control everything? She'd show them.

When she arrived back, Nick was waiting.

'Mum's being deliberately difficult,' he said, his voice hushed, gesturing towards Gloria in the bedroom before Kylie had even shut the door.

'Wow, thanks for letting me know,' said Kylie.

Nick sounded stressed – but he did stress easily. Nick had always been sensitive, buffeted by waves of emotion often related to his performance on the field. He was the tantrum-thrower and the infectious giggler of the family, and both the despair of a close loss and the exhilaration of a come-from-behind victory seemed to unmoor him. He was much better at controlling his emotions now that he was retired from football – or at least, much better at hiding them.

He raised his head to look at her. 'You've got your own problems, I know. Your job disaster. Tansy told me.'

Kylie thought back on this week, which had been going for five months already, and it was only Wednesday. 'And she also told you about Colin, I guess.'

Nick nodded. 'But that's not a disaster, it's only a mild inconvenience. He was as boring as a box of rocks. But I thought you liked him.'

Kylie closed her eyes tight and watched little flares of light appear on the inside of her eyelids. Then she opened them again. 'Well, I didn't. I'm not sure what I saw in him in the first place. I'm quite relieved. I would've ended it myself, probably, before long.'

'If you say so,' said Nick. 'You have been a little bit irritable lately, you know that?'

'That's the most stupid thing you've said in days.' She washed her hands then took an apple from the bowl in the kitchen. Caesar sat up in his bed expectantly but Kylie ignored him and took a bite.

'Not irritable, got it. You know, Kyles, it might help to get things off your chest. Talk to someone.' Nick nodded sagely, rubbing his chin. 'Not me, obviously. I have somewhere I need to be. But someone.'

Kylie didn't need to talk to anyone. Kylie needed people in her life to start behaving: Colin, Gloria, Pharmacy King. She needed the disasters in her life to begin to repair.

'You should see all of this as an opportunity, Kyles. You need to set higher standards. Why are you still working for Tim anyway? You're in a rut. A safe, boring rut.' Nick spoke airily, as though he were a professional anarchist rather than someone with a government job. 'At least date someone worthy of you. Someone with a bit more . . . spine. Someone a bit . . . sharper. In fact, I think I know the perfect person.'

'Absolutely not. I've been single for five minutes. I'm not dating anyone, especially not some retired footballer.'

'How did you know he was a retired footballer?'

'Nick. Who else do you know?'

'You're very quick to dismiss someone you've never even met. Patrick Gaumond is his name. Google him.'

'I'm not the kind of woman who stalks people,' she said, which was a huge fib because she totally was.

'You don't want a night away from Mum, out of this house? With alcohol?' Nick plucked the apple from her hand and took a bite. 'Because that seems like a good idea to me.'

It was true that the kitchen walls seemed closer than they were this morning, and any minute now Gloria would call out wanting a pee, or more clothes hauled downstairs from her never-ending wardrobe, or a cup of tea made by someone who once worked for Prince William. Kylie thudded her head several times against the side of the refrigerator.

'Maybe this Patrick could text me first,' she said. 'We could text each other. To see if we click.'

'Ha ha, no,' said Nick. 'Nothing in writing until you agree. I know you. If he uses "their" instead of "they're", he's doomed. Okay, that doesn't make sense in speech but you know what I mean.'

'No, then. I'm not going on any dates. No way.'

Nick lay one hand on her shoulder, kindly. 'I get it. You're devastated. I've had my heart broken more times than I can count! You're feeling vulnerable, fragile, betrayed. You're worried you'll never recover.'

Kylie laughed in a way that sounded less like an expression of mirth and more like an anxious seal. 'I do not feel any of those things.' She sat down at the table in front of the piles of papers and twirled her pen around her thumb, then twirled it back the other way. 'I am not devastated about Colin. I could not care less about Colin.' Kylie groaned. 'Fine. Tell this Patrick to pick me up here. Friday night, seven.'

'Confident, considering Friday night is not usually for first dates and it's incredibly short notice – but I can work with that,' Nick said. 'Oh, and Kylie? Don't be so hard on Mum.'

Why did everyone assume she was hard on Gloria? Kylie thought as Nick left. *If anything, it was the other way around.*

In the late afternoon, Kylie used the upstairs toilet to pee – but there was only a thin, sharp dribble. A UTI now? *Now?* She felt like punching the wall. She'd been too busy running around after everybody to drink enough water, so she went downstairs and skolled a large glass. If she still had it tomorrow, she'd have to get antibiotics, which was another job she didn't need.

Then she spent a ridiculous amount of time brushing Caesar's supermodel coat. At the rate he shed, she could make a new dog in a matter of weeks. Then Tansy arrived with groceries and chatted with Gloria for a while. On her way out, she stopped to talk with Kylie in the kitchen, while avoiding Caesar threading between her legs.

'Don't tell Mia and Lachie you have a dog,' said Tansy. 'Especially not one with more toys than them.'

'I don't have a dog. It's temporary.'

Caesar looked up at Kylie, offended.

'You're your own worst enemy, you know that? Looking after Mum is more than enough for one person. Why would you take on extra work?' Tansy folded her arms and leaned against the kitchen bench.

What a stupid question! Kylie opened her mouth to say, *Because no one else does things right* when Tansy continued.

'How about lunch on Sunday, at ours? Bring Mum. Don't bring the dog. It'll do both of you good to get out of the house.'

Tansy, Simon and the children lived in a tiny two-bedroom flat and Gloria had all this space, yet Schnabel family lunches and dinners were always held at Tansy's. Tansy and her family, and Nick, Kylie, and Gloria, and lately their half-sister Monica, plus Colin, made nine, all huddled in the flat's tiny lounge room or in the communal backyard that Simon had landscaped on weekends in exchange for a reduction in the rent. It was ever thus. It was never questioned. Kylie wondered if it was an accommodation made for her or if the whole family felt as uncomfortable in Gloria's house as she did.

'I don't think the old girl'll make it up the stairs to your place with that moon boot.' Kylie sat on a kitchen stool and started flicking through one of the pharmacy journals she'd brought from home.

'Well, we can't have lunch here,' Tansy said. 'You don't cook, and of course Mum didn't cook even when she had two functioning feet. You're alike in that way.'

Kylie jerked her gaze up from the magazine. 'I *beg* your pardon?'

'I said that neither you or Mum cook. We could have it here and order pizza, I guess. Or I could come over early to start cooking? Simon could—'

And then, on an impulse so odd that she felt apart from her body, as though she were floating two feet overhead and watching herself, Kylie said, 'Of course I can cook. I haven't yet starved to death in my own home.'

Tansy paused. 'You cook for yourself at home, yes. You make tofu stir-fries, and chicken breast with salad. Fish twice a week, as per the guidelines. All very . . . nutritional. Cooking for a lunch, a social occasion, requires something a little less boring. Food that, you know, tastes good.'

Kylie felt she had been somehow transformed into a muppet. It was as if someone else's hand was physically inside her body animating it, forcing her mouth to open and these incongruous words to come out, yet she kept speaking. 'I can cook *delicious* food. I can cook the most delicious food you've ever tasted. In fact, you should all come over here for lunch and I'll make a feast.'

'Are you joking? What would you cook, exactly? Because the kids can be picky—'

'A *feast*, all right, Tans? I will make a *feast*.' *Help! Someone stop me*, Kylie thought, even as she heard the words come out of her mouth.

'You won't be too tired, looking after Mum all week?'

'I worked my way through uni. I've been tired before.' Though in reality, she already felt the kind of exhaustion that she imagined belonged only to surgeons in war zones and K2 mountaineers. Yes, logically it had been barely one day, but life with Gloria had a weird effect on time in the same way the pandemic had.

'I hate to play the mother card,' said Tansy, 'but being tired in the service of your own choices is different. There's a different exhaustion that comes when you lose your agency. When you're operating on someone else's agenda.'

'Oh, because only mothers . . .' Then Kylie stopped. She was too exhausted to even snap at her little sister, that's how exhausted she was. She'd run around after Gloria all day, and then, every time she'd become frustrated, she'd taken Caesar around the block for a pee. Caesar had gone for three walks already and had begun to turn his back when he saw Kylie with the lead.

'Kylie?' Gloria called out. 'My foot is itchy. I think that dog has given me fleas.'

'You don't have fleas!' Kylie yelled back. 'We've been through this. Your foot is sweaty in the boot, that's all. Your other foot is fine!' She rested her head in her hands.

'Maybe it's an allergy, then!' Gloria yelled out. 'A dog-hair allergy! Sometimes allergies only affect one foot, it's possible!'

Kylie thumped her head on the kitchen counter.

'Mum is amazing, Kylie, don't forget that.' Tansy folded her arms. 'Don't be so hard on her, Kylie.'

Kylie raised her head. 'I'm not hard on her. And besides, I'm only here for one more night. I phoned the agency this morning. They're sending over a nurse first thing tomorrow. And it shouldn't be this hard to invite your family for lunch. You text Monica and tell Nick to bring the drinks. I'll look after the food. Sunday, one o'clock, and that's final.'

Soon all this would be over and Kylie's life would be her own again.

Later that night after Gloria and Caesar were asleep, while Caesar's sage chicken and rice, made without the assistance of a Thermomix, was cooling in the fridge, Kylie stretched out with her laptop on the bed in Tansy's time capsule of a room to consider potential résumé fonts. Tansy's posters of Hanson and James Van Der Beek were still blue-tacked to the wall above Kylie's head, which made her wonder if she and Tansy were related after all because she could think of nothing less heart-throbby than any of those boring cheesy pale idiots. And Tansy had lived at home until she married Simon! That means her bedroom was like this until she was in her mid-twenties. What was she thinking?

Underneath the posters, the walls were still pink and the gold-rimmed mirror above the white dresser remained in place. When Kylie, Tansy and Nick were small children, Gloria had painted their bedrooms herself, dressed in white overalls with a 60s pop singer headband. Pink for Tansy, blue for Nick, purple for Kylie. Their bedrooms were magazine-worthy – every kid's dream. Even then, Kylie was conscious that Gloria was decorating them for herself. Like many grown women, Gloria yearned to relive the childhood she'd never had.

It was sweet of Nick to set her up. Sweet, but deluded. Kylie found Nick's friend Patrick's Twitter feed, which mostly consisted of thoughts and retweets about football and in-jokes she didn't follow. He liked electric cars, which was a big tick. She found a fundraising page – he was running a marathon for an environmental charity. Another tick. Some old stuff about his football career. His profile photo was – well, yes, okay. He was hot, that much at least was true. He seemed professional, ambitious. He even had a LinkedIn page. He probably had his very own lanyard.

Patrick did seem like her kind of person. Someone organised, with goals. Kylie allowed herself a small moment of possibility – and then she felt a twinge in her abdomen. Tomorrow, her period would be four days late. She felt bloated, headachy, crampy. Her phone was in her hand and part of her wanted to google *failure rate vasectomy*, but she stopped herself. Her period would probably come tomorrow. She refused to worry about nothing.

THURSDAY

Chapter 16

There is nothing more pleasing than bestowing the gift of order upon those poor unfortunates who are administratively challenged.

Standard Operating Procedures, or SOPs, were one of Kylie's superpowers. She'd drawn them up for every task in the pharmacy as well as for significant family events. Nick and his friends still talked about the one she issued everyone for his twenty-first! Nick had even stuck it on the fridge with a fridge magnet from the local real estate agent! No one had ever seen anything like it!

So that night, instead of sleeping, Kylie sat on the couch in her pyjamas, hunched over her laptop in the dark, writing an SOP for managing Gloria's ankle, imaginatively titled: *Management of Gloria's Ankle*. Each stakeholder – every Schnabel and the Larsens also, as Tansy had, for reasons beyond Kylie's comprehension, taken Simon's surname – was identified by their initials and assigned specifics tasks. TL would take over grocery shopping; SL, responsibility for Gloria's garden. NS would be Gloria's social secretary, a job for which he was born. MS would handle communications, and ML and LL, as joint Vice-Presidents in Charge of Cheering Nana Up, would zoom her on alternate days and bring homemade get-well cards on the weekends.

And KS's role? She was CEO, obviously. She would provide supervision over all these portfolios and keep everyone on track.

It was amazing how much better Kylie felt once every little task was safely spreadsheeted and emailed to everyone. She dozed, then woke at 5 am, slicked with sweat in soaked sheets, pulsing with heat radiating up her torso and a sinking nausea in her stomach. She needed cold, desperately, urgently. She fought the urge to stick her head in the freezer and nestle her face into the peas. Had she caught Covid again? Or something else? Or was it just boiling in this room? In the bathroom upstairs, she splashed water on her face and took her temperature with Gloria's olde-worlde mercury thermometer. No, no fever. Surely Gloria couldn't have turned the heating on, at this time of year?

She would feel better after a cool shower, but before she turned on the taps, the sick feeling passed as quickly as it had come. It was the unfamiliarity of everything here that was making her feel so weird, she decided. Gloria's strange striped toothpaste rather than her mild white one; Gloria's hand cream, which smelled like rose-flavoured motor oil, rather than her citrusy, waxy brand. When she was home, everything would be back to normal.

At least she was awake in time to keep an eye out the window and intercept the front door before it rang.

On the step a little after 7 am was Ramona from the nursing agency: a young, thin Eastern-European woman with a sharp face, arched eyebrows like two upside-down Nike swooshes, two dark plaits and a deadpan expression that reminded Kylie of herself. Ramona wore a pink polo shirt, black pants and sensible white shoes. No make-up or jewellery. In her short sleeves, her arms were muscular and defined. She was the very definition of sober competency. Anyone would be lucky to have her looking after them, even Gloria. Kylie liked her at once.

'Bad luck, mother breaking ankle,' Ramona said, looking around Gloria's museum house.

There was much to look at. Among the rose-glass single-stem vases and the onyx trays inlaid with mother-of-pearl and the various crystal decanters containing various brown liquids crowding Gloria's coffee tables and ledges was a range of tennis trophies of shiny plastic women frozen in obscure positions belonging to Gloria, and similar shiny plastic frozen men with footballs belonging to Nick, all crowded in with assorted unidentifiable attempts at pottery (gifts from Lachie) and various framed drawings of Gloria (from Mia).

There were no plastic women depicting Kylie because she was not athletic, and there were no school projects made by her children because she didn't have any. Kylie was well represented, though, by photos of her in her cap and gown with Gloria at her various graduations and award ceremonies.

The photos summed it up. Tansy was the kind one with the kids, Nick the charismatic athletic one and Kylie had always been the smart one. That was her role, not only in Gloria's photo gallery, but in the family.

She had to get this job disaster fixed, and fast. Otherwise, who even was she?

Ramona paused in front of the mantel above the fireplace, where there were dozens of framed photos of young Kylie and her siblings, as well as more recent ones with Tansy's children, and Gloria posing with doubles partners from each decade of her life, both women and mixed.

'Your . . . father, is this?' Ramona said, picking up one of the photos. 'Is very handsome, but familiar somehow?'

Kylie shrugged. 'One of those faces, I guess.'

But that wasn't it. After Gloria and David divorced, anything that couldn't be donated or relegated to hard waste underwent a ceremonial burning in one frenetic afternoon. Gloria sorted everything into piles and the three kids ferried loads to the cinder-block incinerator that was still at the end of the cement path in the backyard despite the councils recent prohibition against burn-offs. Wedding photos, cards and mementos, David's old tax returns and university records – everything burned, becoming soft black flakes that swirled in the air and dotted their faces and clothes.

The family photos taken when the children were young though, couldn't be replaced – which led to a crisis. In those years before Photoshop, what could be done about David, who was in the centre of many of the said photos and who Gloria wished dead several times a day in a variety of painful ways? Facing the grinning face of her ex-husband every day in her own home was untenable.

Gloria's solution had been to cut out a range of Kevin Costner heads of varying sizes from different magazines and glue them over similarly sized David heads. Now the family photos lined up on the mantel were of Gloria and Kevin, standing proudly behind their children, young Kylie, Tansy and Nick.

Ramona seemed unperturbed by the unexpected Kevin heads. Kylie took this as a good sign. Either she was oblivious or she was unflappable – both of which would stand her in good stead, looking after a reluctant Gloria.

'And dog?' said Ramona. 'What I do with it?'

Caesar was still sleeping in his bed near the dining table, exhausted from yesterday's walkathon, yipping softly and moving his legs like he was barking at intruders in his dreams.

'He mostly just sleeps,' Kylie said. 'Let him out in the backyard for a pee once or twice, that's all.' She gave Ramona a quick summary of the Caesar-related rules, then led her to the bedroom.

'Brace yourself for turbulence,' Kylie said to Ramona. She knocked on the door and peeked in before swinging it open. 'Mum? Are you awake?'

Gloria *was* awake, sitting up in bed, arms crossed, wearing her moon boot, a blue leopard-print chiffon skirt, a purple cashmere sweater and blood-red lipstick. Her crutches were leaning on the bedside table. Where she thought she was going and how long it had taken her to dress on her own, Kylie couldn't imagine.

Kylie introduced them.

'That young woman better not be a nurse, Kylie. Because I told you that under no circumstances do I want or need a nurse.' The expression on Gloria's face resembled a cubist painting that might be found in a modern art museum entitled *I breastfed you for eight months and this is the thanks I get*.

Kylie threaded her hand through her hair and tugged it. 'I've got to go to work, Mum. And Ramona is not only a nurse, she's highly qualified, extremely sought-after, and has rehab experience. Just give her a chance.'

'You not even know I here,' Ramona said. 'I sit on couch, you yell if you need me.'

'There you go,' Kylie said. 'Can't be fairer than that.'

Gloria smiled with what seemed like genuine affection and shook her head. '*Kylie, Kylie, Kylie.* You think you've won, don't you?'

'It's not about winning, Mum. It's about you having the best possible care.'

Gloria inspected her manicured nails and ran the pad of her thumb over the shiny red polish. 'My darling girl, how brave you are. Always throwing yourself at brick walls, fighting the world, trying to make everyone fall in line. That's the way you were at the pharmacy, the way you were with Colin.'

'I'm trying to do what's best for everyone, Mum,' said Kylie. *And yet*, she thought, *for some reason, people still complain.*

Gloria continued. 'I see. And this insistence on getting your own way, where do you think you get that from? I've been getting my own way since before you were born. I've just learned to be a little more . . . strategic over the years.'

Kylie opened her mouth to reply, but Gloria spoke to Ramona. 'None of this is your fault.' Gloria patted the side of her bed. 'Welcome! Rehab experience, Kylie said? Tell me a little about yourself.'

Ramona gave Kylie a brief, enquiring glance. Kylie nodded; Ramona sat. Gloria asked her about her nursing career, explained the specifics of her ankle and asked if her backhand was single or double-handed. Ramona, relaxing, was confused about the backhand question but asked to see Gloria's X-rays and began describing specific movements, using words like dorsiflexion and proprioception.

Kylie watched for a few minutes in case Gloria drew a weapon, but they were getting on well.

While Ramona and Gloria were chatting, Kylie wandered back to the lounge room and peered again at the photos on the mantel. She spotted a more recent shot that she recognised – it was taken last Christmas with Gloria's actual camera, of everyone who'd been there for lunch. Gloria and Nick, so similar, glowing and vital in the centre, with Kylie and Tansy on either side of them. Colin was on the far end next to Kylie and Simon stood on the other side next to Tansy. Tansy's children Mia and Lachie were in front, still wearing the paper hats from their crackers.

Except the photo was now lopsided. Colin had been cut away and the white backing paper was visible against the edge of the frame.

The shot had been taken in the backyard of Tansy's block of flats before they began to eat their picnic lunch. Gloria had arranged for one of Tansy's neighbours to act as photographer while she orchestrated everyone into position, moving Simon and Colin on the outside of Gloria and her children and grandchildren. Now that Kylie thought about it, she realised that in every photo with Simon in it, and/or Colin – in fact, every photo with every partner any of them had brought home since they'd began dating – non-family members were always standing on the far edges of the group.

She'd assumed this placement was something to do with height – although Nick, the tallest in the family, was always in the centre. Only now did she realise that Gloria had learned her lesson when covering David's head with all those Kevins. The partners were on the outside so that Gloria could literally cut them out if they split with her children. If Kylie went to the kitchen right now and checked through Gloria's bin she would no doubt find skinny photo strips of Colin forcibly excised from the Schnabels with the good scissors.

Kylie found this reassuring. She and Tansy and Nick had always been close – three tight satellites revolving around the planet that was Gloria. As the father of Mia and Lachie, Simon was almost one of them – an honorary Schnabel – but the Colins of the world could always be trimmed away.

As Kylie dressed, she became aware of something odd. Her trousers were unusually tight around her middle. Over the last week or two, she'd noticed red elastic marks on the white skin of her abdomen, but now there was no avoiding it. She was gaining weight. Kylie did not gain weight. Colin had been a bad influence, with his insistence on eating for pleasure. He was always wanting to go for Vietnamese because he fancied a pho, or open a bottle of red wine of a different variety when they already had a bottle of another variety open. Colin loved pancakes for Sunday breakfast and pizza on Friday nights and he was forever tempting her with a taste of whatever he was eating. Sugar and salt and fat made him happy – which was ridiculous, because giving food the power to change your emotional state is what leads to unhealthy decisions. Food should be treated as fuel, because it was. As soon as she was back in her own house, making her own choices without Colin, her body would right itself.

She ran a brush through her hair, keenly aware of Gloria downstairs, unchaperoned with an unsuspecting Ramona. Thinking about it, the hairs on Kylie's arms stood on end. Introducing Ramona *had* gone well. Too well. There had been something lurking in Gloria's smile when she said, *Kylie, Kylie, Kylie.*

Downstairs, she pulled Ramona aside and began to explain her fears.

'Every woman thinks their mother is difficult one,' Ramona said when she walked Kylie to the door.

'Yes, but mine is . . .' Kylie began. 'Not *difficult*, exactly. More like . . . Gloria, Mother of Dragons.'

'But if she is mother of dragons, that makes you . . . dragon.'

'I'm not . . . it's just an expression.'

Ramona patted Kylie's arm and nodded in a comforting way. 'Listen, you go to work, relax. We soon become friends, you see.'

By the time Kylie had settled Ramona in, she was running late for work. Just last week, this would have left Kylie with a creeping, itchy panic. She would have cursed every red light and cursed Colin because on the rare occurrences she had been late, it was his fault – he couldn't find his keys and had parked her in, or he'd switched off her alarm by accident or begun some conversation that he said was important but really could have waited.

Now she was late and there was no Colin to blame, not anymore, and Kylie couldn't stand any more responsibility. She almost followed Ramona's advice and relaxed.

Chapter 17

This was why Kylie should never relax.

She checked the time on her Fitbit just before pushing open the pharmacy door. Considering everything she was juggling, it was a miracle she was only a little late. In fact, for one brief, fragile moment she felt infused with satisfaction. She was calm, she was accomplished. Gloria was being looked after by someone competent who wasn't Kylie; she had a date tomorrow night that looked promising; when she peed this morning, it had stung less due to her diligent water consumption; and providing she kept Caesar breathing until Sunday, she would almost certainly retain her job. She'd taken every problem the week so far had thrown her and lobbed it back. Her life was returning to its usual orderly structure. She was back in control! On the drive to work, she almost put the top of Gloria's convertible down. Almost, but not quite, because that would imply that she approved of such an impractical, indulgent car.

Her phone rang. It was Tansy.

'Thanks for the SOP,' she said. 'It's been ages since you did one. I'd almost forgotten.'

'I did a seven-page one for Christmas, remember?' said Kylie. 'Lachie was Head of Tinsel.'

'Oh, yes. But wasn't Colin in charge of tinsel?'

'Not originally. In the first draft, I had him down for mixers but he went completely off-piste. Decided we needed a different brand of tonic water and refused to buy the soft drink from Aldi.' Kylie shook her head. 'So I demoted him to tinsel and moved Lachie to crackers.'

'It's all coming back to me now,' Tansy said. 'So did Mum's nurse show?'

She did, Kylie told her. Everything would be fine.

'Great. Listen, I've got yoga tonight. Why don't you come?'

'Join a herd of women in Lululemon and one obligatory middle-aged man in a tie-dyed singlet and a headband namaste-ing to sitar music with their ankles behind their necks? No thanks,' said Kylie. 'Besides, I'm not flexible.'

'That's a ridiculous reason to say no. That's like saying you can't have a shower because you're dirty.' Tansy's voice was thin on the line; she was also driving. 'How about we take a meditation course? There are lots of studies showing that meditation is excellent for stress. I asked Mia to google it, so I could support my case.'

'Firstly, I'm not stressed, and second, can you see me in lotus position, chanting om and focusing on my chakras? No. Where is this coming from?'

'Nowhere! Nowhere at all!' Tansy said.

There was an unexpected pause.

'You've been under a lot of pressure lately. Not quite yourself,' Tansy said. 'It might be nice to try something new.'

Honestly! Nick with his date, and now Tansy with these random classes! Everyone was trying to boss her around all of a sudden, when the last thing Kylie needed was *something new*.

She made her position on hippy classes clear to Tansy, then said goodbye as she parked. The pharmacy, before her in all its faded glory, was its usual, un-new self – familiar and solid. In that instant, it was difficult to imagine that she would ever be cast out.

Her good vibe lasted until the moment she stepped inside. Before the door had even closed, Gail zigzagged into her path as if she'd been waiting to pounce. Her arms were folded, and in one hand was her notebook. 'Kylie,' she said, smiling. 'So happy you could join us.'

This is why smiles are worth nothing, Kylie thought. They're set dressing, that's all. They do not accurately reflect a person's intention. She made agreeing noises while on her way to the storeroom to stash her bag.

'Remember what I said about Pharmacy King being like a family?' Gail followed, almost stepping on Kylie's heels. 'You wouldn't steal from a member of your family, would you?'

'Of course not,' Kylie said. 'I only ever steal from strangers.'

Today Gail's hair was pulled back into a butterfly clip and her glasses were round and electric blue, connected to a plastic chain around her neck. Her pale throat was soft and had several large skin tags at the base.

'But seriously, every time you're late, you're stealing from us. Punctuality is one of our core values at Pharmacy King. Perhaps you could remember that, going forward.' Gail made another small mark in her notebook.

Honestly! Kylie checked the time again on her Fitbit. 'Tim's here to fill scripts, isn't he? Besides, it was only ten minutes.'

'Yes, but that's not the point. And it was . . .' Gail produced her phone from the pocket of her cardigan with a flourish and looked at the screen ostentatiously, '*eleven* whole minutes. Eleven minutes every day means you're stealing almost an hour per week from the company. I understand that Tim has run a loose ship but you should be aware that stealing is theft.'

Stealing is theft, is it? A familiar glow of anger worked itself up Kylie's chest and she felt her face redden. She had been the first to arrive for decades. It was she who opened the door and flicked on the lights and switched on the urn and switched off the answering machine and ran a vacuum over the carpet and adjusted the counter displays. She was working Saturday to make up for her day off yesterday. This . . . reprimand . . . was patently unfair.

In the storeroom, Kylie took her white coat from the hook. 'Listen . . .' she began – but then she noticed a tall young woman in a Pharmacy King uniform standing there, in Kylie's spot, in Kylie's dispensary. The woman smiled at Kylie. Her smile was not perfect in that white, even, morning-show-host way. It was a little lopsided, and one of the eyeteeth wasn't facing the same direction as its neighbours. A dimple appeared in her left cheek. Yet somehow it was the very definition of *welcoming*. When she smiled, the room felt sunnier.

'This is Emily,' Gail said. 'She covered for you yesterday. Tim and I are going through the inventory, so I asked her to stay for the week.'

Kylie wasn't sure exactly what she'd been expecting, but it wasn't this. Emily was young. *Very* young. And she glowed. Her hair was naturally dark and shampoo-commercial glossy and her skin was clear and even-toned. It was no wonder she hadn't found a full-time job. The hair, the face, the general demeanour was obviously unsettling. The world was biased in favour of attractive people, that was obvious, but a pretty face could only get you so far in the professional world. The Emilys of this world were unused to hard work. They lacked resilience and grit. Besides, that smile was clearly covering up something. It was highly probable that Emily coasted on her looks, hoping they'd obscure the fact that she was an intellectual and moral lightweight.

'That's not necessary,' Kylie said. 'I don't need any help.'

'It's sensible to have a contingency plan. In case of . . .' Gail shuddered briefly, and her eyes filled with disappointment at the vagaries of the world, 'unreliability.'

'I'm so happy to meet you, Kylie!' Emily said. 'Gosh, your systems are amazing.'

Yes, they were – but still, Kylie scanned Emily's face for evidence of sarcasm. She found none. Despite herself, Kylie felt the glossy, smiling Emily somehow made both the pharmacy and herself seem hopelessly rustic. Kylie's cheeks began to burn again at the dowdiness around her – the overcrowded shelves, the scuffed and faded carpet, the waistband of her trousers tight on her stomach.

'I'm sorry to hear you're having trouble finding full-time work,' said Kylie.

Emily beamed even warmer. 'Thanks! None of the offers I've received have been exactly right. I've been overseas for a while and ever since I got back, it's been a struggle to find my place.'

Overseas! How frivolous! Probably on a gap year, swanning around Ibiza or something. Clearly, Emily wasn't an eldest child with a single parent and two younger siblings to look after, a mortgage to pay and a pharmacy to save for. It wasn't that Kylie hadn't travelled. She had travelled. She'd been on a beach holiday, with Colin. Phillip Island was amazing! People travelled from right around the world to see the penguins. And it was so close! Besides, Kylie didn't like being away from home for extended periods. Who knew what could happen without her supervision?

'I'm picky, I guess,' Emily went on. 'I don't just want any job. I'm looking for a real community. A family atmosphere,' said Emily. 'Not that I didn't love my time working for Médecins Sans Frontières! Being on the frontline really changes your perspective, you know?'

'Emily ran a hospital pharmacy in an Ebola outbreak in Liberia,' said Gail.

'Just the tail end of one,' said Emily. 'It was a privilege. And refreshing! No one cared about my Dean's Medal for Excellence or my Pharmacy Student of the Year Award there. To them, I was just one of the team.'

'But you're so young!' said Sandy. 'Weren't you scared of being out of your depth?'

'Sometimes!' Emily's smile pivoted to bashful. 'But you can't control everything, you know? At some point, you've got to roll up your sleeves and give it a go! There are no guarantees in life.'

'Kylie?' said Gail. 'You look a little red.'

The burn in Kylie's cheeks was now a steady, hot throbbing that began in the skin at the top of her chest, then seared up to her ears and across her scalp in shivering waves. A sudden nausea curdled the back of her throat. She was beginning to feel . . . uncomfortable. Sweaty and faint. Could she have eaten something dodgy? Had she been in the sun yesterday? Yes, but she always wore SPF50. She held the back of her hand to her forehead like a Bronte heroine.

'I'm fine,' she gasped.

'There's so much I can learn from you, Kylie,' Emily continued, beaming, 'with all your years of experience. You've been a pharmacist for almost as long as I've been alive!'

'That's a little confronting.'

'I *love* being a pharmacist. You too, right?'

Kylie swallowed. 'I guess. Listen, Emma—'

'It's Emily.'

'Right, Emily.'

Just then, Sandy interrupted her. There was a customer standing in the far aisle near the dispensary wanting advice and a prescription filled.

'I'm in the middle of something,' Kylie said. 'Could you ask Tim to see her?'

'I'll do it!' squeaked Emily. 'Happy to!'

'The customer asked for Kylie specifically,' said Sandy.

'For heaven's sake, don't make her wait any longer!' said Gail. 'We can discuss this later.'

Kylie took a deep breath to steady herself. She felt better – the sick feeling was gone already, passed over her like a wave. She felt protective towards these women who waited for a female pharmacist, especially the young ones. If they were this embarrassed discussing their period pain or thrush or incontinence with Tim despite his experience and kindliness, what must the rest of their life be like? Were they mortified at the checkout, watching their tampons creep along the conveyer belt? The vulnerability behind their eyes told of some past horror: pads stolen by kids at school when they were twelve and thrown like a ball over their head; a bloodstain on the back of their skirt at work and no one saying anything.

The customer waiting for Kylie wasn't young, though. She was a tall, powerfully built woman with sleek silver-grey hair parted on one side and she had no obvious vulnerability behind her eyes or anywhere else. She wasn't a regular either. How she'd known to ask for Kylie specifically was a mystery.

She needed scripts filled for HRT, she said, but her regimen was giving her trouble.

Kylie looked at the scripts. They weren't especially complicated or obscure, and the customer herself didn't seem in any way impaired. Yet Kylie found herself explaining how oestrogen patches work and how to apply them, and the superiority of progesterone gel-caps over tablets and why her doctor had likely chosen them, and giving general advice on sleep hygiene, diet and exercise. After a good ten minutes of this, the woman interrupted her.

'Is there something wrong with my medication?' she asked.

'No,' said Kylie.

The customer tilted her head like a parrot. She wore an A-line black smock and sandals, both expensive. Her lip gloss was pearlescent and softening. It definitely wasn't one of their dowdy brands.

Kylie blinked. She could hear a distant chirping – it was her mobile, behind her in a drawer in the dispensary. She ignored it.

The woman glanced around at the shelves. 'And what else would you recommend for menopause?'

'It depends on your symptoms,' said Kylie.

'I'm menopausal, that's my symptom.'

'That's a stage of life, not a symptom,' said Kylie. 'Some women have many symptoms, some have very few or none.' Her phone stopped chirping. *Probably spam*, Kylie thought.

'What do you take yourself?'

Kylie felt her eyebrows nestling into her hairline. *Herself?* What did she take *herself*? She was forty-three! Her hair was still jet-black – dyed, yes, but as natural-looking as black hair could be, on someone of her complexion. She was in good shape, she stayed out of the sun, her ankles were still up to wearing heels. Women still had babies at her age. Lots of women. *I'm much too young to be approaching the change of life*, Kylie thought.

The *change* of life.

The very name told Kylie she did not want to do it.

'Nothing,' Kylie said. 'I'm years away.'

'Oh,' the woman said. 'Sorry. I just assumed you were my age. Anyway, do you not know the common complaints of an average menopausal women? What else do I need?'

What else do I need? Nothing, Kylie was sure. If she were choosing for herself she'd pick ibuprofen capsules (fast release) for the insomnia headache that was right now nestling like a seed between her eyes, an aluminium tube of hand cream that smelled like oranges, and a crinkly sheet mask that improved the skin not one jot but was worth every penny because it gave harried women an excuse to lie down with their eyes closed for twenty minutes.

The customer was waiting for Kylie to recommend something. She should just recommend something. *For once, Kylie, take the path of least resistance.*

She adjusted her face. 'Every human is unique. Nobody is *common* or *average*,' Kylie said. 'The medication you've been prescribed *by your doctor* should help. If things don't resolve after a few weeks, I'd be happy to recommend some over-the-counter products.'

'Vitamins? Herbs? Would you recommend a diet shake? A night cream with collagen to fight the seven signs of ageing?'

'Which sign of ageing would you like to fight? Increased confidence? Hard-earned wisdom? Restaurants becoming too noisy all of a sudden?'

'How about something to help me sleep?'

'Are you having trouble sleeping?'

'I didn't say that.' The woman puckered her shiny lips as though she'd sucked on something sour. 'You should use your clinical judgement and recommend something.'

'Sorry, the psychic pharmacist is only here on Thursdays,' said Kylie.

The shop phone began to ring at the front counter, cutting through the tense silence.

'I'm standing in your store. Are you really not going to sell me anything other than the prescription?' the woman said.

Just then, Sandy interrupted. 'Phone for you,' she said. 'Said you didn't answer your mobile.'

'I'm with a customer. I'll call them back.'

'It's urgent, they said.'

Urgent! Kylie's brain filled with possibilities – Gloria, on her way to hospital having fallen down the stairs, or being arrested after attacking Ramona with a racquet. Or perhaps she'd locked Caesar in a cupboard as she'd threatened. Anything could have happened!

'I'm sorry, I have to answer. My mother's unwell.' Kylie moved towards the front counter.

'You're not seriously going to take that call,' the woman said after her, hands on her hips. 'I'm a paying customer.'

Kylie looked back at her, eyes hooded. 'I'll be one minute. Sandy, perhaps you could compliment the paying customer's handbag while I'm gone.'

'It is very nice,' said Sandy.

'Unbelievable,' the woman said.

At the counter, Kylie turned to face the front window and put her hand around the receiver. She felt all her muscles tense. 'Everything okay, Mum?' she said into the phone.

'It's not Mum,' said Nick.

Kylie groaned. She could feel the customer's gaze boring into her back from the other end of the store. If Gail saw Kylie ignoring a customer in favour of a personal call, it would be her second black mark of the day.

'What, Nick? I'm in the middle of something.'

'I'll be quick,' said Nick. 'It's about the open day.'

Of course it was. He would be trying to get out of it, Kylie could guess. Trying to dump all that extra work on her. She had a sudden memory of a cartoon from their childhood: Wile E Coyote digging a gaping pit in the road and camouflaging it with a sheet, waiting for an unsuspecting Road Runner. This conversation right here, it was a metaphorical pit. Kylie would not fall into the pit because she was not a controlling person. Nick was a grown man. He could manage on his own.

'Nick, it's nothing to do with me.'

'Sure, of course. But Mum's just emailed me a big list of stuff to hire so I'm just about to put in an online order.'

'But it's already Thursday!' Kylie squeezed the phone. 'The open day is Saturday! Can they deliver by then?'

'Well . . . they can't guarantee it. But it'll probably be okay, right? "Can't guarantee" means almost certainly, ninety-five per cent.'

'No! "Can't guarantee" means no, Nick! You'll have to drive out to the store and pick it up.'

'Yeah, can't. I'm busy today and tomorrow.'

Do not tumble into the cartoon pit, Kylie, she thought.

'I don't know what you expect me to do about it,' said Kylie. 'I'm working tomorrow too.'

'I know that! God. I've got it under control. The trouble is that Mum has almost no supplies. She donated all her old stuff and needs to hire new everything. But don't worry! The kids can share racquets. Besides, Mum probably has spares packed in boxes in the garage. Some of the strings are a bit dodgy, but it's just for kids, right?'

'Those old things? They're falling apart! They won't do! And the kids can't *share* – no one does that anymore. It's hard enough to get parents to pay tuition in advance. Mum needs to look like a professional, serious business.'

'I'm sure it'll be fine. Not your problem, right?'

Absolutely right. Kylie would not get involved, she would tiptoe around the pit. Outside the front window, three teenagers on skateboards zipped along the footpath. She looked down at her knuckles, tight on the phone. 'If you place the order in advance, I can probably nip out to the store first thing tomorrow morning and pick it up.'

'That's kind, but absolutely not! I know how busy you are, and as you said, it's not your problem,' said Nick. 'Although it would really help. Are you sure?'

Kylie was sure. This one little job didn't change her concrete resolution because picking up a few racquets and balls wasn't really being *involved*. She could manage it before the pharmacy opened, even listen to a podcast about compounding while she drove. It was practically work, if you looked at it like that.

'Oh, and Kyles? I'm not exactly sure how to *run* the day? Mum will be there to do the admin and talk to people but I don't want to let her down. Any chance you could knock up one of your SOPs?'

Of course Nick wanted a SOP. Who wouldn't? Knocking up a quick SOP, also, wasn't really *involvement*. Not technically. She could draft up something tonight after dinner. It would probably take her all of twenty minutes and that would be the extent of her *involvement*. Finished. Done and dusted. After that, Nick was on his own.

'Yes, yes.' She was relieved, proud of herself. She had avoided the pit. 'I'll do an SOP.'

'Awesome,' said Nick.

In Kylie's peripheral vision, she noticed the customer with the handbag standing at the counter, paying Sandy for her HRT and huffing dramatically. Kylie tucked her head down as she left. There were no other customers. The pharmacy was quiet.

Kylie rang off just as Gail appeared beside her. 'Is everything all right?' she said. 'That customer looked a bit cross.'

'Some people just look like that,' said Kylie.

Chapter 18

Kylie's half-sister, Monica, met her for lunch. It was something they did once or twice a month – Kylie's rare proper lunchbreak – in a cafe with tables. Today, they sat outside on the footpath bench, each with a juice and a spinach and feta roll from the pie shop in a paper bag on their laps.

'We could have cancelled, no drama.' Mon took a slurp of her juice. Her hair, once buzzcut to her skull, had grown into shoulder-length pink waves with a severe, blunt fringe. Her clothes had veered towards urban groove but now, despite living in the suburbs, everything seemed hand-woven – it was as though Monica was a city girl when living in the country and a country girl since she'd moved to town. As part of her rustic revival, she'd spent the summer dying organic hemp with onion skins and turmeric in the bath in her share house and for Christmas had given everyone t-shirts tie-dyed with coffee grounds. Everyone had loved them, but mainly for the look on Gloria's face. Kylie still had no idea what to do with hers.

'Earth to Kyles? I said we could have cancelled.'

Kylie had been staring at the pharmacy, gauging how many customers entered and left. She turned to look at Mon. 'Of course not. It's good to see you.'

'It's a shop, Kyles. They're quite permanent. It won't disappear if you turn your back.'

It might, Kylie thought.

Had they really known Monica for only a year? It seemed longer. Sometimes it seemed *much* longer. A few years after David left the family, he remarried and moved to a farm in East Gippsland. They'd seen him occasionally – school events and uni graduations, and at Tansy's wedding and Mia's and Lachie's christenings. He'd sent cards and presents for birthdays and Christmases. Then early in the pandemic, Gloria received a letter to tell her that David had died. It was unexpected and shocking. Because of the lockdown restrictions, he'd been buried in a small ceremony in the town where he'd lived on a farm with his second wife and daughter, Monica.

It hadn't taken long for the wheels in Gloria's head to turn. Last year when larger gatherings were allowed again, Gloria concocted a belated memorial service for David to serve a scheme of her own, and dragged the rest of the family and some of their friends into it. Monica came to the city for the memorial and met them all. She'd stayed with Tansy and Simon for a few weeks while finding her feet, then moved to a share house in Coburg.

Kylie hadn't known what to expect when Monica first showed up. How does one act around a surprise half-sibling in her twenties? Kylie felt more like Monica's aunt than her sister. In the beginning, the relationship had been solidly driven by Monica. As a child, she'd often wished for siblings, she'd told them. She babysat Mia and Lachie, she helped Gloria with her garden. She also had a brief affair with a friend of Tansy's, which proved awkward for everyone but had petered out. Monica had been determined to insert herself into the family – and was successful. It seemed like she'd always been one of them. Even Gloria liked her.

'Thanks for the SOP.' Monica snorted. '"Management of Gloria's Ankle". Hilarious.'

'I wasn't aiming for hilarious,' Kylie said. 'I was aiming for efficient.'

'Right, of course. Are you okay?' Mon said.

Kylie brushed pastry crumbs off her pants. Normally she brought a salad from home but of course Gloria had no ingredients, and no containers either. Kylie couldn't believe the cost of that roll! 'Of course. When have I not been okay?'

'About Colin, I mean. Tansy told me.'

This family. Always in each other's business.

'If you don't want to talk about it, that's cool.' Monica took a bite of her spinach roll.

'I can talk about it,' Kylie said. 'Why wouldn't I want to talk about it?'

Yet she didn't. Instead, she looked across the road, where a blue car was backing out of a driveway. In the house beside that, a woman in a pink dressing-gown with a mug in her hand was on her way to the letterbox. Further up the footpath, a man in a hi-vis shirt armed with a device was walking from house to house. All these strangers, going about their normal lives, probably with normal partners.

Mon cleared her throat. 'Poor Gloria. An ankle, that's tragic. She called me yesterday. Which is something she does. Lol. Mostly to talk about her Instagram account.'

Kylie's attention jerked back to Monica. 'Her . . . what?'

'It's looking ace – she's already got followers.'

Before Monica moved to the city, she was building a career as a social media influencer. Away from her mother's photogenic livestock, though, her posts became more suburban and pedestrian. Gone were the cute chickens and baby ducklings, and her mum's sourdough starter and jars of jams were no more. Monica's followers fell away. And living in Melbourne was expensive! She was just at the point of having to move back to her mother's when Simon asked her to do some social media marketing for his new landscaping business.

Monica's posts were fresh and friendly and soon Simon's plant supplier noticed, and so did a couple of Simon's clients with small businesses of their own. Now, six months later, Monica was earning okay money as a freelance social media consultant, running accounts for cafes and independent jewellery designers and home cookie manufacturers and footballers' wives.

'I hope Gloria is paying your normal fee. I'd be invoicing her extra if it were me. An annoyance mark-up,' Kylie said.

Monica was smart and hardworking with a stylist's eye for arrangement and colour, and her love for social media was entirely pure. Monica saw only its power to form online communities, subvert the messages of the powerful and connect people across distance, culture and circumstance. Unlike Kylie, who believed it reflected the downfall of society.

Monica rolled her eyes. 'Of course. It's not my first day on earth.'

'Good. If you're spending time at Gloria's whim, you deserve to be paid.'

'Sure, of course. But I can't charge her,' Monica continued, 'like, actual *money*, because she's *family*.'

'Jesus Christ,' said Kylie.

'It's all good! She's going to pay me in tennis lessons. She *wanted* to pay me, seriously. I had to insist she didn't,' Monica said earnestly, as if today was indeed her first day on earth.

Kylie knew that Monica was young and her childhood had been sheltered, but still. How could a grown woman not notice that she was being manipulated? It was beyond Kylie's understanding, the gullibility of people, the way their egos made them vulnerable to flattery and reverse psychology. When would Monica wise up?

'That's what she wanted you to think,' said Kylie. 'She's taking advantage of you. Just say no.'

'But I don't want to say no. I like helping Gloria. In fact, I'm not busy right now. What can I do to help?'

Nothing. Not a thing, Kylie told her. The Gloria problem was now solved, thanks to Ramona. If only the pharmacy disaster could be solved so easily.

For the next few hours, Kylie kept her head down. She gave an elderly couple a booster shot and pointed out a sunspot that should be checked by a GP, then took Mrs Lee's blood pressure, then discussed different anti-inflammatory creams with a personal trainer who was overdoing everything, and all while Emily hovered. Every now and then Gail returned from the storeroom where she was going through the inventory with Tim to watch Kylie with narrowed eyes and make little notes in her book. At one point when there were no customers, Kylie walked the shelves with a basket, picking out supplies for Gloria: painkillers, vitamin C, dry shampoo, several different ankle bandages. In the Family Planning section, she paused in front of the shelf of pregnancy tests. All those brands in their pink or blue boxes. In-stream and cup, digital and packaged with ovulation predictors. Results in two minutes, one minute. Early. Earlier.

It was a ridiculous thought. A completely unnecessary waste of money. Periods were not normally considered late until the seven-day mark. Hers was only four days late.

And yet.

Kylie couldn't recall her period ever being late before, not since she was a teenager. If nothing else, a test would put an end to it, once and for all. Give her peace of mind.

She looked from side to side. Sandy was restocking the contact lens solutions, Gail and Tim were in the storeroom, Emily was checking the trays in case there was a prescription she'd overlooked. Fast as a cat, Kylie snatched one of the pregnancy tests and dropped it in her basket. She hurried to the cash register and rang everything up herself, then she paid, packed it all in a paper bag and stashed it in her locker.

For the next hour, Kylie managed to get to most of the customers and scripts ahead of Emily.

'Kylie, let me help you!' Emily said. 'That's what I'm here for.'

'I've got it, thanks,' said Kylie.

'Emily managed a team of ten in a tiny field hospital and worked beside operating theatre personnel on a daily basis, saving lives in a war zone, Kylie,' said Gail. 'I'm sure she can handle a few prescriptions.'

'Stop, Gail.' Emily giggled softly, like rain falling on a tropical beach on a moonlit night. 'You're embarrassing me.'

Just after lunch, the store phone rang again. *If it was Nick again*, Kylie thought, *he'd regret it.*

Sandy answered it. 'It's for you,' she mouthed to Kylie. 'Your mum.'

Gail's head appeared in the doorway to the storeroom, as if she'd been waiting. 'You should know that we discourage personal calls at Pharmacy King,' she said.

'Noted,' Kylie said as she walked to the counter.

'I never make personal calls.' Emily tossed her long hair from one shoulder to the other. 'Except for once, when I had malaria. That was the delirium talking.'

Again Kylie turned her back on everyone and hunched over the receiver. 'Mum? Is everything all right?'

'Yes, yes, absolutely fine,' Gloria said. 'Right as rain. You weren't answering your mobile.'

Phew. Everything was fine. That was a relief.

'How's your day been so far?' said Gloria.

Kylie grunted. 'Haven't stabbed anyone so far.'

'Excellent. Just one thing,' Gloria said. 'And no rush at all, but Ramona is heading off. Right now. She won't be here when you get home tonight, sadly.'

Oh no.

'Mum. What did you do?'

'Nothing that didn't need to be done,' said Gloria.

Chapter 19

If Kylie left work immediately, she could make it home in time to catch Ramona. Which was obviously vital. Without Ramona, how could Kylie work full-time, perfectly, to impress Gail, and also look after Gloria at the same time? She needed to apologise for whatever Gloria had done or said and change Ramona's mind about leaving.

On the other hand, leaving work now would only make Kylie look even less reliable, especially compared to Emily, the smiling superwoman pharmacist.

Her mother or her job. Kylie groaned, she tugged at her hair. She didn't even try to explain things to Gail, who wasn't the boss of her. (Yet.) She told Gloria to have Ramona wait for twenty minutes and told Tim she was taking the rest of the day off.

'Fine with me,' said Tim. 'I hope Gloria's okay.'

'Yay!' said Emily. 'I mean, I'm sorry about your mum. Family comes first.'

'We usually require a week's notice in writing prior to requesting a personal day,' said Gail.

'Noted,' Kylie said to all of them, as she grabbed her handbag and her shopping from her locker.

'You can't be in charge of everything, you know.' Sandy leaned against the front door and opened it wide for Kylie.

'Why not?' Kylie muttered as she passed. 'Why can't I?'

Gloria's house looked normal from the outside, but Kylie ran up the path as though there was a fire.

'Mum?' she called as she let herself in.

There was no answer. She wandered through the house to Gloria's room to find her lying in bed in her dressing-gown, reading. In blatant violation of Gloria's own decree, Caesar was lying on top of the covers across her lap. Caesar raised his head lazily and growled at Kylie.

'Now, now, darling,' Gloria stroked Caesar's head. 'It's just Kylie.'

Unbelievable. Kylie dropped her bag on the floor and pinched the bridge of her nose, hard, as though her brain was at risk of leaking out. 'What about the rules, Mum? The dog is not allowed on the furniture, that's what we discussed.'

'Rules exist for a reason, Kylie. And that reason is to identify people who lack the imagination to think for themselves so the rest of us know whom to avoid. Ramona?' Gloria called out. 'Kylie's home.'

Ramona came out of the kitchen, wiping her hands on a tea towel. 'Kylie,' she said, 'I am very grateful for this job. But also, I quit.'

'Tell her the big news,' said Gloria.

'There's bigger news?' said Kylie.

Ramona grinned and leaned forward with her hands on her knees. 'I go to Cairns. Tonight!'

Gloria ran her fingers through Caesar's fur and smiled at Kylie angelically. 'She goes to Cairns tonight!'

'Tonight?' said Kylie. 'Cairns, in Queensland?'

'Turns out,' said Gloria, 'that Ramona has a fiancé.'

'*Had* fiancé,' said Ramona.

'They'd split up over the silliest thing,' said Gloria.

'Your mother, she is very wise,' said Ramona. 'We fight. I have been very unhappy. Very, very unhappy. But Gloria is right! We are young, we are in love. We should be together! He wants to drive to beaches in a Kombi, learn scuba, whatever. I phone him. I will go. Gloria, she inspires me.'

Kylie never drank to excess. It was messy, mindless. It achieved nothing. But in that moment, she wanted nothing more than to be wildly drunk and swaying, beyond the point of caring about anything. 'You can't just throw your career away for a partner!' Kylie said.

'Can.' Ramona looked at Gloria with wet eyes. 'Not every patient is kind like Gloria.'

Gloria sniffed. 'Young love! It's inspiring. Besides, one must have a certain internal fortitude to deal with patients. Ramona is too kind-hearted.'

Kylie looked from Ramona to Gloria and back again. How could she have been so wrong about Ramona? Had Kylie culturally stereotyped her? Had she imagined that Eastern Europeans were solid, stoic, unimpressionable, when in fact Ramona was as giddy as a schoolgirl, unable to resist Gloria's wiles?

'Be sensible,' Kylie said. 'You have a good job here. What are you going to do for money?'

'Gloria fix already,' said Ramona.

'I made a few calls.' Gloria shrugged, modestly. 'There are a number of tennis schools in Cairns looking for someone with Ramona's physical therapy experience.'

'I have clients lined up!' Ramona held her hands to her heart. 'I will be making *same* money in much less time, and cost of living is less! And all thanks to Gloria.'

'I just want you to be happy,' said Gloria.

Kylie felt a steel band tightening around her forehead. *Happy*! What a ridiculous concept. If that was what mattered in life, no work would ever get done by anyone, anywhere! Besides, Gloria did not care about Ramona being happy. She cared only about getting her own way, which meant not having a nurse. This was a direct challenge to Kylie's authority.

Kylie turned to Gloria. 'You think this is over.' She felt her nostrils flare. 'It's not over.'

Gloria smiled beatifically. 'We'll see,' she said.

After Ramona gathered her belongings and left to catch her flight, tearfully grateful, Kylie felt her seed of a headache begin to sprout long tendrils along the centre of her forehead.

'I have a life, you know. I have work commitments. I could just stop helping you,' Kylie said. 'Where would you be then?'

'I am very grateful for your help, but *helping* does not mean *controlling*. But of course, you are free to do whatever you want.' Gloria was calmness itself, laying on the bed like a Zen monk beside her novice, running her fingers through Caesar's fur.

She was infuriating!

Kylie grumbled and muttered and stomped for a while. Then she helped Gloria pee, then took Caesar out to pee, then made Gloria a cup of tea, which lately involved making three or four teas and bringing them all to Gloria on a tray so she could choose the cup with the correct steepness. Then she found some food Gloria would eat, then did the dishes, then unclogged the laundry drain.

Then Kylie headed back to the bedroom. Gloria was propped up in bed wearing her cat's eye reading glasses, a number of bottles of nail polish beside her on top of the covers. She glared at Gloria from the doorway.

'You manipulated Ramona for your own purposes,' said Kylie

'Oh darling.' Gloria chose one bottle and shook it, then she extracted the brush, removing the excess polish against one edge, and painted the longest of Caesar's nails a neon pink. 'That's nonsense. I merely took the trouble to find out what would make her happy and helped her achieve it. Her family's in Europe – she has no support. I was just trying to make the world a better place for one woman.' She was concentrating on each of Caesar's nails, painting them pink in turn. When she was done, she blew on them. 'Ramona is in love! She didn't want to be a nurse in the first place, I could tell. She wasn't even wearing scrubs.'

'She didn't have to wear scrubs! She wasn't here to remove your spleen.' Kylie lay down on the bed beside Gloria and folded her arms on her chest. 'What happens now, Mum? You need help and I have to work.'

Gloria shrugged. 'I'll manage.'

It was all too much. Kylie should have tried something easier than looking after Gloria, like solving the homelessness crisis or mediating between North and South Korea. Kylie was almost ready to admit defeat.

'You're killing me, Mum,' she said. 'Seriously.'

Gloria frowned, and looked at Kylie over her glasses. 'Have you gained weight? Around your middle.'

'What?'

'You look different, that's all. Very nice, but different. It suits you.'

Have you gained weight? What kind of a question was that, coming from your own mother? Kylie wriggled up from the bed, huffed to the door and marched to the kitchen.

'It was just an observation,' Gloria called after her. 'No need to get snippy.'

Snippy? Kylie was not *snippy*. Yes, apparently she had gained weight around her middle over the last few weeks, but staying with Gloria certainly hadn't helped, beginning with the packet of Cheezels at the hospital. Also, there was barely anything to eat in this house except frozen peas and pickles from the Cretaceous era, which led to inappropriate snacking. Exhaustion made people eat more, as did frustration. Kylie needed to be back in her own house, back to her old rhythms.

She would not give up. Tomorrow morning, she'd ring the nursing agency again and brief them differently this time. More . . . honestly. Ramona had been insufficiently prepared for dealing with Gloria. She'd imagined her as a stereotypical mum, someone like her own mother perhaps. Traditional mothers were cuddly with short auburn hair with grey roots and wire-frame glasses. They were fond of Words with Friends and baking caramel slices and watching that nice Professor Alice Roberts explore historic towns on SBS. Kylie had told the agency over the phone that Gloria was a children's tennis coach, so no doubt Ramona had imagined someone like a school lunch lady, gently lobbing balls at concentrating little boys with glasses and little girls with knock-knees, patiently building their hand-eye coordination and their confidence.

This time Kylie would specify she wanted someone with a qualification in psychological warfare. Someone utterly committed to nursing with no secret passions to do anything else or be anywhere else. Someone who was not *in love* and was immune to any kind of manipulation.

Tomorrow, another nurse would arrive and Kylie could leave and go to work, and Gloria and the new nurse would get on so well that Kylie could work all day. Then, as Gloria improved, Kylie could begin to sleep in her own bed.

A snack would make her feel better. She opened the fridge, then closed it again.

Who was she kidding? Once Gloria had her heart set on something, nothing and no one would change her mind. All at once, Kylie felt impossibly weary, as though she were holding up the world by herself. She leaned against the fridge and held her face in her hands.

Kylie had arranged to go the movies with Alice that night, Thursday, but midafternoon she snuck up to Tansy's bedroom and called the vet clinic to cancel. She couldn't leave Gloria at home by herself, she told Alice. As well as her high-maintenance mother, she had somehow temporarily adopted a high-maintenance Pomeranian and she needed to finish her job application and Nick's SOP. Besides, she was groggy with exhaustion. She wouldn't be able to keep her eyes open during the film.

'Lucky you. I love Pomeranians,' Alice said when she took the call. 'I wouldn't mind an early night myself. It's our monthly Spay Day, which is exhausting. I'm right in the middle of castrating a German Shepherd now.'

'Sounds fascinating.'

'From most people, that would be sarcasm,' Alice said. 'But I know you mean it.'

Kylie did mean it. Alice's clientele was wildly different from hers but she envied Alice's ability to personally intervene. Veterinary medicine was direct, hands-on, tactile. Alice touched her patients, looked them in the eyes and took their measure. Kylie knew how important her own work was, how much her customers relied upon her. Still, the sticking of labels onto boxes of drugs prescribed by someone else seemed remote and tepid compared with holding a small mewing or barking creature in her hands.

'Just a sec while I exteriorise this testicle,' Alice said.

Kylie looked at the ceiling. After a few moments, Alice came back.

'Okay, done!' she said cheerily. 'What were you saying?'

'That I don't feel lucky. I feel like I'm in Dante's tenth circle of hell – parental frustration.'

'You should count your blessings. I'd give anything to take a week off work and spend time with my mum, the darling. I'd make shortbread. We'd play Scrabble and watch old episodes of *Vera*.'

'Gloria doesn't eat shortbread,' Kylie said. 'If you can't make a toastie out of it, it's a biscuit, it's not bread, she says. Scottish people need to stop lying to themselves about the amount of sugar they're consuming.'

'Oh.'

'And she did have a Scrabble set once. But she played with Mia and Lachie when they were younger and used four-letter words so Tansy confiscated it. And she doesn't like *Vera*. She hates her clothes. Gloria's favourite movie is *Kill Bill*.'

'Right,' said Alice. 'I forgot who we were talking about for a minute. You need to rethink your expectations.'

'I didn't expect her to inspire her nurse to quit!'

Alice hesitated ominously. 'Listen, if you're really desperate, I know someone who can start tomorrow.'

'It's pointless. She won't have anyone.'

'Unless Gloria's bite is literally worse than her bark, I've got the perfect nurse for you.'

'Seriously? Who?'

'Well.' Alice spoke slowly, drawing out her response. 'Someone who is currently unemployed, is experienced in aged care, and bar work, and labouring, is happy to do anything, is always cheerful and who owes me big time.'

Kylie had a long night ahead. Alice was her best friend, but Kylie had no brain space for nonsense. Her thoughts were uncharacteristically foggy today, yes, but it didn't take a first-class degree with honours to work out what Alice was implying.

'Alice. This is my mother we're talking about. I'm cross now, but I really do adore her. Please don't say Leo.'

'Leo,' said Alice.

Chapter 20

After Kylie finished talking with Alice, she tackled Nick's SOP for the open day.

Nick wasn't a baby anymore. His irresponsible phase was over, mostly – it had been years since Kylie had helped him prepare a speech for breaking up with someone, or loaned him money, or picked him up in the early hours hiding outside a party in a distant suburb because he'd accidentally run into someone he'd accidentally shagged. Kylie didn't want him to feel patronised, so the open-day SOP ended up much abbreviated compared with Nick's famous twenty-first birthday one, which was seventeen pages long with three appendices and an index. For this SOP she decided against attaching a map with the route from his place to the tennis centre, and she'd skipped the detailed instructions, with illustrations, of how to attach the net. The actual exercises and games – well, he could sort those out on his own. He was a former athlete and great with kids. That kind of thing was in his DNA.

Even this simplified version, though, took Kylie longer than she'd anticipated. There was so much at stake. Yes, Gloria would be there to supervise but in these days of Google reviews and Facebook posts, professional reputations were at the mercy of anyone with a grudge. Not to mention health and safety issues! Tennis racquets could be dangerous. One errant swing to the face of one child, one broken nose, and who would sign up to be taught by Gloria? No one, that's who.

After she finally finished Nick's SOP, Kylie turned to her job application. Her résumé, untouched for decades, needed sprucing. Under *References*, she put: *To be supplied on request,* so she could surprise them by giving Brian's name in the interview.

Applying for any job was tedious but applying for her own was humiliating, infantilising. And the application itself was just the beginning. The next step would be sitting in an interview answering lame questions in front of a panel of bored strangers with the muscles in your forehead hoicked up and your cheeks deliberately indented to give the appearance of a *welcoming demeanour* while explaining where you saw yourself in five years – the grown-up version of *what do you want to be when you grow up?*

The last time Kylie had held a résumé in her hand was in Tim's pharmacy all those years ago. She could shut her eyes and see the two chrome-tubed rattan chairs against the wall near the consulting area, where customers sat while waiting for prescriptions. She could see herself so vividly, as though she were still sitting in the left one that Wednesday afternoon twenty years ago, waiting for the interview for what would be her first job out of university.

See how skinny she was in her first proper suit, a merlot-coloured single-breasted she'd bought on sale at Cue? She loved that suit. She wished she could wear it every day, even Sundays. For the interview, she matched it with new heels that left gaping blisters on the ridges of her heel. You couldn't tell she was nervous because even then her facial expression was a cross between Kristen Stewart and Grumpy Cat. On her lap was a plastic folder with a spare copy of her application. She'd printed out references from her favourite lecturer and from her boss at the uni library where she worked part-time. She'd tried to think of everything.

She expected to be called into an office out the back somewhere. That was how interviews usually went, with the hiring manager sitting across a wide, intimidating table.

Tim hadn't called her anywhere. Instead he'd come out from around the counter during a quiet moment between prescriptions and he'd sat beside her as though they were two commuters waiting for a late bus. He took the résumé, asked a few questions about dispensing specific items and what she liked most about working with medicines and people. Tested her knowledge of basic contraindications and warnings. She remembered his gentle manner, the deliberate way he ran his finger down her résumé, reading the list of her subjects.

With grades like these, Tim had said, *you could work anywhere you want. Or stay in academia. Drug research, maybe.*

She hadn't answered. She didn't know how to explain her narrow horizons without making it seem a weakness, something she could overcome with a little gumption. That was a faulty interpretation, of course. Narrow horizons were a strength because it was easier to make everything perfect when there were fewer things to worry about.

Tim had nodded thoughtfully. *It's not the most exciting job. Community pharmacy. Some days can be slow. A little routine, for a young person.*

I'm not looking for excitement, Kylie had said. *That's the last thing I'm looking for.*

Tim had smiled. *You've come to the right place.*

She'd started working for him as soon as she graduated, in her suit and flight-attendant heels.

At first, Tim encouraged her to relax. She needn't wear the suit, he'd said. He was a jeans man himself – if he wore a suit to work, everyone would ask him who'd died. And those shoes! She'd be on her feet most of the day. Surely she could find something more comfortable. She hadn't yielded. Her suit was like maroon wool-blend armour. She doubled down and bought another and later, when she could afford it, another. Not pastels – she didn't go the full Hillary – but a mix of single and double-breasted in different fabric weights, all dark colours. She kept wearing the heels and in time her own feet formed calluses in the perfect spot; her remarkable body protecting the tender parts of her. She brought her own lunch she packed the night before and she took home all the trade magazines and journals to read in bed before turning out the light. Weekends were for professional development courses. After a while, Tim grew to accept her as she was.

Tim, she soon realised, had worried about hiring a graduate in case she'd wanted to introduce new products, change things.

She never had. Over time, they'd become . . . if not *friends*-friends, then good *work*-friends. Kylie went to Tim's wedding to Chris, when that was finally allowed. She was the one who'd hired Sandy when Maureen retired and she chose the locums when one of them had a day off or were on holidays, and when Tim had his hip replacement. She and Tim trusted each other. The world outside might have changed in the last two decades but here, tucked inside the pharmacy, nothing ever did.

Now, though, the past didn't matter. The only thing that mattered were the numbers in Gail Osborne's spreadsheet.

Could Kylie really blame Pharmacy King? It might seem just moments ago to her, but now the chrome on the chairs was peeling and the rattan was unravelling, and she sometimes worried that the chairs wouldn't take the customers' weight. The shelves were beginning to rust at the joins and the carpet was patchworked with stains from leaking hand cream testers and baby food and other substances that Kylie didn't like to think about. Soon Pharmacy King would park a skip on the street outside and bring in shopfitters and painters and designers. Everything here that was reliable and trustworthy would be thanked for its service then dumped and replaced with the new and the shiny, with the white and the bright and the neon.

Those chairs – and everything else that remained – were destined for the scrap heap. Whatever happened, her life was going to change.

Her fingers went to her stomach. She couldn't deny it any longer – there was something weird and hormonal happening to her body. Her fingers then went to her phone, where she googled *failure rate vasectomy.*

The results of her search? It was rare, but it was possible.

Her blood chilled. As horrific as it seemed, there was a slim chance she might be pregnant.

FRIDAY

Chapter 21

Kylie woke on the couch in her bra and undies after three hours of sweaty sleep to a persistent buzzing and the terrifying conclusion that she'd gone blind in the night. Perhaps a lack of sleep could do that to a person. Perhaps right now the blood flow to her amygdala was shrinking to a trickle and her heart was on the verge of giving up.

She wasn't blind, though, and the buzzing wasn't in her head. Caesar was asleep on her head like a fluffy orange Cossack hat. It was a miracle she hadn't been smothered. Caesar was not impressed at being woken and settled back on the couch while Kylie scrambled to find the source of the buzzing. Her forehead was itchy now as well as sweaty. She possibly had fleas. All at once, she recalled her googling from last night. She couldn't possibly be pregnant. Could she? That would be a disaster. And . . . to Colin? That would be a disaster of unprecedented proportions.

That buzzing would not stop.

'What, Mum?' she yelled into her phone. 'For the love of god, what do you want?'

But the buzzing wasn't coming from her phone. It was the front door.

'Kylie?' yelled Gloria from the bedroom. 'It's the front door.'

Caesar, disturbed again, stood on the couch and turned a little circle to resettle, grumbling, as if to say, *Will you two keep it down?*

Kylie staggered to her feet, wrapped the sheet around her and pincered to the door on her aching feet. Waiting on the front step was a man at least two inches shorter than her. His hair was soft and floppy and his beard was scruffy – naturally so, not deliberately like the trendy bartender who made their martinis the night of Gloria's fall. He wore fresh blue scrubs creased in large squares like they'd just come out of a packet, what appeared to be orthopaedic shoes, some kind of hippy braided bracelet around his left wrist and, over one shoulder, a black backpack.

'You must be kidding,' Kylie said.

Yes, Alice had promised to arrange it. Leo had changed, she'd said. Grown up. *The cavalry will come, I promise.* Kylie hadn't actually expected him to show – although he did look different than she recalled. His hair was too long and curled, with burnished gold tips that told of sun and salt water and hours of wasted time. His eyes were a vivid cobalt blue, although that might have been the effect of the scrubs.

'Kyles.' He inhaled sharply and leaned on the doorjamb. 'It's been ages. You look . . .' he paused, searching for the perfect word, '. . . awesome. How have you been? Still running the world?'

Leo was indecently pleasant for that hour, and physically relaxed to the point of drowsiness. His face was entirely without lines and his arms dangled loose on his shoulders, like a puppet.

'Fine, and if by "running the world" you mean having a career, then yes. What have you been up to, Leo?' She tried to make her voice sound as though she wanted to know.

'Oh, stuff.' Leo looked at her with measurable empathy, as if he knew all her troubles. 'Are you seeing anyone?'

It struck Kylie that Leo's voice was altogether lacking sharpness and timbre. She had known him since they were kids. She'd listened to Alice's recitations of his every false step and bad decision; his dropping out of school and backpacking for months, every time he'd been sacked for no-shows. Gloria needed a sergeant-major, someone who would bark at her. Leo sounded like the host of *Play School* reading *Where Is the Green Sheep?*

'Look, Leo. I'm sorry to have wasted your time, but this isn't going to work. Mum's decided she doesn't need help after all. She was very firm about it and it's important to respect that.'

Leo looked up at her like a puppy. 'Can I ask her, at least?'

She knew Leo to be a kind boy (he'd always be a boy to Kylie, despite being in his mid-thirties now). It was not his fault that he was born without a rudder. Or an engine. Or any form of propulsion or steering that would enable him to achieve anything. Even making it to Gloria's house by himself at this hour seemed wildly out of character. She was a woman dressed in a sheet, getting rid of someone who'd come all this way to do her a favour. *Be non-judgemental, Kylie*, she thought. Sure, Leo probably had nothing better to do with his time – he was likely spending his days standing outside Coles as a chugger for Greenpeace, or dealing weed. Still, he'd shown up here, in the suburbs, early in the morning with his new scrubs and dopey smile. He didn't deserve to be rejected out of hand.

She shrugged and led him to Gloria's room, dragging the sheet behind her like bride with an unwieldy train, past the couch where Caesar was scratching Kylie's remaining bedding into a more comfortable bed for himself.

'Nice Pomeranian,' Leo said.

Caesar raised his head with an expression of utter disdain.

Kylie knocked. Gloria was sitting up in bed, still in her dressing-gown. She looked at the two of them over her book, wearily. 'Kylie, not this again.'

'Yes, this again. Mum, you remember Leo? Alice's brother.'

Gloria shook her head, frowning.

'You've met him before, Mum. When Alice and I lived in the share house, when we were at uni? He often visited.'

'I was still at school, Mrs Schnabel. Once you bought me an ice cream,' said Leo.

'Oh yes.' Gloria sniffed. 'I didn't recognise you – your skin is much better now. Hello.' Then she went back to reading her book.

Leo chuckled. 'Puberty hormones, hey. I was pretty zitty as a kid.'

'Mum,' said Kylie, 'Leo's offered to give you a hand for a few days, but it's completely up to you.'

'No offence, Leo, but I neither want nor need a nurse.' Just then, Caesar leaped onto the bed and curled up beside Gloria. She wound her fingers through his fur. 'We don't like strangers in our house, do we, Caesar?' Then, to Leo, 'You can see yourself out.'

Kylie opened her mouth, but Leo spoke first.

'Sure, no worries. I don't want to get in your way.' He didn't seem perturbed. He gazed kindly at Gloria propped up in bed. 'I get it. You're an independent woman. Relying on other people, it's rubbish.'

'Rubbish, exactly,' said Gloria. 'Bye bye now.'

He nodded as if, in Gloria's place, he'd also send himself away. 'But seeing as I'm here already, I might as well make myself useful before I leave. What do you need, Gloria? I make a fantastic eggs Benedict.'

Oh no, Kylie thought. *Don't say tea. Don't say tea*.

'Tea,' Gloria said with a cruel smile. 'White with one.'

Well, that's the end of that. Leo didn't know enough to be afraid.

'Tea it is.' But Leo didn't head to the kitchen right away. Instead he unzipped his backpack, reached inside and pulled out a Pantone colour fan deck, the kind used by interior designers. He flicked his thumb over the long rectangular leaves until he chose two which he separated from the others, then he walked over to Gloria and offered them for her inspection. 'How strong?'

Gloria's eyes widened. She peered up at him, then down at the deck through her glasses, then pointed at a tan rectangle that looked to Kylie indistinguishable from the tan rectangles on either side of it.

'Yep, you're a 2314C. I might have guessed. You wouldn't believe how many people are 2317C! I mean, why bother, right?' He gave a soft chuckle and folded away his fan deck. 'I prefer to use loose tea, if you have any? I mean, tea bags are okay in a pinch but they aren't the same quality of leaf. And I'd rather use a pot? Tea in a bag can't circulate in the water in a cup, and also warming the cup first isn't the same as warming the pot. Because the pot has a lid, the heat is retained.'

'I'll just show you—' Kylie began.

'I'll find everything, no worries.' Leo held up one palm to her in an authoritative motion. Then headed off in the direction of the kitchen.

'Did he just tell me to stay? That was . . .' Kylie began when he'd left.

'Commanding. That young man knows how to look after someone,' Gloria said. 'How strange, I had him confused with someone else. In my mind, Alice's brother was an odd little boy who barely finished school and was always hanging around you girls. When did he study nursing? I thought he worked in a food co-op and rode one of those delivery bicycles. That boy had such a crush on you, Kylie. Or was that someone else?'

'Someone else,' Kylie said.

'He was wearing scrubs, did you notice?' Gloria went on. 'Obviously a theatre nurse.'

'Ah . . . I'm not sure he's *actually* a theatre nurse.' Still in her sheet, she wriggled over to the bed and sat beside Gloria.

There was sound of cupboards opening in the kitchen, then water running. This Leo experiment would end in disaster, Kylie felt it in her bones. She could imagine how the day would progress. She'd be at the pharmacy, concentrating on something important, with Gail looking over her shoulder and making notes in her little book and Emily telling everyone how she personally cured an entire village of leprosy, then Gloria would phone and she'd have to drop everything and scramble back here because Leo had vanished either due to his own chronic unreliability or because of some scheme of Gloria's, and she and/or Caesar needed to eat and/or pee.

'Listen, Mum, if you're not comfortable I can send Leo away. I don't want to leave you here alone with someone . . . odd.'

Gloria moved Kylie's hair away from her face. 'How did I raise someone so suspicious? That is a young man of exceptional character, I can tell. You should watch yourself, Kylie. Paranoia can creep into your brain like a slug – you must be alert to it. Weren't you going to pick up the equipment for tomorrow before work? I think Leo and I will be fine.'

Chapter 22

Yes, Kylie had promised Nick she'd pick up the open-day supplies, so she decided not to worry about Leo. But not because she was confident in his ability to look after Gloria. Now that the possibility of being pregnant had seeded itself in her brain, it was difficult to worry about anything else. Kylie had never wanted children. Being the eldest sibling in a single-parent family had been more than enough, thank you very much. Were she pregnant, it would be a disaster of a scale that would dwarf her other three disasters of work, Gloria's ankle and Colin.

Wait.

Colin.

If Kylie was pregnant, did she have to tell Colin? Was that the ethical course of action? After all, he need never know, because her decision was straightforward. She didn't want to call him. She wanted to never speak to him again. Although if she were pregnant, which she wasn't, it would equally be his responsibility. It would be more his responsibility than hers, actually, because the failed vasectomy was his. And if she were to keep it, which she wouldn't, after he recovered from the shock, Colin would be okay as a father. He was affectionate and gentle. He had a short attention span, true. Also, he could be anxious. Avoidant. A little wimpy. Kylie suffered from none of these flaws, thankfully. She could compensate for all of them.

Snap out of it, Kylie, she thought. There was no point agonising over a hypothetical problem that would likely never come to be. Instead, she would keep moving, think of other things. By 8 am, she was on the road in the convertible. The morning traffic was light; the day was cool and clear.

The sports store out on the highway was the size of an aircraft hangar. Sports of all kinds reminded Kylie of being a teenager in the house with Gloria and Nick and their obsessions – the pair of them going for runs or out on their bikes or bonding over tournaments of any and all kinds on TV at all hours. She hadn't grasped the finer details but she remembered conversations over breakfast about personal bests and most valuable players. Nick's childhood bedroom was and remained a poster-clad shrine to his heroes – serious men with their arms crossed, looking down upon his shelves of signed balls, collected after games in all weather. Kylie could remember being assaulted by the unique aroma of boys' trainers every time she passed his door.

This will only take a little while, she thought. She didn't want to spend any more time surrounded by athletic gear than absolutely necessary.

Kylie's hopes of a quick getaway were shattered though as she pulled into the carpark. It was fast filling with SUVs and, if the stick-figure families plastered on the back windows were any guide, many children were likely to be inside. Both an inflatable wavy-arms guy and a huge sign out the front told her that a meet-and-greet breakfast event for AWFL Demons was just about to start. Kylie had forgotten it was school holidays.

Wait . . . it was school holidays? That meant Nick wasn't working today after all. Kylie smacked the steering wheel. He should be the one doing this! Her brother was incorrigible.

Inside, the store was cavernous and bright – a shrine to wanton physicality. Most of the space was filled with towering shelves and bins with all kinds of equipment and clothes – a wall of shoes, another of cricket pads, a corner filled with dozens of basketball hoops – but in a clearing was a huge freestanding cardboard bullseye and a large net full of footballs.

At last Kylie found an attendant who took down the reference number Nick had texted her. The special hire orders were in the back, he told her. It would take a little while to find someone to fetch it.

'Can you hurry?' she said.

'We're short-staffed and it's a big day,' he said, nodding at the bullseye. He suggested she should take Gloria's notice down from the bulletin board while she was waiting.

Bulletin board? Kylie vaguely remembered the concept. When Gloria had said *a notice had gone up*, Kylie had assumed she meant on Facebook. But sure enough, on the wall near the front door among flyers for lost skateboards, croquet mallet repair and netball players wanted for a Wednesday night mixed league, was Gloria's notice advertising her open day as 'fun for children of all ages'. It even had little strips on the bottom for ripping off with her phone number, as though it were the twentieth century and she was selling a lightly used Betamax.

Gloria had done well, though. Almost all of the little strips were gone.

Kylie took down the notice and folded it. She found a seat at the end of a row of folding chairs and as she waited, the store began to fill. Staff were dressed as umpires, and the MC – a grinning television commentator – began instructions for a handballing competition, shepherding pre-teen girls in guernseys and shorts into lines while parents hovered, looking sleepy, or annoyed, or both, drinking coffee from keep cups and looking at their phones. The girls came in different varieties: keen girls, grouping around the net of balls, and shy ones who stayed within a foot of their parents, and some that were keen but trying to look bored, and others that were bored and trying to look keen. Several were taller than Kylie, with legs that seemed engineered for football. A few looked terrified, like they wished they were anywhere but here, and one seemed on the verge of tears, but all the girls were quiet and orderly and patient.

'I wish I could control them like that,' said one of the dads, standing up the back.

Then the MC asked the girls to line up and they began to handball on cue, one by one, aiming for the target. Some were nonchalant, sailing the ball towards the hole with practised ease. Others were etched with concentration, teeth gritted, hands jangly. Some of them shivered as they waited their turn, excitement visible under their skin. Some were born sharp-shooters and others couldn't have hit the back of a barn, but even the ones who'd failed in the first round stepped up for another attempt without hesitation. They were fearless, all of them, and kind – the way they patted the unsuccessful on the back and cheered for the winners of each round.

As Kylie watched, something inexplicable overtook her, filling her with a warm, bright fire. Those girls. Their shiny limbs and shiny faces. They were magnificent.

Kylie could not tear her gaze away. How beautiful they were, how majestic. They were young women, really, on the verge of adulthood. Their lives were before them and they could do anything, and they would. They would change the world. The pride their parents must feel, it was overwhelming.

'Which one's yours?' a voice said beside her.

Kylie started. She hadn't even noticed the woman sit down. Her hands flew to her stomach. This question that she'd been asked so often – all at once, she couldn't find an answer.

She was saved by the sales assistant, apologising for the delay and asking her to drive around to the loading dock.

Back at the car, she took the roof down for easier packing. The assistant appeared from the back of the store, and stood beside a half-pallet of boxes with a clipboard in his hand.

'Which ones are mine?' said Kylie.

'All of them,' he said.

There must be some mistake. She took the list from him – three pages of it. Not just balls and racquets for (the majority of, Gloria predicted) children who would arrive without one, but spare shoelaces and spare strings, overgrips in a variety of colours and designs for children whose parents had bought them a racquet that they could 'grow into' but was too big to effectively hold, bags to carry said racquets and balls, microfibre towels for sweaty little mitts, mini-nets, a first-aid kit and a number of wire ball holders to be positioned around the court. There were sign-up sheets and a credit card machine and boxes of juggle scarves and bean bags and small blow-up beach balls for games for the littlies, and a box of promotional headbands and another of wristbands as giveaways.

Gloria, not unexpectedly, had gone overboard.

'We don't usually accept orders at such short notice,' he said. 'If it wasn't for Gloria, we would have said to pick it up on Monday. You'll be right to pack it yourself?'

Kylie looked at her Fitbit. It was past ten o'clock already – she'd been so absorbed in watching the girls that she hadn't noticed. Her week had been a broken record of predictable failure after failure – she was cursed and there was no use fighting it. She was out of options, torn in half. She rang the pharmacy and told Sandy she wouldn't be in until after lunch.

It was almost eleven by the time Kylie was back at Gloria's garage, unpacking and sorting everything for tomorrow. The garage was, like the rest of the house, unchanged since Kylie was a child: the workbench still on one side and above it, dusty jars of screws and nails attached to the wall by their lids. A beer fridge stood in the back corner. Somehow Kylie had to find room to organise all this new gear.

She heard someone calling her name. It was Nick, walking up the drive wearing designer trainers, slim-fit chinos and a blazer. The fact that he was here, and the cost of his outfit, made Kylie want to smack him in the back of the head.

'You thought I wouldn't realise it was school holidays?' she said.

'Yeah, sorry. It slipped my mind.'

'I bet.'

Nick began strolling around the garage, idly opening and closing boxes with one hand and swinging a racquet with the other. 'Did you count the stuff when you picked it up? Because you can't trust the store, that's what Mum said.'

'I'm checking it now. You could have come with me this morning, if you're so concerned.'

After a few minutes of watching her, Nick leaned against the convertible and tilted his head back. 'This. Is. So. Boring.'

It *was* boring. Gloria's open day wasn't an easy, fun couple of hours whacking balls to (at?) small children. In reality it was a much bigger deal. Kylie was once again glad she had stuck to her resolution and refused to become involved.

Nick took a ball from one of the boxes and hit it against the bare garage wall with the flat of his hand. 'Kids don't need all this stuff, surely.'

'Right?' said Kylie. 'Normal people start to act like doomsday preppers when they have kids. Mia and Lachie have so much *stuff*.'

Nick nodded. 'I thought about having a word to Tansy about it but you know what she's like.'

'So touchy.'

'She's like, "you have no children, what do you know?" As if only parents can have opinions about parenting.'

'I know!'

'And Simon takes everything personally,' said Nick 'He was an only child, you can tell. Used to everything going his way. No siblings to toughen him up.'

The ball had bounced against the wall and back towards Nick in a perfect arc and he hit it back against the wall again, and again. And again. He had been a professional athlete, yes, and handball against a garage wall wasn't the most demanding of physical pursuits, yet even in this, there was something captivating about the way Nick's body moved. His lazy feet stepped with ease and grace, effortlessly arriving in the perfect position to return the ball, and his balletic arms swooped to connect with the ball at the height of its bounce. His eyes and his brain and his body all worked seamlessly towards his goal with the same grace as Gloria, in both her everyday movements and on the tennis court.

'How about giving me a hand tomorrow?' Nick said.

Kylie lifted a box and moved it a few feet to one side, like a witness in *Law & Order* who, for some inexplicable reason, keeps working, nonplussed, while being questioned by the detectives about some horrific crime. 'N. O. I do not play tennis.'

'Yeah, that's right. You're unco.'

'What?'

'You're terrible at anything physical.'

'What? Where did you get that idea? I most certainly am not.'

'Then why don't you play sport? Or do any proper exercise at all? Walking doesn't count. It does nothing for your aerobic fitness.'

'Walking does count. And I've had more important things to think about than sport.'

'You're busy now, I get that. But after Dad left, when Mum started to get serious about coaching, she taught Tansy and me. Tansy isn't brilliant, but she can hold her own in a social game. You were in high school by then, sure, but you flat-out refused. You'd rather stay home by yourself than hang out with us.'

'I'm not sporty. Never have been.'

'It wasn't tryouts for Man City. It was hitting a few balls around a court with your mother and sister and brother. Was it part of your conscious rejection of everything to do with Mum?'

'My *what*?'

Nick bent to reclaim the ball, then he picked another two from the open box and began to idly juggle the three of them. 'You know.'

'I don't know.' Kylie put down the racquet she was cleaning and turned to face him. 'Why don't you explain it to me?'

'Kylie, whatever choice Mum makes about her life, you make the opposite one. If she says something's black, you'll say it's white.'

Kylie folded her arms and leaned back against the car. 'At least I didn't become a professional athlete merely to suck up to her. If she was a chef, you'd be up to your elbows in cookie dough right now. If she was a dancer, you'd be a ballerino.'

'A ballerino?'

'A male ballet dancer, doofus.'

'No one but you knows what that word means. You are such a nerd.'

'And you're a grown man still desperate for Mummy's approval.'

'Am not,' Nick said, catching all three balls against his chest.

'Oh please! *Mum, darling* this! *Mum, angel* that! *I would've brought flowers but there was a nuclear accident on the way to the florist and I had to personally rescue a busload of old age pensioners using three paddle-pop sticks and a tube of hand sanitiser!* I've changed your nappies, so I know exactly what went on in there. You are still full of it.'

'Will you shut up about the nappies, god. It's been thirty-six years and you're still talking about my nappies.'

'Because changing your nappies scarred me for life. And *you* shut up.'

'Make me.' Nick began juggling the three balls again, easily. He stepped closer, still juggling, until he was standing right in front of Kylie.

'If one of those balls touches me . . .' said Kylie.

'Not touching you,' said Nick, as each ball sailed up and down in the air centimetres from Kylie's face.

'So help me . . .'

'Still not touching you.'

The tennis balls floated in front of her face, up and down.

'In one minute, I'll be touching the both of you,' Gloria said from behind Nick. 'Don't think I can't.'

Gloria was at the garage door with her crutches and the heavy boot, her face a storm. The tennis balls fell from Nick's hands and bounced harmlessly away. Both he and Kylie stared at the cement floor.

'She started it,' said Nick. 'I was minding my own business.'

Kylie turned to him. 'You little suck.'

'Kylie! Honest to god, I turn my back for one minute,' said Gloria. 'I expect better from you. You know how important this open day is to me. And Nick, Kylie has told you she doesn't want to help, so leave her alone.'

'It's not that I don't want to,' Kylie said.

'It's that she's terrible at sport, and she's no good with kids,' said Nick.

'Neither of those things are true,' said Gloria. 'She's having a very busy week. She's been here looking after me, and she's been terribly upset with that Colin business.'

'What?' said Kylie. 'No, I haven't. I've hardly given him a thought. Honestly, Colin who?'

'Her job disaster, then,' said Gloria. 'Show a bit of sympathy, Nicky. She's on the verge of unemployment.'

'I'm really not,' said Kylie. 'I'll fix it. Don't worry. I have it all in hand.'

'See? She's not helping because she knows she'd stuff it,' said Nick. 'No one would sign their kids up if Miss Grumpy's there.'

'I'll have you know that I am terrific with children, and at tennis.'

'Kylie, it's fine! It's good for Nicky and me to do something together, just the two of us,' Gloria said. 'Mother–son bonding time.'

'Right. This is a special day for me and Mum. You'd stuff it anyway. I am doing this on my own and that is final,' said Nick.

'I'm the eldest, I outrank you,' Kylie said. 'I'm coming. You can't stop me.'

'Mum, tell her she can't come. You picked me first,' said Nick. 'This is so unfair.'

'Are you sure, Kylie?' said Gloria. 'It's completely up to you.'

She nodded. How dare Nick tell her what she could and couldn't do?

'If you're sure? I guess you can share,' said Gloria.

'I'll have to change my SOP,' said Kylie. 'But that's fine.'

After Nick left, Kylie sent a text to Tim saying that something had come up with Gloria and she couldn't work tomorrow. She received a thumbs-up emoji in reply. Then she pulled up YouTube and was soon lost down a rabbit hole of warm-ups, forehands, backhands and drills. She went over foot positions for each stroke, rehearsing until they were rote, and practised changing grips until every movement was second nature. Then she cleared some boxes away from the garage wall so she had a bit more width to practise on.

Kylie knew she had certain practical disadvantages compared with Nick. His was an equal-opportunity charm that affected men and children, and possibly animals and inanimate objects, as well as women. Kylie lacked both Nick's golden touch and Tansy's no-nonsense warmth. To compensate, she would work harder. Try harder.

She began padding the ball against the wall with a racquet, gently at first. After a while, she found it came easier. She was deliberate, focused. She hit the ball, it hit the wall, then bounced, then she returned it. Again. And again. So far, so good.

She held the racquet perfectly and concentrated on every stroke and every swing. She would run wonderful exercises tomorrow, no one could stop her.

When she came inside again, she crept upstairs, avoiding Gloria and Leo. Sitting on the single bed in Tansy's room looking at James Van Der Beek and those Hanson twerps, she texted Alice to tell her that Leo had arrived and all was well so far. Privately, though, she thought it couldn't last. Leo was too, too . . . Leo-ish. He strolled through the world as though nothing bad would ever happen. Gloria would soon find some way to get rid of him.

All at once, she stopped texting to listen.

What was that weird sound, coming from downstairs? Was somebody being strangled? Or was Gloria . . . *laughing?* What on earth was happening down there?

Kylie leaned back against Tansy's bedhead. She'd just rest here for a moment before she headed into work.

Kylie's mouth was stale and clammy. It took a moment to recall where she was. Her brain was woolly. She was vertical instead of horizontal and when she opened her bleary eyes the sunlight was lower through the window. Her face felt tight and sore. There was drool down one side of her face and on Tansy's pillow.

Oh. My. God. She'd fallen asleep.

How could she have fallen asleep? And how long had she slept?

She checked her Fitbit – it was after five.

This wasn't possible. She'd slept the entire afternoon away. How could that have happened! She was supposed to have been at work hours ago. How would she explain this to Tim? To Gail?

And what had finally woken her? Had the front door slammed, the sound of Leo bolting like a prisoner on day release? She didn't think so. Kylie leaped to her feet, checking her pockets for her phone. There were no missed calls, no notifications at all.

She crept down the stairs. Gloria looked up from where she reclined on the couch, sipping a cup of tea that was obviously acceptable, while Caesar slept on her lap.

'She's up!' Gloria said, as if waking was a thrilling novelty, as if Kylie didn't do it every day.

'Mum. Why didn't you wake me?'

'You obviously needed it. You must have been exhausted. And don't worry, I know how you are about things like that so I called Tim for you.'

Kylie felt a chill. 'You what?'

'I rang Tim. He was fine.'

Oh no. This wasn't school, where your mother phoned the absentee line – which had never happened to Kylie anyway except in Year 6 when she'd had her tonsils out. She would seem not only unreliable but cowardly, hiding behind her mother's skirts. This was the kind of thing that was recorded on your permanent record. It was unthinkable.

'We had a lovely chat,' continued Gloria. 'In fact, he said to tell you not to worry coming in at all today because it was probably too late to make a difference anyway, whatever that meant. He'll see you on Monday.'

Kylie ran one hand through her hair, gripped it near her scalp and pulled. Too late to make a difference to her job application, is that what he meant? *Too late* in a good way, or in a bad way? Then Kylie noticed that everything seemed . . . fresher. There were vacuum marks on the carpet and the scent of Mr Sheen hung in the air.

'Is . . . everything okay?' she said.

'Why wouldn't it be?' Gloria said. 'Don't be such a drama queen, Kylie. The world can cope without you for one day.'

That was obviously ridiculous. If she wasn't so discombobulated, she would have laughed. 'Where's Leo?'

'In here,' he called from the spare room, where he was de-casing a floral pillow next to Gloria's stripped bed. 'I thought I'd put a load on. Nothing like fresh sheets to make someone feel better.'

'Isn't he thoughtful?' said Gloria.

There was no point ringing Tim now – the pharmacy was already closed. And what could she possibly say? Besides, Patrick was picking her up for her date in an hour and a half. Kylie still felt that daytime sleep daze; muddle-headed and dopey. What she needed was exercise. Her body would begin to feel like itself again, instead of this alien shell.

In fact, she'd go for a run. Lack of exertion was probably what was making her body feel so strange, and she could also show Nick how wrong he was about her fitness, and her coordination.

In the back of Gloria's wardrobe Kylie found pairs of sports shoes of various brands, all of them new-ish. She chose the pair that looked the biggest, that would fit her if she wore thin socks. She found a new pair of workout tights with the price tag still on, a clean t-shirt, and a tight crop top she could wear over her normal bra that should eliminate bounce (or as much as was possible anyway). She changed into her mother's clothes in the upstairs bathroom. She laced up the shoes, tight.

Downstairs, Gloria was still on the couch with her leg up, now playing cards with Leo. They lifted their heads. Both of them had mud masks on their faces – they looked like two Willards about to rise out of the water to kill two Kurtzes. Caesar, having orange fur on his face in place of skin, reclined with two discs of cucumber over his eyes in lieu of a mask.

'What, Kylie?' muttered Gloria, her mouth immobile under the mask.

Kylie did not reply. She headed out the front door, and as she did, she wondered how long ago it was that she'd been for a run. It had been quite a long time, but in her twenties she'd run often. It was like riding a bicycle. She was fit. She had always been fit. Nick was completely wrong about walking being unrelated to aerobic fitness. A short run around the block would be easy.

Should she stretch first? That's what she used to do when she ran regularly. She reached down to touch her toes and pull backwards on her foot. It seemed she couldn't reach as far as usual. For some reason, her hamstrings were tight. She loosened and retied her shoes again then off she went, running down the drive.

Wow, cement is hard! was her first thought. It reverberated through her feet and up the long bones of her legs so she felt the shudder in her knees, fighting a desire to stop that was almost overwhelming. She forced herself on, gingerly, taking great care when she placed each foot. If she were to roll an ankle now she would be even more similar to Gloria – two ducks hobbling around on one leg each. That would be more than she could stand.

By the time she reached the corner it was clear that something had gone terribly wrong. This bore no resemblance to her earlier running. This was a gaping, quaking embarrassment. She noticed nothing of her surroundings, not a tree, not a house. In only a few minutes her face was a burning scarlet and her lungs were heaving. Actual stars began to orbit around her head as though she were a cartoon character hit in the head by a falling anvil. She thought she might be sick.

Somehow she made it around the block and back to Gloria's like a gazelle – not a graceful, bouncy gazelle, but one that was a hundred and ten in antelope years and absolutely over avoiding cheetahs and instead looking for a quiet place to lay down and die.

Kylie hoped none of Gloria's neighbours had seen her. She shuddered in the back door and peeked around the corner to check the coast was clear, then she limped up the stairs. Blood pounded in her ears and there was a distinct possibility she had peed herself a little bit. Kylie had no idea whose body this was. Despite the more than twenty years between her and Gloria, they were both unable to go for a simple run. Gloria, though, had a better excuse.

What had happened to her? She was forty-three years old, not seven hundred. It was not linked to the very, very low possibility of being pregnant. Perhaps she was coming down with something.

Upstairs in the bathroom, Kylie put her head under the water and gulped then wiped her mouth with the back of her hand. Then she froze.

Before her in the mirror was her mother.

Or at least, the mother she remembered as a teenager. The shape of the eyes and their colour and the way they tilted down at the corners were the same, as was the shape of the face and the jowls that were once straight as a ruler and were now as soft as a cotton ball. Gloria's hair was a dark blonde and the woman in front of her had black hair, but apart from that, the same. Although – she leaned closer to the mirror – lighter roots were beginning to show. *Grey* roots.

It hurt. The whole thing hurt, growing less like herself and more like someone else, and she couldn't hold the gaze of the woman in the mirror anymore. When she looked down at her hands, splayed flat on the bench in front of the sink, they were also achingly familiar in appearance. Fingers spread wide and stiff, as though measuring something invisible. She had seen those hands a million times in her childhood: flat on tennis skirts as they were being ironed, stretched wide around teacups.

Kylie's hands, her face, her body – they belonged to someone else. They belonged to a mother. Her mother.

Her hands began to shake. Being back in this house, it was doing her head in.

Chapter 23

Unbelievably, Kylie was wearing make-up, which went against everything she believed. It was Gloria's fault. She had thrown her hands in the air and nagged and exclaimed and sworn and insisted. Yes, Kylie had come back from her run with her face red and blotchy, but what was the big deal? If Patrick didn't like her the way she was, a normal human woman with normal human skin, it was fine with her. In the end, Kylie had allowed Gloria to apply a tinted moisturiser, mascara, a nude lipstick and neutral eyeshadow – but only after negotiating a concession from Gloria. If Leo didn't work out, as Kylie still expected, Gloria agreed to have another nurse look after her during the day. It was an acceptable deal.

Now, Kylie was upstairs, checking her face in the bathroom mirror. At least it was the kind of make-up that didn't look like make-up at all.

'Kylie!' Gloria called from downstairs. 'Your date will be here soon!'

Yes, yes.

The next 21st-century dilemma – what to wear. Kylie had only casual clothes and her work suit with her so she borrowed the longest and stretchiest of Gloria's dresses. It was fancier than her own clothes. Would Patrick think she'd worn make-up and dressed up to impress him?

Who cared what Patrick thought? Why should she be interested in the opinion of some rando ex-footballer she hadn't even met yet? She shouldn't. Was she wearing a dress because she'd been so deeply scarred by the end of her relationship that she'd contrived to change herself rather than face rejection? Colin had loved it when she wore dresses. He'd wanted her to grow her hair; he'd given her a Zara voucher for Christmas and had been disappointed that Kylie planned to keep it until winter and buy herself a warm jacket.

Or was the *refusal* to change in itself a reaction to splitting up with Colin? Was wearing a dress a reaction, or a refusal to react?

Being a modern woman was exhausting. There was so much societal pressure, and pressure from everyone around her, to look a certain way, act a certain way. All this second-guessing yourself, and third-guessing, and fourth. She was determined to keep her own sovereignty, to ensure the north star she set her sails on was her own.

Tonight she would be herself. But she would also wear make-up and Gloria's dress.

Yes, this whole thing was Nick's idea but despite that, Kylie was mildly excited. It might work out. Patrick might be just what she needed. After all, what was her option – stay here on a Friday night with Gloria?

'Kylie!' Gloria yelled from downstairs.

'What!' Kylie bellowed back.

'Are you in my bedroom? Are you taking my gold Glomesh clutch? Because I'm not sure it's really *you*.'

Kylie groaned. How can a bag be 'you' or 'not you'? Kylie was many things, but she was almost certainly not a bag. She didn't want to take the stupid bag anyway, because it wasn't 1976.

'Kylie!' yelled Gloria.

'Jesus, what!'

'Your date's here!' Then Kylie heard some muttering, before Gloria yelled again. 'Patrick, that's his name.'

Kylie stalked to the top of the stairs and yelled, 'God, Mum! I know his name!'

She clomped back to Gloria's bedroom where she took out a small, inconspicuous black bag from the wardrobe. Then she upended Gloria's gold Glomesh clutch on the bed and scooped everything she'd already put in it – the tissues and sanitiser and lipstick and credit card and keys – into the black bag. She straightened Gloria's dress – a classic black sleeveless knit – and gave herself a once-over in the mirror. Quite frankly, she looked amazing. Leo had volunteered to stay late so Kylie didn't have to rush home to look after Gloria. In this moment, right now, all was right with the world.

When she reached the landing though, she could hear Gloria mid-conversation with Patrick, which could not be good. She squatted down so she could spy on them through the railings.

'. . . anyway, not only did I have to fake my orgasms – *Oh, god, yes, more* – throughout that entire marriage, I had to fake my whole life,' Gloria said. She was sitting at the dining room table with Caesar on her lap.

'And your ex-husband never suspected?' said Leo.

'Never. All that smiling! I would have made a fabulous weather girl. It's exhausting. And quite painful, right here.' Gloria stabbed herself in both cheeks with the long red nails of her index fingers, making temporary dimples. 'Never again.'

'Some people can be utterly oblivious to what's really happening right in front of them,' said Leo.

'He's a nice little fella,' said a male voice, presumably Patrick. 'Can I pat him?'

Kylie assumed he was talking about Caesar but from this angle, he might have been patting Leo. She moved down an extra step so she could see better.

'What is he?' Patrick said.

'A Virgo, I think,' said Gloria. She buried her face in Caesar's neck. 'Aren't you, you little cutie?'

'I can't imagine you married, Gloria,' said Leo.

'I adore being single,' Gloria said. 'I'm not so sure Kylie does though. She's just split up with someone, did Nick tell you? None of us liked him but of course we didn't say anything. She's very sensitive and takes everything the wrong way. Regardless, now she's at the perfect age to find a man because all the good ones are back on the market after getting their first divorces.'

'Oh,' Patrick said.

'It's all in the timing. She can swoop in and scoop them up! Divorced men are already housetrained. Lonely. Desperate to overcome their overwhelming sense of failure after ruining their marriage, which was supposed to be forever. Profoundly damaged. They're perfect, really. Not that you're not perfect! Damage isn't essential.'

'Phew,' said Leo.

'Although what undamaged men talk about on dates, I couldn't imagine! In my experience men can't really relax until they've told you all about their emotionally crippling relationship with their father. You haven't been married, Patrick, correct?'

'Never married,' he said.

'Me neither,' said Leo.

Kylie moved one step down for a better view. Patrick was attractive, certainly. Neck entirely free of beard, comprehensible when speaking, knuckles untattooed with *LOVE* and *HATE*, as far as she could tell. *So far, so good.*

Next to him, Leo was leaning against the kitchen bench like he owned the place, eating a banana.

'How much older is Kylie than Nick?' Patrick said.

'Oh, years and years,' said Gloria breezily.

'And how much older than you, Leo?'

Leo laughed.

'Oh, Leo's not one of my children.' Gloria smiled.

'Right, sorry,' said Patrick. 'I didn't think Nick had a brother! I would have remembered.'

Okay, this was becoming creepy. The last thing Kylie needed was another random relative – she'd only just recovered from the arrival of Monica. Besides, she knew quite enough people already. If she had to fit a new person in her life, someone would have to die.

She straightened and went down the stairs, nonchalant, as though she hadn't been eavesdropping.

'Kylie, I presume?' Patrick said.

Now that she was closer, Kylie could see that Patrick had that ex-footballer look, like all of Nick's friends. He was long-limbed and shaved-headed and square-jawed and wore a black V-neck knit and jeans that looked expensive. He also had a nose that had been broken, which should have been a flaw but instead made him look sexy, like a gangster in a Guy Ritchie movie. Definitely one of Nick's crowd.

'You look . . . awesome,' said Leo.

'You do!' said Gloria. 'And it's so nice to see that dress! I haven't worn it since my great aunt's funeral in 1995.'

'Thanks, Mum. I think.' Kylie checked she had her keys and headed towards the door.

'Lovely to meet you, Gloria,' said Patrick. 'And you too, Leo. And, Gloria, thanks for the advice about trimming my box hedge.'

'"Trimming my box hedge".' Leo snorted, then took another bite of his banana.

'And I'll certainly consider taking up tennis.'

'You really should,' said Gloria. 'I'd be happy to give you a few pointers. That feeling, the thwack of a new ball against tight strings, the way it reverberates up your arm. It relieves all my stress. Without it, I would have stabbed someone in the neck by now. I'd be in prison serving twenty to life in an orange tracksuit.'

'I'll keep that in mind,' said Patrick.

'Where are you going?' Gloria said.

'We're having Indian,' Patrick said. 'Kylie chose the restaurant, but I love India. It's my happy place.'

'Excellent. Kylie? Do you need some condoms?' Gloria said.

There was a moment's pause. Leo stopped chewing. Even Caesar lifted his head and stared at them. His paws were stretched out in front of him, his nails a sparkly pink.

'Wow,' said Leo.

'Are you drunk?' said Kylie. 'And . . . why do you have condoms?'

Gloria gestured to Kylie. 'She's a prude, like her father,' she said to Patrick. 'I prefer to live in the real world. Safety first, that's my motto. My recent misadventure' – she pointed to her ankle with one of Caesar's paws – 'has reinforced that you can't be too careful. A young man like you should value the ability to plan ahead above all else.'

'As much as I appreciate your optimism, Mum,' said Kylie. 'I think we'll be right.'

Chapter 24

Patrick drove, in his Tesla. They chatted for a while about the car and its weird lack of instrumentation on its non-existent console, about the boundless future of electric vehicles and the wonder of going out for dinner – such a small thing, but glorious. About the things they'd missed, the things they resolved to never take for granted again but inevitably had.

'So,' Patrick said. 'Has your mum always been the shy, retiring type?'

'All my life,' Kylie said.

'And Leo and your mum are . . .' His pause was heavy with implication.

'Ew, god no. She pays him.' Kylie paused for a moment. 'God, that sounds worse.' She explained that he was the brother of a friend, looking after Gloria temporarily. 'And you're a friend of Nick's?'

'There were mitigating circumstances,' Patrick said. 'We played football together.'

'Really? I went to most of Nick's matches – we all did. I don't remember you.'

'Wow, thanks.' He smiled. 'I spent a bit of time in the VFL, though I actually played more games than Nick. In total. I'm a property developer now, actually.'

'Of course you are.' Kylie crossed her legs, then crossed them the other way.

Patrick looked at her.

'Not that there's anything wrong with that. I just meant that you're obviously not a teacher like Nick.'

'Why obviously?'

Because of the car, the black knit, his general hotness? None of her brother's teacher friends were hot; Kylie suspected that Nick enjoyed being the person in a group to whom all eyes were drawn. Corralling small children was a surprisingly down-to-earth job considering most of his cohort were brand ambassadors or reality television contestants. But then the Tesla pulled up in front of the restaurant and Kylie was spared from explaining.

She'd chosen the Indian place next door to the pharmacy. Why, she wasn't sure. She'd been under pressure when he texted, and she hadn't wanted anywhere near her house, anywhere she'd been with Colin. Inside, the air was heavy with the scent of spices and the garlic warmth of bread. The lighting was low, which leaned date-ish but the atmosphere was cheerful. This would be a calming, relaxing night away from Gloria. There wasn't a thing to worry about. The waitress sat them at a table for two, against the wall on the right-hand side.

'So,' Patrick said. 'No kids?'

Kylie raised her eyebrows. 'Not that I know of.'

'Me neither. Freedom is too important to me. Starting new businesses, travel. I'm always on the move.' He gestured around the restaurant and sighed longingly. 'I love India. It really speaks to me.'

'Oh?' said Kylie.

'It's more than just the Golden Triangle, which is all most tourists see from their air-conditioned minibuses. Seriously, get among the locals, experience the real India! It's like *Slumdog Millionaire* out there, people, not *Eat Pray Love.* Eat with your hands, use a squat toilet. Have you been?'

Kylie hadn't been to either India or a squat toilet.

'You haven't lived! Skip the Taj, though. Too many tourists. Honestly, they ruin everything.'

'Aren't you a tourist?' said Kylie.

'Me? No, no. I'm a *traveller.* I *travel* beyond the Golden Triangle. *Way* beyond. For example, I had the best holiday of my life in Goa. Magical place. Although the surfing is really just for beginners. Longboarders, bless them.' He chuckled.

'Longboarders are bad?'

'Hopeless! Old blokes in their fifties swaying up the wing of a jumbo. People say Goa isn't the real India. That's rubbish. They have cows right on the beach! And the massages! They find all your sore spots with their elbows, it's torture. But so good. Service is rubbish in this country. Resorts here have a lot to learn.'

'Right,' said Kylie.

'And the food! Amazing. Although I think the best Indian food I've ever had was in Singapore. You have to get off the beaten track, obviously. Little India, in the side streets. I still remember one fish-head curry. They serve it on a banana leaf, you eat it with your fingers. So authentic. Awesome stuff. Super hot, blows your head off.'

'Sounds messy. The exploding head, I meant. Not the fingers.'

'All credit to the Poms, though. Chicken tikka masala is practically the national dish. Poms love tikka sauce on everything, to be honest. Not authentic but still amazing.'

'Right.'

'Travel is awesome. It really broadens the mind.'

Kylie was sure it did. Where were the menus? That waitress was taking forever.

'The last few years have been hell, literal hell.'

'For nurses and doctors, and parents trying to homeschool?' said Kylie.

'For travellers,' said Patrick. 'I have to be free. Next on my list is getting back to Japan. I cannot wait. No one can drink like the Japanese – and I've been to Munich for Oktoberfest! Japanese whiskey, unbelievable. And the streets are so clean. And no tips! They just won't accept them, chase you out onto the street with the money in their hand. People leave their bikes out without a lock, it's ridiculous.'

Kylie said she'd heard that.

Then no one said anything. For a little while, Kylie thought that perhaps time had actually stopped but then the waitress returned with menus and laid napkins on their laps.

'Any chef's specials?' Patrick said. 'You know, off-menu? For . . . locals?'

'No,' said the waitress.

'I love it spicy. The more authentic, the better,' he said.

She didn't reply.

'India, it's kind of my spiritual home,' Patrick continued. 'Where are you from?'

The waitress flicked her long dark ponytail over her shoulder and pressed her pen on her notepad. 'Nunawading,' she said. 'What would you like?'

'I'll have a Kingfisher. A bit hoppy for a lager, to be honest. If I wanted hops I'd order an IPA, but when in Rome, right,' said Patrick. 'Kylie?'

'Me too,' she said instinctively. Then, that horrible nagging thought appeared from the back of her brain where she'd stashed it. 'Ah, no. A mineral water, please.'

They ordered the on-menu, non-locals, non-authentic banquet for two. While they waited for their food, Kylie continued to listen to the gospel according to Patrick. In the beginning, god may have created the heavens and the earth but shortly after that, at least in Patrick's view, he made the glorious Qantas 747 and sent it winging its way over the teeming waters to somewhere other than here. Patrick had walked on the Great Wall ('Not the one closest to Beijing, which is fake as. Practically rebuilt in the eighties. I walked on the real one'), taken a prank photo with the Leaning Tower of Pisa ('Not my usual thing but Mum loved it. Loosen up, Patrick, right?') and seen Victoria Falls from a cruise on the Zambezi ('Not a cruise full of Americans on an all-inclusive package tour, a local one. You have to know someone'). He spoke as if the world was a mammoth bingo card and he, a sharpie-wielding winner crossing the globe while crossing off countries. Kylie guessed that once Patrick finished playing football, he needed something else on which to release his competitive spirit.

Eventually when the entree platter arrived, he said, 'And you're a pharmacist?'

Kylie jumped in her seat, startled. She'd forgotten for a moment that Patrick was a real person rather than a spectacular deep-fake she was watching on YouTube, or a piece of conceptual performance art. *That's right*, she thought. This was a date. Interaction was required, albeit only occasionally.

'Yes,' she said deliberately. She picked up one of the samosas with her fingers. It was hot, crisp and plump, sandy-coloured and heavy for its size. She took a bite.

'And what's your endgame?' Patrick poured water for Kylie and himself.

'My what?'

'What do you plan to achieve with your life? I'm asking, because most people are content to waste their lives as passive consumers of popular culture.'

Kylie, who ten minutes ago felt exactly the same way and was in total intellectual agreement, who had reluctantly, sulkily sat through Colin's mindless television and juvenile movies, all at once felt this was a pompous and ridiculous position as soon as it came out of Patrick's mouth.

'You don't like popular culture? None of it?' She dipped an unbitten corner of the samosa in the minty yoghurt. It was amazing. Or as Leo would say, *awesome*.

'I do watch the ABC. *Insiders* mostly. *Foreign Correspondent*, of course. But yeah, I'm an outlier, I know. Anything designed for mass consumption is rubbish. Modern music, for a start.

And don't talk to me about what passes for drama. I mean, *Game of Thrones*? What even *was* that? Someone trying to rip off Tolkien? Popular culture encourages people to become consumers of life. Spectators rather than participants. It's too passive for me. I want to *make* a movie some day, not *watch* movies. Literature, the same. I only read classics. Preferably Russian. Nabokov, Bulgakov, Asimov . . . all the ovs, basically. Those guys really knew how to tell a story.'

'Right,' said Kylie. She knocked off the rest of the samosa then reached for a crispy, golden nugget on the platter. 'Ooh, pakoras. Yum.'

Patrick cleared his throat. 'Well actually, I think you'll find it's a *bhaji*, sometimes mispronounced as *bhaja*.'

Kylie thought back to their earlier conversation, in the car on the way here. *I actually played more games than Nick. In total*, he'd said. Aha. He's compensating for his less-than-stellar career. Nick behaved the same – although he had been successful, albeit briefly. Nick had been the best at ball skills in his baby team at Auskick, then the best player from the first day he started in the Under 9s. After that, he was better than every other kid through juniors and in every school team. Once Nick turned professional though? Kylie imagined that Patrick went through the same experience. There's nothing like a big pond to make a man feel like a little fish who needs to drive an expensive car. Nick never recovered from the sudden realisation that talent alone was not enough. Hard work and luck were also required to be successful at anything – one was no good without the other two.

That's why smart people stay in their own ponds, Kylie thought. There was nothing to be gained from going out on a limb.

'The word pakora – or more properly *pakoda* as they say in the south – is an umbrella term meaning any vegetable dipped in batter and deep-fried.' Patrick took a swig of his Kingfisher. 'Although it's only an authentic bhaji if it's made with chickpea flour. Otherwise it's just a fritter.'

Kylie gazed longingly at the beer. Something about Patrick's authentic-bhaji, no-popular-culture ethos made her want to act entirely out of character: lay on her own couch, eating chicken Twisties from a bowl resting on her chest and watching the most popular of popular culture, the kind that would make Patrick run screaming into the night. Something made for teenage boys with superheroes and lots of violence but no effects of said violence, no swellings or bruises or gaping wounds. Something that ended in the plucky underestimated underdogs overcoming overwhelming odds to swelling orchestral overtures.

But she wasn't at home on her couch. She was here, with Patrick. She might as well have a little fun.

'Fascinating. About the pakoda, I mean.' Kylie leaned on one elbow as she chewed. 'Tell me more.'

'Well, actually, keeping the name but using inauthentic ingredients is actually part of a broader issue of cultural appropriation of food. Don't get me started on what passes for Chinese food in this country. Not many people realise this, but China is actually made up of a whole lot of regional cuisines.'

'Amazing,' said Kylie. 'And which one is deep-fried ice cream from?'

Patrick stared so hard, Kylie could imagine his eyeball dislocating and bouncing across the table, landing with a splash in the green yoghurt sauce. 'It's from nowhere, Kylie!' he said. 'It's not Chinese food!'

'Wow, really? I've definitely had it in Chinese restaurants. Are you sure?'

'Of course I'm sure! Pizza is another example. The stuff we have here isn't *pizza*. *Pizza* has to come from Naples and it's just tomato and cheese and basil, that's it.'

'Pineapple, though, surely?' said Kylie. 'Pineapple isn't only for authentic Chinese food, like sweet and sour pork, right? I could never eat a pizza without pineapple. It really sets off the barbecue sauce.'

Patrick spluttered his beer on the table. He wiped his mouth with the napkin, wiped around the edge of his glass and took a deep breath in, then out. 'Anyway,' he said. 'Enough about food. Let's talk about something else. I was asking about your plan.'

'I haven't given it a lot of thought,' said Kylie. 'But at this stage – one more piece of tempura, then I'll move on to the orange chicken.'

'It's not . . . I meant your long-term plan.'

'You mean, after this? I'm not sure dessert is included in the banquet.'

'Can I make a humble suggestion? Run a marathon by the time you're forty. Talk about life-changing! I remember my first marathon. The energy of the crowd carries you. It's an intensely emotional experience, all these strangers willing each other over the line. Supportive. Non-judgemental. I'm under four hours on a good day. Very happy to give you a few pointers.'

'No thanks. I'd be shocking at it.'

'Everyone's shocking at the beginning! Dare to fail, Kylie!'

Patrick had more suggestions for her life goals. *Many* more. Before he was halfway through his monologue, the waitress from Nunawading cleared away the entrees and brought curries in gleaming copper bowls, rich and thick with cashews and spinach and cheese, and fluffy yellow rice, and golden blistered bread that smelled like heaven. Kylie was tempted to call it 'naan bread' to see if Patrick would remark that the word *naan* actually means bread, so 'naan bread' actually meant 'bread bread', but she was reluctant to turn the conversation back to food.

'Okay, new subject!' he said as they ate. 'What's your career goal? I'm sure you don't want to work in a pharmacy forever.'

'But I do want to work in a pharmacy forever. I want to get better and better at my job until I'm perfect.'

'Wow. You must really love it.'

Kylie paused, naan in hand. 'I don't know if *loving* your work is really a good idea. I mean, *love*? You know what love did to Romeo and Juliet, right?'

Patrick leaned on his elbows and steepled his fingers. His eyes were a gentle brown, enquiring and patient. 'It's just that Nick told me how smart you were. I assumed you had plans for something remarkable before the last two quarters.'

'The last two quarters?'

'Of your life. Before the final siren. You've got a giant inside you, Kylie.'

Kylie looked down at her top. 'I've got a what?'

'Not literally. It's from my favourite book. It means that people contain more than they know, and they shouldn't settle for less than they deserve. The giant, you've got to awaken it.'

'I'm ambitious to eat this delicious palak paneer, that's all. And I'd like some more poppadums.'

She turned to look behind her for the waitress. That's when she saw Tim, at the front counter.

Chapter 25

Kylie could have chosen a dimly lit cocktail bar on the other side of town for this date but she hadn't, because dinner with Patrick was nothing to be ashamed of. He wasn't a minor member of the Trump family or someone from *Love Island*. And Kylie liked Tim, and her job – it wasn't that.

The problem was, how would it look being out at dinner after her mother rang in for her absence today? Like a little kid caught having a sickie, that's how. Tim would think less of her. And what excuse did Gloria give for her absence? Kylie hadn't asked.

Yet here Tim was, and here she was. Kylie should have realised that she wasn't the only person from work who'd noticed the new Indian restaurant next door.

'Christ on a Cruskit.' She turned back around quickly.

'Um . . . what?'

'Don't look, but that's my boss.' She indicated behind her with her head.

Patrick craned his neck to get a better view. 'What, him? The old guy with the grey hair?'

'Does "don't look" mean something different where you come from?'

He straightened again. 'Not looking. I get it, you don't want to see him because you hate working there and he's a giant pain in your arse.'

'Not at all,' Kylie said. 'The job is great, he's great. I'm just thinking back to the words of the great Doctor Egon Spengler, "Don't cross the streams".'

Patrick frowned. 'Is that your . . . urologist?'

Kylie was struck with sudden inspiration. Gloria lived in the 1980s, didn't she? She fished around in Gloria's handbag and sure enough, inside was a gold olde-worlde compact. She clicked it open. There was a tarnished mirror in the top half and a cracked and dried-out disc of powder in the bottom half that. She peered in the mirror. Tim seemed to be waiting for takeaway. Now she could clearly see when he left.

'Is . . . everything okay?' said Patrick. 'You don't need to powder your nose. I actually prefer women who don't wear make-up.'

'Uh-huh,' Kylie said, still peering into the mirror.

'Make-up just seems, I don't know, insecure to me. Because it's basically a lie, right?'

'Right,' Kylie muttered into the mirror.

'I'm looking for *honesty* in a woman, you know? *Authenticity*. Not someone who covers their real self.'

Kylie lifted her gaze from the mirror. 'What? Sorry. I'm a bit distracted.' She clicked the compact closed again and dropped it on her lap.

'It's fine if you want to go over and say hello to your boss. I don't mind.'

'But I don't want to go over and say hello.' She smiled, deliberately. 'I'm entirely happy in your company.'

'Good. Great. Have some naan – just rip off a bit with your hands. Generally I prefer paratha or chapati, but this is amazing. Do you know that some people call it "naan bread"? But actually, naan is bread. Calling it naan bread is a tautology, like ATM machine. Or PIN number. It's hilarious how many tautologies people use in everyday language.'

As instructed, Kylie ripped herself a piece of naan then kept ripping, absentmindedly, until it was suitable only for sparrows.

'LCD display,' Patrick said.

Kylie looked at him. 'What?'

'Another tautology. The D in LCD already means display. Liquid crystal display display. When people use tautologies in their speech, it's a sign of a lack of logic. If everyone fixed their illogical language, better thought processes would follow. Orwell said that. Don't get me started on RAT tests! Would you like a beer?'

'Yes. No. No, thank you.'

She was quiet again, ripping and thinking.

Patrick coughed. The waitress came. Patrick ordered another Kingfisher. 'Kylie?' he said.

'Me too,' she said. Why had she not ordered one earlier? If she were pregnant, by some disastrous chance in a million, there was no question of her keeping it.

'Usually girls have lots of questions about what it's like to play professional football,' he said.

'Girls?'

'Sorry. Women.'

'Well, if I did have any questions about professional football, which I don't, I would have asked my brother by now.'

Patrick chuckled like Kylie had said something cute. 'Well, my career panned out a little differently from Nick's. I didn't make such a splash at the beginning, sure, but I had more games. Longevity, that's the key to success. The life of a professional footballer is not for everyone.'

'Right,' said Kylie.

The Kingfisher came, cold and beaded. Kylie took a long, cleansing drink, then took another quick peek in the compact. Tim was still there. Honestly, how long did it take to cook takeaway?

Patrick shrugged. 'Anyway, back to you. You're in a rut. Nick told me. You're not living up to your potential. You need a new challenge.' He spooned another dollop of palak paneer on her plate. 'Have some more of this, it's fantastic. Don't use a fork! Pick up the rice pilaf with the naan, that's how they do it.'

Patrick said rice pilaf, which was a tautology! He'd handed Kylie the perfect opportunity to correct him, but she simply stared at the curry. She'd lost her appetite for petty point-scoring as well as for food. Things really were dire.

'Change is good, Kylie,' Patrick said. 'Embrace it. That's what Eckhart Tolle says. Or was it Seneca?'

Kylie took another quick peek in the compact. Tim was no longer there. *Phew.*

Patrick cleared his throat. Kylie looked up. Tim was standing beside their table.

Up until that moment, she'd been having fun. She hadn't been entirely oblivious to her behaviour – part of her was aware she was being unkind to Patrick, and that she enjoyed being unkind. She had judged him unworthy, which made him fair game. Patrick was unaware and unoffended, yes, but his ignorance was no excuse – it made her behaviour worse somehow, his clueless hopefulness.

The truth was, he was more honest than her, and he was braver. Patrick was being himself, his unselfconscious and real and pompous self, sitting before her with his heart in his hands. He was one person, and he was showing himself to her. She was playing the role of a woman on a date, but really she was two people – the unkind, mocking one and the one observing her unkindness and feeling ashamed of it.

Now the world had turned and karma had bared its teeth and her own day of judgement had come.

Tim looked sad, as though he were a parent about to say, *I'm not angry, just disappointed.*

'Kylie. This is a surprise. I'm glad you're feeling better.'

'Much better,' she managed. She somehow found her tongue to introduce Patrick and – thankfully, blessedly – moments later the waitress appeared with two steaming, aromatic plastic bags for Tim.

Tim said goodbye, but just before he left them, he turned back.

'Whatever way it goes, you'll land on your feet, Kylie,' he said, his voice soft. 'I don't have a doubt in the world.'

Kylie's memory about the rest of the evening was fuzzy. She almost certainly heard Patrick explaining (to her, a pharmacist) how antidepressants work, and also (to her, a homeowner) the best way to buy a house. He also gave her advice about – was it strength training when you're middle-aged? Or effective complaining when you're enraged? Maybe it was both. She couldn't even enjoy asking Patrick ridiculous questions, such was her remorse. Also, she couldn't stop thinking about what Tim had said.

You'll land on your feet wasn't said to someone successful, or even someone who'd had a close shave. It was said to people in dire circumstances who'd figuratively fallen off something – a cliff or a skyscraper – and were hurtling towards the ground, arms and legs flailing, struggling to swivel in midair like a cat.

Patrick didn't seem to notice anything amiss in Kylie's lack of chat. When it came to enjoyable conversations, he found another person surplus to requirements.

Kylie had fallen, it was apparent.

Needless to say, Gloria's condoms were not required. When Patrick dropped her off at Gloria's, he told Kylie that he'd had a great night. She narrowed her eyes and examined his face but her satire detector did not ping.

She let herself in and kicked her shoes off at the door. She expected the house to be dark and quiet but the kitchen light was on and the house was full of the spicy warmth of frying onions. Random bangs and clanks echoed down the hall.

She discovered Leo standing in front of the stove with his back to her, wearing pink headphones and stirring something in a pot with a wooden spoon. He was wearing a t-shirt and trackpants and bopping away to silent music, entirely at home in Gloria's kitchen, the cream and mission-brown tiles a backdrop to his wildly daggy movements: part teen-girl hip sway, part disco finger. The vulnerability of someone lost in solitude – watching him felt like a violation. Kylie briefly considered leaving and coming back again, louder, to give him a chance to stop. If anyone ever came upon Kylie dancing like that, she'd have to move to another country.

'Hey,' she said.

Leo continued stirring and jiving, excruciatingly. Faint steam came from the pot.

She leaned against the kitchen counter and rapped it with her knuckles. 'Hey,' she said again, louder. This time he slipped the headphones around his neck. He didn't look even slightly embarrassed.

'Kylie. Hey. Which superpower would you choose: invisibility or flight?' he said to her.

'What?'

'Invisibility or flight? Gloria said invisibility, and that's just crazy.' Leo turned down the flame under the pot and half-covered it with a lid. 'But you can't tell her. She won't be told.'

'I thought you'd have gone home hours ago,' Kylie said.

'I mean, seriously! She'd rather be invisible than zoom around like a bird.' He wiped his hands on a tea towel and puffed up his cheeks. 'It's up to Gloria, I guess. She's a grown woman, you can't tell her what to think. How was your date?'

'Leo. Why are you still here?'

'I wanted to make sure Gloria was okay. And make soup. It's nearly ready. Have a taste.' He transferred the wooden spoon to his left hand, fished a soup spoon from the drawer, dug it into the pot and offered it to Kylie.

'Thanks, but no.'

He raised the soup spoon again. 'Seriously, let me know if it's got enough salt, or whatever.'

'It's got enough salt if you followed the recipe.'

'Recipe?'

Of course Leo wouldn't have used a recipe. He was not that kind of person, never had been. He held the spoon, waiting. If she didn't taste his stupid soup, she'd never get him to leave. She took the spoon, blew on it and sipped it. It was delicious: green and smooth and creamy.

'It's fine,' she said.

'My specialty. Or one of them. Broccoli, but with a little smoked paprika and lots of cheese. It's the mullet of soups: business at the front, party at the back.' He took the spoon from her and dropped it in the sink. 'How was your date?'

'It was fine.' She set her mouth. 'You can leave now.'

'I'll clean up first. Besides, it needs to cool a bit. The soup.' He switched off the burner. 'Then I'll pop it in the fridge. Then I'll go.'

He was nervous, she realised. It was obvious in the way he gripped the wooden spoon, in his insistence on her tasting the soup. What had happened since she'd left? Things had been looking so promising between him and Gloria.

'I hope Gloria wasn't too tough on you.'

'What? No. I love looking after people, and she's a complete sweetheart.' He winked at Kylie. 'Besides, I've been working in aged care for a few years now. I've picked up a few tricks of the trade.'

'Didn't Alice tell me you were unemployed?'

He rolled one arm at the shoulder joint, then massaged his neck with the other hand. Kylie could see his muscles moving under the cotton of his scrubs. He'd filled out since he was a kid, that was apparent.

'I work for a while, until I save some cash, then I quit and go surfing for a while. Then when I run out of money, I get another job. Too easy.'

She could have guessed as much. Leo hadn't changed, not really. He still had no work ethic, no sense of commitment, no motivation to climb any professional ladder. It was almost as though he thought that life should be enjoyable and that work should fit around having fun.

'Do you surf?' he said.

She raised her eyebrows. 'Do I look like I surf?'

'Oh, but you should at least try!' He leaned back against the kitchen counter and bent his hands backwards at the wrist, flexing his forearms. 'I'd love to take you, Kylie. Any time.'

Kylie declined his offer. Of course she did. Could she imagine herself surfing? Not in a million years. She looked around while Leo returned his focus to the soup. The kitchen felt smaller than usual. Small and hot.

'Well,' she said. 'I'm going to bed now. Good night.' She turned and left before Leo could reply.

Once she reached the lounge room, though, she felt weird about changing into her pyjamas and settling on the couch while he fluffed about, so she nipped upstairs to wait it out in the bathroom.

Leo was clearly a man with too much time on his hands and, not unrelated, a meandering thought process. After all, what were the ground rules of her hypothetical invisibility? Would her clothes also be invisible? Because if not, her physical presence would be given away by her navy suit walking around without her in it because Kylie wasn't getting naked in public, invisible or not. And what about the process of turning invisible? Was it instantaneous? Would she be able to turn it on and off at will? And if she were to choose flight: how far could she travel? And how high? And could she carry anyone with her, à la Superman and Lois Lane?

And the most important question of all: why was Kylie even thinking about these ridiculous scenarios? This was why frivolous people were so dangerous. The smallest amount of exposure and before you knew it, your very thoughts were running in unproductive, undisciplined directions.

When she heard the front door close, she crept downstairs. The kitchen was sparkling and somehow more cosy than yesterday, yet the only signs that Leo had been there were a fresh tea towel folded over the handle of the oven, a wet dishwashing glove drying on the edge of the sink and the lingering savoury, smokey warmth of the soup.

SATURDAY

Chapter 26

For the first time since Kylie arrived at Gloria's house, she slept soundly and woke relaxed and calm. From her position on the couch, she could see through the high side windows and the sky looked faintly grey, eerie, far away. The only sound was the humming of the fridge, one of the few new things in the house. Gloria's approach to home repairs made Kylie think of the old joke about the fifty-year-old axe with three new heads and seven new handles. The last fridge must have been hopelessly unfixable for Gloria to replace it. She never gave up on anything. Their original family-sized white whale had made a grinding noise, Kylie remembered, punctuated by a random clunk like something metallic had fallen. This new fridge was slimmer, stainless steel and sounded high-pitched and vaguely electrical, as though it was emitting some kind of radiation in the dark. It also had a bigger freezer, better suited to a single elderly woman who didn't eat actual meals but had a vast collection of condiments and a thing for frozen peas.

Kylie climbed the stairs, quietly. In the bathroom she stood frozen, staring at herself in the mirror, the pregnancy test in her hand.

Should she take the test? She should. Of course she should. What could be easier than peeing on a stick? It would take two minutes. Besides, she'd already spent the money. It would be a waste if she didn't take it. Pregnancy tests were scientific miracles – extremely accurate, even at this hypothetically early stage. She could take the test and when the result was negative, which it would be, she could put the entire thing out of her mind and never think of embryos or of Colin, or of what kind of a father Colin would make, ever again.

In the mirror, sensible, logical Kylie nodded back at her.

On the other hand – was testing in the face of such long odds itself a capitulation? Giving in to this rising tide of anxiety and sense of approaching dread could be interpreted as weakness of character. What would Jane Goodall do? Or Mary Wollstonecraft? Of course Kylie shouldn't take the test, because she wasn't pregnant! The possibility of Colin's vasectomy failing was vanishingly small and the thought of herself as a mother was laughable. She should be a Stoic and not give in to irrational fears.

Mirror Kylie agreed. She should trust her body. Give it time. It would right itself.

Or . . . wait a minute. Maybe not taking the test was a sign of weakness? Was she giving an infinitesimally remote possibility credence by refusing to resolve it in such a straightforward scientific way?

And back. And forward. And back again.

This was ridiculous. Kylie was not an indecisive person.

She was on the verge of making two lists, pros and cons, when Gloria called from downstairs. 'Kylie? Where are you?'

That settled it. She couldn't take the test now. Gloria was awake, and the idea of her mother knowing – the idea of any of them knowing – that she, Kylie, the sensible one, had allowed herself to be in this position . . . that was untenable. Kylie could imagine how it would unfold, because she'd seen it over and over. First, the news would spread to each and every Schnabel in a flurry of phone calls, then Gloria would swoop in, organise, mobilise. There would be Schnabel family meetings of concerned faces around Gloria's dining table discussing Kylie's problem and formulating elaborate plans to solve it. Everyone chipping in as though she were a charity case incapable of managing her own life.

Absolutely not. Kylie was the strong one, the one who managed everyone else. No one could ever know.

Downstairs, Gloria was sitting up in bed with Caesar nestled under her arm. 'You're up early,' she said to Kylie.

Kylie climbed over the foot of the bed and lay beside Gloria, who leaned over and peered at her face.

'Oh dear,' Gloria said. 'You have a . . .' She gestured to her forehead, just above the inside corner of her eyebrow, and passed Kylie a small hand mirror from her bedside table.

In Gloria's mirror, Kylie's face was barely noticeable because a pimple obliterated everything else in view. It was almost purple and the size of a small Volkswagen. It was the kind of pimple that had its own postcode and weather patterns.

She sat up and angled her face this way and that, catching the light. How could she not have noticed this herself in the bathroom mirror upstairs? Yes, the lighting was poor and she had other things to worry about, but as soon as Gloria pointed it out, it was so obvious.

'A little concealer and you'll be fine.' Gloria patted her arm. 'Just don't touch it.'

Kylie hadn't woken with a pimple in more than twenty years. She felt faint and slightly sick. Seeing her skin like this reminded Kylie of the horror of puberty. She vividly recalled being accustomed to her angular, sharp girl-body, being familiar with every inch of it. Wishing she could keep it forever. But she could not keep it. Gradually but unrelentingly, it began to slip away from her, replacing itself with an alien shell. The shock of being in the shower and spotting her first pubic hairs – she'd felt helpless, at the mercy of a force more powerful than herself, as though she were being swept away by wild currents.

The pimple was Kylie's final piece of evidence. Something strange was happening to her, physically, beyond all doubt. Something hormonal.

'Kylie? I said, is it cool outside?' Gloria said. 'Will Caesar need a jacket?'

'Are you sure he should come? We'll have enough to worry about.'

Gloria ran her fingers through Caesar's fur. 'Of course he's coming! He's been looking forward to it.'

Kylie shrugged. She helped Gloria shower and dress in her immaculate tennis whites then she took Caesar out for a walk. Everything would be perfect today, she would make sure of it.

It would be a signal, an omen. She knew nothing about tennis, or about children, so today's success would prove to everyone that, whatever happened, Kylie was still in control. She would still have her job, the same job, except with a big company that offered opportunities for career development – and she would also have a lanyard.

'I don't need Colin. I don't need anyone. I am the mistress of my own destiny,' she said to Caesar as she kneeled on the footpath to pick up his poo.

Caesar stood beside her, happily panting. Dogs never express surprise at an apex predator ten times their size picking up their poo. They take it for granted. Dogs have a staggering sense of entitlement.

No wonder he and Gloria got on so well, thought Kylie.

On the walk back, Nick rang.

'Spill,' he said.

'I have no idea what you mean. Did you get the SOP about Mum's ankle?'

'I guess? I haven't looked at my emails. I mean, how was your date with Patrick? I texted you last night and you didn't reply. Is that a good sign?'

'I didn't have sex with your friend, if that's what you're asking.'

'Yes, I know that. I've already spoken to him. Did he say anything about me?'

'This might shock you,' she said. 'But we didn't talk about you at all.'

'But you had a great night, yes?'

Kylie could imagine Nick's eyes, bright and keen. She was seeing him soon, at the open day. He rang because he was impatient to know what happened. He was undeniably invested, had gone out of his way to set it up. She needed to find a way to phrase it that was respectful of the effort he'd taken.

She decided on, 'I wasn't expecting much, to be honest, but I had an incredibly entertaining evening with Patrick. I'm very grateful to you for organising it.'

Nick groaned. 'Oh my god, Kylie! That sounds like a reference for a work experience kid who broke the photocopier but brought in cupcakes on their last day. "Incredibly entertaining"? Seriously? You messed with him, didn't you? Why? You've got so much in common.'

'We've *what*?'

'You're practically twins! He's good-looking, focused, high-achieving and extremely disciplined. Remember how you used to complain about Colin never taking charge? God, make up your mind. What type of bloke do you want, Kylie?'

Yes, Kylie had said that about Colin. Nick was right; Kylie was being unreasonable. Patrick was focused and motivated, yes, but she'd prefer someone motivated towards different goals.

'He thought you were charming. He rang me this morning. He actually said—'

'Actually? He actually said actually? Or are you actually saying actually?'

'—how refreshing it was to be out to dinner with a woman who ate.'

Just then, Caesar lunged at a cat, safely out of reach on top of a fence, and Kylie almost tripped over the lead. 'Does he normally date women who photosynthesise?'

'He's grateful to you. He's been thinking about starting a new business and last night pushed him over the line. You really helped, he said.'

'I live to serve.' She curtsied to no one. 'He didn't say anything to me about a new business.'

'Really? He wants to be a life coach.'

A minute later, when Kylie had finished laughing, she straightened and smoothed her hair. She was remorseful for her behaviour on her date, yes, but she was only human. 'Oh my god, of course he does. Thanks, Nick. I really needed that.'

'This is why Tansy is my favourite sibling, no offence,' Nick said. 'Kyles, this attitude is why you're single.'

'Really. And why are you single?'

'I'm single by choice,' he said.

'Sure you are, buddy,' Kylie said as Caesar darted towards an irresistible tree. 'Not your choice though.'

Chapter 27

In this city famous for its nightlife, even the inner-middle north where Kylie lived had its own ecosystem of nightclubs and live music venues and bars. Weekend midmornings saw the streets dotted with vomit and litter and the odd multitasking creep still off his face but somehow capable of yelling obscenities while peeing on the side of a random building.

Out here in the middle suburbs though, it seemed like a bygone era or the set of a Netflix limited series about a boy discovering his sexuality against a nostalgic, vaseline-smeared past. Out here, the day shone brighter and calmer, and the only people Kylie noticed from the car window were pairs of joggers and pensioner power-walkers and dads with prams and strollers. The children in said strollers, who often looked old enough to drive, sat like miniature royalty as if being pushed by staff was the most natural thing in the world. People walked in a relaxed way. They smiled and nodded to strangers as they passed. Kylie wouldn't have been surprised to see children manning a lemonade stand, or a man with a white cap delivering milk from a horse-drawn cart.

As they approached the recreation centre, Kylie was struck anew by its size and pristine condition. It was lush and green, with eight tennis courts in the centre, next to basketball and netball courts, a baseball diamond and squash complex, and even a public pool, all ringed by a park with cycling tracks, a carpark and a small lake, and access from the highway on the far side. Even the air seemed calm. Across the broad vista of open space, children were riding bikes with training wheels, teenagers were throwing frisbees and a man in cargo shorts was flying a black four-cornered drone, zipping it along the tree line.

'Drones,' sniffed Gloria. She was reclining on the back seat of the convertible with Caesar on her lap. 'The things you see when you don't have a slingshot.'

Nick had already arrived, bless him. The high fences around the courts were decorated with green and red balloons and streamers and signs, coloured to match the surfaces and the surrounds. The nets were up. For normal lessons Gloria only hired two courts but for today she'd booked four. The carpark was almost empty. The few cars belonged to the Rotarians, who had cans of soft drink on ice and the sausage sizzle underway. She caught a sharp whiff of charry, greasy eau de Bunnings on the breeze.

Nick came over to help Gloria out of the car. 'I don't think we have a racquet his size,' Nick said when he saw Caesar.

'He's leaving us tomorrow,' said Gloria. 'I thought an outing would be nice.'

Then Nick noticed Kylie. 'Whoa. I could say that your skin looks like a teenager's but what I really mean is that is an excellent spot. Does it at least pay rent?'

Brothers. Honestly, she longed for the good old days when she could tell him he was adopted and make him cry.

Next to the courts was a cool concrete shelter where Caesar and Gloria could sit. Kylie tied his lead in one corner and fetched water in a bowl and a towel for him to lay on while Gloria, surprisingly agile on her crutches, set out her paperwork and the credit card machine for deposits and then made herself comfortable on a bench near the entrance. Caesar was fidgety and unsettled. Unfamiliar smells, perhaps. All kinds of animals would wander around here at night, indiscriminately weeing. Cats, possums, maybe even foxes. It was no doubt a heady atmosphere for a small Pomeranian, like a young girl at a school dance surrounded by a dozen boys drenched in different breeds of Lynx. *He'll calm down eventually*, Kylie thought. Then she set to work unpacking the car and setting up the cones for the games.

Once these were all in place, Nick nudged her, gesturing to the carpark. 'Look.'

'All these people can't be here for Gloria,' Kylie said, because children were appearing – on foot and disgorging from SUVs, with and without parents – from everywhere. Skinny children and round ones, of all skin colours and hair colours, agile and gawky and everything in between. 'Something else must be happening.'

'No, this is quite normal,' Gloria said from the shelter. 'The more children, the better.'

'Mum, there are too many kids!' said Kylie. 'We can't manage, just the two of us.'

'Really, Kylie, I always have this many. Often parents will only register one kid and the others tag along, or they'll forget to register at all.' Gloria picked Caesar up from his towel and positioned him on her lap. He panted in an especially friendly manner to reward her. 'I usually manage by myself, and there's two of you. Piece of cake.'

'Are you serious? Mum, there are too many!' said Nick.

Kylie had just said that, literally seven seconds earlier, but when Nick spoke, Gloria jerked her head up and looked up. 'Really? I suppose you're right, Nicky. Tell you what, I'll give Leo a call and see what he's up to. He can give you a hand.'

'I thought it was Leo's day off?' Kylie said. 'What makes you so sure he'll even come?'

'Oh Kylie, open your eyes.' Gloria winked at her, a little creepily. 'Leave it to me. I know how to get him here.'

'What's that supposed to mean?'

'She means that Leo used to follow you around like a spaniel when he was a kid,' said Nick. 'And I doubt anything has changed.'

'Exactly,' Gloria said, with her hand cupped around the phone.

Well, that was ridiculous. All of a sudden, Kylie needed to look at her phone. Where was her phone? She was sure she remembered to bring her phone, which should be in her handbag, so she walked over to the corner of her shelter where her handbag was and began rifling through it. Yes, here was her phone, exactly where she'd put it! Of course she hadn't left it behind, that was not something she would do. She flicked the phone open and checked her emails: nothing but a newsletter from a stationery store and another from a language school. She deleted the stationery store one, because she had no need of another planner until next year. The language school email, though, she would keep. This could be her year to finally learn Spanish!

'Flustered, Kylie?' said Nick.

'Absolutely not,' she said.

Because she wasn't, not at all. She'd just wanted to check her phone. Besides, not only was Leo Nick's age, which was obviously too young, he was the absolute opposite of her: an unmotivated, unfocused underachiever. He invited her to go surfing, for heaven's sake! Even mentioning Leo in a romantic context was an obvious attempt of Nick's to deflect attention from what always happened. Kylie would say something – like 'This is too many kids!' – and be totally ignored. Nick would say the exact same thing, and Gloria would snap to attention. It was all related: Kylie's bedroom being instantly repurposed the second she turned her back while Nick's and Tansy's were fossilised in place; Kylie being the one who had to move in when Gloria was injured.

'Leo is on his way,' Gloria said when she hung up. 'Just remember we're here to have fun. I'll chat to the parents, you two look after the kids. Don't be bossy. Kylie, that means you. Be chill. One thing – best not hand out the racquets and balls all at once. Give them out group by group when you're ready to start. Okay?'

Honestly! Bossy? Her? That was rich coming from Gloria, the original back-seat driver who, in telling Kylie not to be bossy, was herself being bossy! Kylie could handle a few kids, that was certain. All this open space, clean air, children happily running about. All those children. Perhaps she should have brought the pregnancy test with her and peed on the stick in the toilet block when they weren't busy. Or not.

'Are you okay?' said Nick.

Kylie nodded.

'Are you sure? Your face seems even more . . .' He waved his palm in front of Kylie, '. . . than usual.'

'I'm fine,' Kylie said, grimacing. 'Better than fine.'

All at once she jolted, as if waking from a dream. There were children milling around the courts, sitting on the ground, looking through their bags. Parents began unpacking water bottles, tying shoelaces, speaking over each other. Kylie didn't play tennis, children were completely alien to her. She should be at work, or if not at work, learning something or achieving something or doing something. How on earth did she wind up spending her Saturday here?

Nick swung his clipboard in a backhand swoop as though it were a tennis racquet. 'Here they come,' he said.

Chapter 28

On that particular Saturday morning, the mothers – and they were mostly mothers, with only the occasional father – queuing with their children were not smiling either.

The mothers hadn't considered early weekend mornings like these in their doe-eyed years of early coupledom, back when babies were only a twinkle in their eye. Oh, they were braced for the months ahead. They knew that parenting a newborn would bring physical, emotional and psychological challenges beyond their imaginings. They hadn't realised that they would spend the next eighteen years driving small whining ingrates to expensive classes that the mothers themselves had gone without at their age. It was a Saturday morning, for god's sake! Some of the mothers hadn't even had a coffee yet.

Kylie was absolutely, positively not cut out for motherhood. She had so many more things she wanted to achieve! The mothers before her were not working on this fine Saturday morning, or taking classes themselves, or accomplishing anything at all.

Motherhood for Kylie would be untenable. These women were exhibit A.

In front of her, the parents had organised themselves into a queue to have their details checked off by Nick, and Kylie watched him being naturally Nick-ish. He made the odd quip to the kids as they waited. 'Who's waiting to be served?', 'Anyone here named An-*nette*?', 'Anyone interested in silent tennis? It's like normal tennis, but without the racquet.' These lame utterances would have been greeted with painful groans if Simon had made them but a handsome face made every utterance seem that much more clever. The fathers had theories about football they needed to share. The mothers giggled at him, nudging their children, some of whom were happily jiggling where they stood while others crossed their arms, stony-faced, as if they would have given a year of their life to be back in front of their PlayStations.

There was one woman in the queue, though, who wasn't paying Nick any attention. She wasn't obvious about it, but every few steps, the woman – weary-looking, with dark circles under her eyes and a chestnut bob with grey roots – was sneaking sideways glances at Kylie. She had a chubby baby – responsible for the thin trail of vomit down the front of her top – balanced on one hip. Standing beside her was a tween girl glued to her phone.

After a while, Kylie could bear being examined no longer.

'Can I help you?' she said to the woman in her flattest tone.

'It's Kylie, isn't it?' She smiled. 'Kylie Schnabel.'

Kylie said it was.

'You were in my class. In primary school?'

The first reply that popped into Kylie's mind was, *Really? What year did you teach?* But that instinct was a sad of trick of time, that you remain unchanged while everyone around you aged. Of course the woman was Kylie's contemporary. She ran the woman's face through her memory, tried to imagine her as a child. Nothing. Nick remembered everyone he had ever met but it was not a skill Kylie possessed.

The woman saw her blank expression. 'Melinda Khoo?' she said. 'In our last year we had Mrs Holt?'

Kylie did have Mrs Holt in Year 6, but . . . Melinda Khoo, Melinda Khoo. Still nothing.

'I did ballet? And had a ballerina party for my birthday?'

Oh, yes! Ballet-obsessed Melinda. She and Kylie had never been close and had gone to separate high schools and not kept in touch, but in Year 6, Melinda Khoo had invited everyone in the class to her party, even the boys. Gloria had rolled her eyes but made her a tutu from pink tulle and David had driven her and picked her up. Kylie had won the game of musical chairs, thanks to her winning combination of underestimated girlish appearance and utter ruthlessness. Her prize betrayed Melinda's mother's expectations of the gender of the winner – a khaki plastic Donatello of the turtle variety, with a purple mask and yellow shell.

'You had a pink cake in the shape of a skirt with a Barbie sticking out the top,' Kylie said.

'Yes! God, I dreamed about that cake for weeks. Mum went all out.'

From nowhere, vivid memories of coloured streamers sticky-taped to walls, nests of balloons tied to chairs and a trestle table covered with butcher's paper and loaded with jugs of orange cordial, plastic cups and plastic plates, one of which held a tower of caramel slice, came flooding back.

'Kylie?' said Melinda.

'Of course I remember,' she said, swallowing. 'Do you still dance?'

'Are you joking? I have zero time for that. The kids take jujitsu and violin and coding. My only hobby is day drinking.' Melinda dropped her voice to a whisper. 'Is that Nick? He was such a sooky little boy, trying to hang around with you every lunch time. He's so tall, isn't he? If I'd realised he'd be here, I would have brought my husband.' She raised one eyebrow. 'Or not.' Then she gestured to the girl standing beside her. 'This is Katherine. Katherine, this is Mummy's old friend Kylie.'

Katherine was a little older than Mia – ten or eleven – and did not look like an obvious candidate for tennis lessons. She looked rather like she'd be voted girl most likely to end up in juvie. Her hair was electricity-socket wild and she wore a miniature leather jacket and camouflage-pattern leggings. Possibly she had a switchblade in her pocket. Her eyes were almost closed. The expression on her face suggested that throughout all of recorded history and across the vast spread of humanity in all its races and cultures, there had never been a more lame way to spend a Saturday than this.

'Hey,' she said, eyes still on her phone.

I feel you, Katherine, thought Kylie.

Melinda jiggled the baby on her hip. 'I have two other boys at soccer this morning. That's four in total. Four! What were we thinking! This is Noah, our surprise caboose.'

Noah, asleep on Melinda's shoulder in a red onesie with white polka dots, also paid Kylie no attention. He had a sweep of dark hair of surprising thickness.

'Katherine has been looking forward to this for weeks,' Melinda said. 'She loves hitting things. Don't you, Katherine?'

Katherine looked up from her phone. 'Seriously, Mother? You are so basic. I told you to call me Rin.'

At this, Melinda sighed with so much existential angst that Kylie could feel it from a metre away, as though the woman would give everything she owned for a time machine, and if she had a time-machine, she would not zip back to Vienna in 1762 to catch Mozart's first gig or to Chawton in 1814 so she could bump into Jane Austen strolling around the village, but instead would go back to the moment she first decided to come off the pill.

'If I'd spoken that way to my mother, she'd have knocked me into the middle of next week,' she said to Kylie blithely, as though complaining about the weather. Then, to Rin, 'When Kylie was your age, she helped her mother like a good girl. She looked after her baby brother all the time without ever complaining. She used to make lunches for him, and for her sister, and walk them home, and check in on them in the playground. You could learn something, missy.'

Rin looked down at her phone again, deliberately and with great malice.

The queue had by now advanced to the point where Melinda was in line with Gloria.

'What about you?' said Melinda to Kylie. 'You're super successful now, I bet. I guess you're a doctor like you always planned?'

Kylie put one hand to her face. 'A doctor?'

Melinda moved the baby to her other hip. 'The rest of us wanted to be princesses, or a mermaid, or mummies or whatever. Not you. You were the only one who wanted to do a real job. Medicine, med school, hospitals – you went on and on about it.'

These days, whenever Kylie was with Lachie and Mia at a function involving other adults, invariably someone would ask them what they wanted to be when they grew up. Kylie understood that even chatty people were sometimes awkward around young children, but still the question rankled. Being a kid was a full-time job in itself! When a child's personality is still forming, the work of understanding exactly who you are begins with discovering your likes and dislikes, and these must rise organically from your temperament. *It's wrong*, Kylie thought, *to force children to pigeonhole themselves too early.* Learning how the world works and understanding your place in it – these were enormous undertakings. She knew some people well into their forties who still had no idea who they were.

Yet when Kylie herself was asked that same question by well-meaning adults all those years ago, her answer had been immediate. Kylie had all but forgotten how confident she'd been about her future career. She'd had no doubt, none at all. The very sound of anatomical words obsessed her. Epididymis, temporomandibular and islets of Langerhans all made her feel like she was casting spells in Latin. She'd practised on Tansy and Nick – taking their temperature, dotting unmarked skin with unnecessary bandaids, mending the holes in Nick's clothes as though they were wounds. She imagined her adult-self concentrating over flesh, lifting an unconscious limb and feeling the weight of someone's body in her hands so often that her future seemed set in stone. Kylie would grow up to be a surgeon, she was sure of it.

'No,' she said. 'I didn't become a doctor.'

'Oh.' Melinda's face fell, as if the disappointment was her own. 'You were so sure. What happened?'

Not every childhood wish comes true. Life. Life is what happened. Her family happened. But Kylie had no idea how to explain that to Melinda, much less to herself.

She was rescued by the sound of a car horn. Tansy was double-parked in her new SUV in front of the shelter, waving to Kylie from the driver's seat. What on earth was she doing here? Not volunteering to help, Kylie was certain about that. She excused herself to Melinda and jogged out through the nearest gate.

As she approached Tansy's car, the back door opened and Mia and Lachie tumbled out. They were talking over each other, each wanting to show Kylie their racquets and tell her about their morning and ask where Gloria and Nick were.

'Wait till I show you how high I can hit it,' said Mia. 'So high.'

'I can hit it miles higher than you,' said Lachie. 'I can hit the sky.'

Tansy wound down her window. 'Fancy two more?' she said to Kylie.

Kylie swallowed and gave the kids what she hoped was a welcoming wave. 'Of course! The more the merrier. Go on and see Nana.'

Mia and Lachie ran towards the shelter. Once they were out of sight, Kylie leaned into the open window.

'A little bit of notice would have been nice,' she said.

'Sorry. Last-minute decision. I couldn't resist the opportunity for some *quality time* with my husband,' said Tansy.

Kylie stepped back from the car. 'Ugh, Tans.'

'Let the record show: woman has sex with husband.' Tansy winked at her. 'We can't all live like nuns, Kyles.' She started to wind the window up, then lowered it again and leaned across the seat, so she could see Kylie's face. 'And look after my babies.' Then she waved and took off, tooting as she pulled out of the carpark.

Chapter 29

It was time to get the proceedings underway. Nick was spending an inordinate amount of time with the mothers at the end of the queue so Kylie grabbed her own clipboard and began issuing racquets. This proved to be a signal – at least three dozen children approached her at once. It was important to check each child's age and height before choosing a racquet of the correct size but there were too many children and too many racquets for her to police them all. And they weren't queuing! Why didn't parents teach their children to queue in an orderly fashion? If Kylie were a parent, that was the first thing she'd do. Before she had dispensed half the racquets, a yellow neon tennis ball whizzed past Kylie's head from an undetermined direction.

She spun around but couldn't identify the culprit. She hadn't even distributed the balls yet! That ball was unauthorised!

'Okay, who did that?' she said to a huddle of studiously innocent faces. 'You could hurt someone. These are not toys.'

'Kylie!' Gloria called out. 'They *are* toys. We're here to have fun, remember?'

'Yes, yes,' she called back.

Then from the corner of her eye she glimpsed small hands reaching into random boxes and helping themselves to the remaining racquets in chaotic fashion. When she turned back, all of the children had a racquet.

'Okay, who grabbed one without asking?' she said. 'Put them back. You need to have the right size and I need to tick you off my spreadsheet, that's only logical.'

It was not logical to the children. No one surrendered their racquet. There was much giggling and swinging and some holding of the illicit racquets behind backs, but zero appreciation of either Kylie's argument or her spreadsheet. She was vastly outnumbered. Nick should stop flirting with those mothers immediately and come help her. The parents who were left – those who hadn't seized upon an hour of free babysitting and hightailed it back to their cars – were on their phones. Things were veering off track. Kylie needed to retain eye contact, to control their attention. To show them who was boss, the way Sam Neill had with the velociraptors.

'Do you need a hand, Kylie?' Gloria called out. 'I'm quite adept with the crutches now.'

'No, I do not!' Kylie yelled back. Then to the children she used her best cheery cool-aunt voice. 'Let's get into a line and I'll give everyone a ball!'

No one got into a line. Instead they swarmed around the box three children deep, and started passing balls back to each other as if Kylie wasn't even there. Before she could even grasp a semblance of control, all of the tubes in the box were empty. Some children had a ball in each hand and another tucked into the waistband of their shorts. Kylie squeezed the clipboard until her fingers turned white. Where was Nick? Nick was nowhere to be seen.

Don't raise your voice, Kylie, she told herself. *Be calm.*

'That's okay, that's fine!' she said. 'Let's get started!'

The children did not want to get started on something as prosaic as a tennis lesson. It was much more fun to chatter, giggle and shove each other. They drifted across the court, pulled on the net and threw their balls into the air.

She waded into the sea of them. 'Let's form into groups,' she said louder.

The children did not want to form into groups. The children were surrounded by small humans their own age who they didn't yet know, and they ignored her. The real world was noisier and more tactile than the two-dimensional small screen that took up their visual field most of the time. They were overstimulated, overwhelmed.

'That's enough now,' Kylie said, a little louder again, cool-aunt voice forgotten.

She looked behind her at Gloria in the shelter. She was in deep conversation with two fathers and wasn't paying any attention to what was happening on the court.

Kylie clapped her hands. 'Let's line up here,' she said. Her fingers went to the buttons on her Fitbit. Perhaps she should set an alarm, because alarms and sounds that came from a device in general, Kylie knew, garnered more respect than mere humans. At least, they did to her.

Before she could set an alarm though, a small boy no older than six took an almighty swing at another boy's bum right in front of her – then dropped his racquet and ran. The victim gave chase and barrelled into another group of kids, knocking one over.

'Stop that!' Kylie yelled.

On the court next door, Kylie watched one boy put his finger up his nose and threaten a girl with it. She squealed and jumped back onto the foot of another child, who then squealed in turn. Others armed with racquets and balls began busily whacking the net and attempting serves. On the far baseline, two boys began fencing with their racquets, left arms extended behind them like musketeers.

Kylie heard someone say, 'This is so lame.' It was Rin.

Then everything happened in a dreadful kind of slow motion.

First, Leo appeared on the other side of the mesh fence around the courts.

'Kylie!' His fingers were threaded through the wire. He wore shorts, a graphic tee of some unknown band and an unbuttoned khaki shirt in the way of grown men these days who dressed like children. 'Wow, you look awesome. What can I do?'

Someone was here to help, finally. And it was Leo.

But then Caesar, already unsettled on Gloria's lap, saw him and barked. From the side of the court, three older girls with their eyes on their phones looked up and recognised each other, and they all squealed at once. From the sausage stand, the head Rotarian – a real estate auctioneer by trade with a voice that could replace a sound system – held up his burnished sausages on a plate and yelled, 'Come and get 'em!' A stray tennis ball bounced fast into the shelter, hitting the wall near where Gloria was sitting and ricocheting against the seat. Overhead, the drone was approaching like an evil, floating Roomba. The pilot was nowhere in sight. It was dipping and weaving, apparently out of control. It skimmed over the top of the shelter, buzzing like the Incredible Hulk of mosquitos.

The happy sight of Leo, the alarming shrieks of the girls, the yelling sausage griller and the overwhelming smell of hot fat and salt, the bouncing neon ball, the menacing approaching drone. Caesar was becoming more and more agitated on Gloria's lap.

'Mum . . .' Kylie called out.

She heard a voice. 'Auntie Kylie, look at me!'

It was Lachie. He was on the other side of the court, kneeling in a four-point stance at the baseline and sizing up the net, which he was clearly planning to hurdle.

Mia was standing beside him, arms folded in recognisable sibling disapproval.

'He's too short,' she yelled to Kylie. 'And he can't jump!'

'Can so!' yelled Lachie.

'Nick!' Kylie yelled, above the general cacophony. 'Don't! Tansy, stop him!'

But neither of the children paid her any attention because they lived in the present instead of being stuck in the past with Kylie. They didn't even realise she was yelling at them. Lachie was not Nick and Mia was not Tansy.

Back in the shelter, Caesar started barking, insistently. Gloria was shushing, trying to calm him. From the corner of her eye, Kylie saw him pull hard in one direction, then back off with equal force. The collar slipped over his head. Another quick movement and he bounded off Gloria's lap and out of the shelter. He ran down the length of the first court and into the next, a streak of Trumpian orange against the muddy-green surface, zipping around the stunned legs of the children, who were now all shrieking.

Lachie, however, was focused, intent upon the net. He took off like a sprinter, dodging some kids in his path – but he could not dodge Caesar. There was a collision of dog and boy; there was yelping. Lachie went flying as Caesar darted out of the way. Kylie watched as Lachie, seemingly in slow motion, put out his hands before him as he fell. Kylie gasped as his left arm took the weight of him. He screamed as he hit the ground.

When a nest of girls nearby heard Lachie scream, they began to scream, and then Lachie started to cry, and then a boy who hadn't even noticed him fall started to cry.

Kylie started towards Lachie.

'Kylie!' yelled Leo. 'Look!'

He pointed to the far corner of the court diagonal to Kylie, where a gate was open. If Caesar reached that gate, there was nothing but a soccer field between him and the four-lane highway. Kylie stopped, torn between heading to Lachie and catching Caesar.

Then, among the general cacophony, Rin yelled, 'I'll get him! Mum, get out your phone and take this is for my Insta!'

Rin darted after Caesar at pace. All the other children took this as a signal. They followed Rin and before Kylie knew it, all the children were screaming and running, some after Caesar and others in no discernible direction, and in the middle of all of this, Lachie was crying. Mia, kneeling, wrapped him in her arms. Several children collided with each other. Leo, on the other side of the fence, ran around the outside of the courts in an attempt to cut Caesar off, should he clear the gate. All this sound and motion made Caesar run faster, frantically dashing across the courts.

'Oh, for heaven's sake,' Melinda muttered. Then at the top of her lungs, she yelled, 'Katherine Grace, you get back here!'

Kylie was momentarily stunned. What should she do?

'Kylie!' Gloria was stretching under the seat for one of her crutches that had somehow fallen out of reach. 'Kylie, Lachie's hurt!'

So Kylie ran to Lachie, shouting at the children to calm down as she passed. They couldn't hear her but even if they could, no one in the history of the world had ever calmed down when someone told them to. Kylie kneeled beside Lachie and he folded into her, holding his left arm with his right hand, sobbing now. Around them, children kept shrieking and running but Caesar darted between their legs and around their outstretched hands as though he were coated in butter.

Kylie watching him, despairingly. He was uncatchable – until he faced Rin.

She did not pursue him the way everyone else did. Instead she paused several metres away and, in an act of perfect spatial judgement, threw herself forward, diving as if she were a leaf upon the breeze, aiming for where she expected him to be. At the height of her arc, at that precise moment between rising and falling while suspended in midair, she reached down, picked up his little body and encircled him against her chest.

Rin, however, was not a leaf upon the wind. She hit the ground. Hard. She rolled with a sickening thump, then skidded to a stop, flat on her back. Then she was still.

Someone gasped. Melinda held Noah tighter. The children froze, Kylie froze, even Lachie stopped crying to stare at Rin in one of those long suspenseful moments before the extent of an injury is revealed.

Caesar began wriggling, vainly, to be free, but Rin held him firm. She sat up, then stood, gingerly. She dusted herself off. The children cheered. Rin, unfazed, bowed and raised one fist, victorious in her triumph.

'Did you get it? Tell me you got it,' she yelled at Melinda as she limped towards the shelter, the children parting for her.

Melinda's face revealed she had not, in fact, got it.

'Typical,' said Rin with disgust.

'What a hero you are!' said Gloria, as she took Caesar from Rin.

Kylie felt herself sag. That could have been a disaster! Lachie hurting himself was bad enough, but one of the other children might have been injured!

Rin turned back towards her adoring crowd and smiled. Revealing a glaring gap where one of her front incisors used to be.

Melinda dropped her head back and stared at the sky. 'Great,' she said. 'Wait until I tell your father.'

Lachie was attended to first – he was soon sobbing again, holding his now-red and oddly shaped arm, being comforted by Mia and sitting on Gloria's lap. Tansy was phoned. Kylie could only imagine what she'd say when she arrived.

'Just as well you're so brave,' Gloria said to Lachie.

Today had proven beyond all doubt that Kylie was not cut out for parenthood. She was not gifted at child-wrangling, nor at dog-herding for that matter.

This specific problem, however, was made for her. All of Kylie's first-aid courses, all of her preparations, had led to this moment. At once, she sprang into action, gathering all the children and offering them ten dollars for whoever spotted, but did not touch, Rin's missing tooth. Nick, who'd just popped back to his car for a moment for a sharpie so he could sign a football for one of the mums, was aghast on his return.

'I left you alone for two minutes!' he said to Kylie.

'It wasn't Kylie's fault,' said Leo, who'd joined in with the children looking for the tooth.

It was soon spotted by a triumphant six-year-old. Kylie rinsed it quickly in the milk from Noah's spare bottle, then gently positioned it back in the gap in Rin's top row. Then she found a new sweatband for Rin to bite down on to keep the tooth in place.

'Kylie always did want to be a doctor,' said Melinda to no one in particular.

'You need to find a dentist, straight away,' said Kylie. 'The sooner it's re-implanted properly, the better the chances of saving the tooth.'

'Fine.' Melinda handed baby Noah to Kylie. 'Here.'

Kylie took him, there was no option. 'What? No.'

'Don't make that face. He's my fourth so believe me, babies are tougher than they look, and he'll go to anyone. Besides, do you know what dentists cost? You owe me.' Melinda dropped a bulging nappy bag at Kylie's feet and gestured to Rin. 'I won't be long.'

At first Kylie held Noah's body away from hers like he was an unstable incendiary device, but then he began to notice she was a different person from his mother. His big eyes blinked. He saw her. His irises were dark, almost indistinguishable from the pupils. There were tiny grains of sleep in one corner. He was surprisingly heavy for his size – a solid little parcel at the end of her extended arms.

Noah smiled at her. He giggled. It was only natural that Kylie brought him closer to her body until he was cradled against her chest in the most natural position in the world, his hot face in her neck. He was the perfect shape, the perfect weight. His lashes were long and black against the brown skin of his cheek, which would be unbearably soft to touch.

Noah looked up at Kylie and laughed, and his fat satin cheeks puffed up and his tiny ears wiggled.

'What's so funny?' she said to him. She didn't even notice when Melinda and Rin left.

Chapter 30

The parents, cranky from the very beginning, soon would be ropable. A few were already grumbling about the chaos they'd witnessed, and the delay. One or two cast sideways glances at Kylie, their arms folded.

So Gloria eased the white-faced Lachie off her knee. As Mia took over cuddling him, Gloria hauled herself up on her crutches. She limped with practised melodrama and an air of leaving-the-side-of-my-wounded-grandson-to-attend-to-you-people. She stood by the umpire's seat and clapped to get everyone's attention.

'Among the many benefits to children of learning a sport,' she announced to the parents, her eyes boring holes into their heads, 'are discipline and self-control, and the skills of being a good winner and good loser. Your children will remember today, possibly for the rest of their lives. Your children will notice the way you behave today. I am . . . *overwhelmed* with respect for you all and your choice to model equanimity and good behaviour. Showing your children that you are in command of yourselves will repay you a thousandfold in the years to come.'

She then delivered her usual rousing speech about tennis lessons being essential to all civilised humans once water, food, shelter and clothing are sorted, about it being a basic life skill like making toast or changing a tyre. She then returned to Lachie's side, in triumphant dignity.

By the time Tansy had arrived, steaming, to take Lachie for an X-ray, Gloria had delegated exercises to the older kids and amused everyone with some blindfolded parent-versus-kid challenges. She also paid for the Rotarians' entire stock of sausages, which was distributed with largesse – some kids had one in each hand and another in their mouths. Free sausages kept everyone happy. The face painter arrived too, late but keen, and soon the courts abounded with tigers and skulls and spider-kids, though what was face paint and what was tomato sauce, Kylie could not be sure.

Caesar, exhausted after his escapade, snoozed, securely leashed in the corner of the shelter. Gloria appropriated a fold-up chair brought by one of the parents and positioned herself as the umpire. She had assumed that Leo could play tennis – because who on earth couldn't? – so she organised for Nick to take the group of older kids and Leo, the younger ones.

It was soon obvious, though, that Leo was possibly the most incompetent person who'd ever held a racquet. He missed returns so comprehensively it seemed he had an invisible ball-shaped hole in the centre of his strings, and every serve was so wide that Gloria was concerned for his vision. Nick was athletically superior to him in every possible way.

Yet somehow as the day progressed, Leo's group became the sought-after one for kids of all ages.

It was because of this – Leo was enjoying every minute. He simply didn't care that his tennis skills reached a new level of incompetence, and because he didn't care, his attempts to hit the ball were hilarious and non-threatening in the kids' eyes. Every time he missed an easy shot, everyone laughed, including Leo himself. His example showed even the most reluctant, self-conscious child how to be spectacularly untalented at something and still have fun.

Kylie, sitting in the shelter with Noah on her lap, took no further part in proceedings. How could she? She was responsible for a baby.

Over the course of the next few hours, Kylie changed Noah's nappy (under Gloria's supervision) and fed him with a bottle from the nappy bag, which he grabbed at ineffectually with his hands and also with his feet. He took several naps. Noah had only one toy with him – a wooden fish with discs in its middle, like an abacus – so Kylie resorted to makeshift amusements: Gloria's keys, an empty water bottle filled with pebbles, her Fitbit, swinging before him like a pendulum. How could Kylie have thought that babies couldn't communicate? Noah could. Each expression that played upon his face told Kylie something. Everything was new to Noah – tennis balls, Caesar, Kylie – and through his eyes, everything seemed new to Kylie also. When she talked to him, he gripped her pinky with his fist. And as for her belief that babies were interchangeable? Noah was like no other baby. He smelled fresh and at the same time, slightly curdled. His dark eyes, tucked beneath the fold of his eyelid, belonged only to him. The rolls on the back of his neck were the purest, softest substance known to science. His arms beat down spasmodically with their own rhythm, like a tone-deaf but determined drummer. His fat legs kicked, and he found each kick hilarious. On his upper lip was a small red swelling and the side of his neck was somehow perpetually damp with drool. Soon Kylie's shirt was also damp.

Before Kylie knew it, Melinda appeared beside her. She was back without Rin, who was at home with her tooth splinted in place. Noah was asleep in Kylie's arms.

'You're good at this,' Melinda said. She stood expectantly beside Kylie, her arms outstretched.

Kylie, blinking, handed Noah over.

The open day was a success by any measure. All of Leo's younger kids signed up for Gloria's regular lessons, as did most, but not all, of Nick's. Kylie left Nick and Leo to pack up. Both Gloria and Caesar were asleep by the time she reached the highway.

Kylie changed gears and steered with her suddenly empty hands. She was thinking and feeling, thinking and feeling. Her mind revolved around chubby legs and the softest skin and perfect, perfect lashes. Kylie was a different creature from who she'd been this morning. Sometime during the afternoon when she hadn't been paying attention, a key had been inserted into a lock. Pins had pressed against tumblers and a barrel had rotated. Had she listened, she might have heard a mechanical whirring, then a clunking sound.

By the time Kylie was trying to sleep on Gloria's couch that night, it was too late to stop it. Something deep inside her had shifted.

SUNDAY

Chapter 31

Kylie did not sleep at all on the couch that night. She was worried about Lachie, yes – Tansy had texted last night to say his arm was broken *thanks very much for supervising, Kyles* – but there were other things, also, on Kylie's mind. Her hands were tingling and her blood was fizzy. If she had woken with her period, all of this would be moot. But there had been no period. She was seven days late today, which was officially medically late.

Yet the pregnancy test, upstairs under the bathroom sink, remained untaken.

That was because everything was now reversed.

Now there was something wrong with Kylie's arms. They were empty, unanchored. If she relaxed, they would float up towards the ceiling of their own accord. She forced her hands to the swell of her abdomen, below her navel. She had no control over her body, that much was clear. She was almost certain of what had happened – what *was* happening, right now, growing and changing inside her – yet she couldn't bring herself to form it into words. She could only glimpse the idea of it from the corner of her eye, lest it vanish.

Just days ago, that was because she dreaded the test being positive. Now, she dreaded it might not be.

If she was right, there was so much to be prepared in her own home. Things to buy, things to clean. The spare room should be painted and new furniture bought. The cupboards needed locks. Look how easily Lachie had broken his arm! She needed non-slip rugs, a safety gate for the door, some kind of playpen. A leash. Door catches and door stoppers and plastic triangles for the corners of tables. And Tupperware, that's what people in her position found useful.

But she was getting ahead of herself. First things first: Gloria was reasonably mobile, as she proved yesterday, and Leo could pop in every day. Kylie was no longer needed here.

Before either Gloria or Caesar stirred, she packed all her clothes and toiletries and piled the sheets and pillowslips from the couch into the washing machine. Her joints were even stiffer than usual this morning and her feet ached as though they were never meant to carry her weight, but that was to be expected after yesterday's exertions. There were a few dishes draining from the hurried omelette she and Gloria had shared last night. She put them away. She fluffed the cushions and mopped the kitchen floor. Now no one could tell she'd ever been here.

Kylie was collecting Caesar's toys, scattered under every piece of furniture – a premonition of her future? – in a blue Ikea tote when she saw her workbag sitting beside the couch where she'd dumped it. Way back on Monday, months ago, Gail had given her some documents about the conditions of her likely future employment with Pharmacy King. Kylie sat on the couch, fanning the pages on the coffee table. She read them, then read them again, these torturous specimens of corporate waffle in six-point type. Once she sorted out the parties of the first part from those of the second, it was clear: Pharmacy King had reached an agreement with Tim guaranteeing that if Kylie did not continue her employment, her leave entitlements would be paid out. All of them. Annual leave, and long-service leave, and sick leave. If she stayed, though, her new employer would take over her entitlements. And they would waive the usual twelve-month wait required for parental leave. Her stomach fluttered.

This meant that things could be managed. If Kylie was right about the changes in her body, and Kylie was never wrong, things were manageable in a practical sense. She pressed the heels of her palms against her eyes until stars appeared.

When the sheets finished washing, she carried the basket on her hip outside to the Hills hoist. The backyard, Kylie realised, hadn't been touched all week – even though she had sent out the *Management of Gloria's Ankle* SOP that clearly detailed Simon's responsibility for said garden on Thursday! How absolutely typical. Three days, and he'd done nothing. Kylie had no idea how Tansy put up with him. It was a good thing for everyone that Kylie was here.

In the garage she found gloves and a floppy hat, and a fork, trowel and weeder set. She would start with the garden beds then move to the bindies on the lawn. Gloria's front yard had 1960s street appeal, with its spirit-level-flat box hedge along the front and others spiralled like corkscrews. The backyard was more private, less fussy. It was huge, the way everyone's backyard seemed to be in her childhood. High fences, buffalo grass. Kylie's house had only a courtyard with no greenery to speak of, but here was somewhere a child could play.

When they were kids, there was a swing-set in one corner, and a clear plastic inflatable pool with bright tropical fish on the outside. She had vivid memories of being in her primary-school uniform and running laps of the house with Tansy and Nick, calling out, *Mum, Mum, time us!* Kylie could see a young Gloria in hotpants and a halter top, evening drink in one hand and an old-fashioned silver stopwatch in the other, waiting at the finish line, which was the concrete path to the incinerator. Kylie always won. Tansy would be in last place, far behind but not caring. Nick, so much younger, close and straining to catch her. Nick tried to match his big sisters at everything – handstands and cartwheels and climbing trees.

Tansy and Nick and she were indivisible still. The idea of not having them, of being alone in the world, was inconceivable to her. She couldn't imagine the experience of growing up as an only child – although perhaps even that could be managed with a little ingenuity. Parents' groups, day care, camps. A father would want to be involved, even a father who hadn't planned for a child – say, a father who'd had a vasectomy. Probably it would take that kind of father a little while to get used to the idea, but then he would rise to the occasion and would bring with him another set of uncles and aunts and grandparents, all of which would help an only child make lasting connections and learn interpersonal skills.

Around midmorning, Kylie was kneeling on a cushion pulling weeds from around the azaleas, lost in thought, when Gloria came to the side patio.

'Kylie?' she called out. 'What are you doing?'

'What does it look like?' she called back.

'Don't be rude. Do you want any breakfast?'

Kylie didn't. Gloria could manage on her crutches for a little while, because every weed and withered branch offended Kylie. It was chaos out here! It was as though her mind couldn't rest until everything was put right, in its place.

A little later, she heard a voice coming out of the side door. It was Monica.

'Mon, hi,' Kylie said. 'This is a surprise.' She kept her gaze on the weeds and her hands moving.

'Yeah, sorry, I'm a little early,' said Monica. 'I thought I'd visit Gloria and see if you needed a hand.'

'Hand at what?' said Kylie, concentrating on a weed that, she just knew, would leave its roots behind if she pulled too hard.

'Making lunch?'

'Lunch?' said Kylie.

'Everyone's coming, yeah? That's today, right? Tansy texted me.'

Kylie fell backwards onto the grass. Her gaze went to her wrist to check the time on her Fitbit, but the only thing there was an indentation where the band used to sit. She must have taken it off at some stage and forgotten to put it back on. Her Fitbit was missing and a head, and only a head, of a weed was in her hand.

Ten minutes later, Kylie and Monica were in Gloria's car, zooming to Coles.

'So.' Monica was resting her hand on the side passenger window, seemingly for no other reason than to leave smudge marks on the glass. 'You forgot about lunch, right?'

'No. No, no, no,' said Kylie. 'Yes.'

'Gloria is so brave! That ankle must be killing her.' Monica shook her head in wonder, and the pink curls flicked across her face in pretty waves. 'So you're cooking for everybody. Instead of Tansy doing it, like normal. Wild. Can I give you some advice?'

Kylie indicated to go around a corner. She kept her gaze straight ahead.

'This is just like Bridie McGally, from the CWA back home,' said Monica.

'You're going to make me ask, aren't you?' said Kylie. 'Fine. How is this like Bridie McGally from the CWA back home?'

'Well!' Monica turned to her. 'Bridie is an amazing cook, in general. Her passionfruit sponge, I can't tell you. Passionfruit in the sponge, as well as in the cream, as well as the icing! Triple passionfruit! But she wasn't really a jam-maker, right? Just not her thing. I'm not being mean, everyone knew it. Gummy. Sometimes scorched. Then one year, bam! Her apricot is the best out of all the entries. Unbelievably good, because it had been a bad year for apricots and everyone else's was rubbish. She wins for the first time ever! Everyone is shocked! But it turned out . . . drum roll, Kyles . . . that jam had been sitting in her pantry for twelve months because she made it last year!'

'So it's . . . old jam?'

Monica looked at Kylie as if all at once concerned that someone who knew so little about the world was behind the wheel of a car. 'Jam doesn't get old, Kyles. That's the whole point of jam.'

'Oh. Right.'

'No, everyone else's were made with that year's inferior apricots. Boom! She was disqualified!'

'Not sure what you're getting at.'

'Fakery loses every time, Kyles,' Monica said, strumming her fingers on her knee. 'Not everyone's into cooking. You do you, babe.'

'But I can cook. I'm an excellent cook.'

'Just get pizza delivered, seriously. We'll eat it on the couch. We Schnabels, we love you just the way you are. No one's going to care.'

Kylie kept her eyes forward and focused on the traffic. In that moment, she felt not forty-three, but a hundred at least. They might be half-sisters but there were things in Kylie's past and her nature that she could never explain to Monica.

'It's complicated,' she said.

'Hey, are you okay?' said Monica. 'Your left eye has gone all twitchy.'

'I'm fine,' she said.

'How's your job application coming along?'

She answered Mon with a vague grunt. It was impossible to believe, but until Mon asked, Kylie had not thought about her job application once all morning. She had not thought about Tim, or Emily, and had only thought about Pharmacy King in the context of her leave entitlements. Her family was coming for lunch in a couple of hours and until now, she'd also forgotten about that. The changes that were happening in her body had taken all her focus. She simply had no bandwidth to worry about anything else.

Focus, Kylie, she thought. 'How old are Mia and Lachie? Five and three?'

'Nine and six,' said Monica.

'Still. Babies don't eat much.'

'They're not babies.'

'Children, I mean. Babies don't eat anything. They drink milk, which makes them very cheap to run,' muttered Kylie to the steering wheel, as though babies were hybrid Toyotas.

'What?'

'Mia and Lachie probably count as half a person each, is what I mean. Enough food for seven, realistically. You, me, Nick, Tansy and family, and Gloria. That's eight, right?'

'Eight, yep.' Mon counted on her fingers. 'Usually would be nine, but no Colin.'

All at once, the brakes screeched. Monica lurched forward against her seatbelt and raised her hands to the glove box as the car lurched to a halt in the middle of the street. Kylie had stopped to avoid a car ahead that was turning right into a driveway across the flow of traffic.

'Whoa, Toretto,' Mon said. 'Drive it like you stole it.'

'Yep, no Colin,' Kylie said. She tooted the horn and raised her hands at the driver in front in the universal symbol for questioning stupid decisions. 'Honest to god, I'm not psychic, mate,' she said. 'I could have had a kid in the car! Use your indicator!'

The car turned; Kylie accelerated.

'You must miss him. Colin,' said Mon. 'It's only natural.'

Kylie zipped through the gears and cornered.

'Lunch will be better without him, for sure,' Monica said. 'Remember that barbecue at Tansy's, when you told him he was drinking too much? The look on his face. I thought he was going to snap his wineglass in half.'

'I'm sure I never said that. Although, drinking too much is a risk factor for heart disease.'

'You did, though, Kyles? You were just helping, I know. Like his haircut.'

'His haircut?'

Monica nodded, vigorously. 'He looked so much better once you made him go to your hairdresser instead. It doesn't matter how long they'd been friends, a bad cut is a bad cut.'

'Right.'

'And as for his new job – you shouldn't feel guilty about that. So he hated it, so what? We've all had jobs that we've hated. Power through, tough it out. Don't complain all the time.'

'How did you know that Colin hated his job?'

'He told me? At Lachie's birthday party. He was miserable every day, that's what he said. But that's not your fault! Everyone should be so lucky to have someone like you to give them some direction.'

Kylie had thought exactly that, over the last few days. How lucky Colin had been to have her, how stupid he'd been to let her go. But hearing it from Monica was a completely different thing.

'Such a loser, right?' Monica said. 'To have done that to you.'

No, Kylie thought in a sudden flash. Colin wasn't a loser, and, yes, she missed him. She missed seeing his face so peaceful beside her in bed in the morning and she missed sitting on the couch with him watching something stupid on television at night. He loved to touch her skin, she would miss that. The little circles his fingers made on her arm. He had let her have her own way, time and time again, had taken her direction, had done precisely what she wanted. He had been in love, and she had found herself a project. He was weak, yes, but she had been equally at fault.

She needed to tell him about the baby. He was a good man. He would want to be in their lives.

'I've said too much, haven't I?' said Monica. 'Sorry.'

'No,' Kylie said. 'I'm the one who's sorry.'

'You have a list, right?' said Monica as they pulled up in the supermarket carpark. 'You're definitely the kind of person who would have a list. Rip that sucker in half. You can start in fruit and veg and I'll start in frozen.'

Monica was right that Kylie was a list person. Not now, though.

When Kylie had volunteered to cook, she had every intention of buying a fancy magazine and leafing through it, then stocktaking Gloria's pantry and making a comprehensive list of everything she'd need, which would be everything. She'd imagined herself as a Sylvia or a Poh or maybe even a Stephanie, laying earthenware platters filled with steaming, rustic peasant foods and some kind of Asian salad in front of her astonished family. She would plate things! Plate, as a verb! She would buy pomegranate molasses, whatever that was! And make something with eggplant! Kylie was forty-three. It was beyond time to work out how to cook eggplant because if everyone's eggplant turned out like hers the single time she'd attempted it – greyish cubes of squeaky sponge – the eggplant industry would have shrivelled to nothing long ago. She imagined herself triumphant and everyone's mouths agape, because Kylie was perfect at everything and there was literally nothing she couldn't do.

At least, that had been her intention.

Now, though, jogging towards the supermarket with the shopping bags from Gloria's boot and Monica beside her, it was too late for anything fancy. There was certainly no time for unravelling the mysteries of eggplant. Kylie found herself moving instinctively, working on her muscle memory alone, with no thinking required. Inside the supermarket, Kylie darted along the front towards frozen foods, dodging the shoppers queuing at the registers. Monica grabbed a trolley and followed her up and down the aisles, careering the trolley to keep up, dodging meandering couples and stackers kneeling by the bottom shelf as though proposing to a four-litre tin of olive oil. Frozen peas and chocolate ice cream first, then tins of peaches and corn, and macaroni then oats and a bottle of Thousand Island dressing, which Kylie was a little surprised they still made.

She zipped past shelves of baby food and baby biscuits and baby comestibles of all kinds, and in front of them, a heavily pregnant woman was standing with a trolley and a jar of greenish goo in her hands. There had been pregnant women in the world before today, but Kylie had never noticed one before. On autopilot in the fruit and veg department, she chose an iceberg lettuce, two tomatoes and one solitary carrot. And finally, in the meat section, sausages – several trays.

Kylie felt powerful, in the zone, super-human.

Monica, however, was astonished by Kylie's choice of ice cream ('Cheapest plain chocolate in a plastic tub,' she said. 'Bold choice.') and lettuce ('crunchy water') and she handled the macaroni with the reverence of Howard Carter excavating Tutankhamun's tomb. ('Wow. It's just like pasta but boring and not even pretending to have anything to do with Italy.') In the cold section, Monica turned her nose up at Kylie's choice of milk, butter and cheese.

Kylie ignored her.

'Shall we get some camembert? Or brie? To have with bikkies and a quince paste, for starters?'

'Soft cheese has a risk of Listeria. Absolutely not.'

'Kylie, babe. What's with all the tins, seriously? It's peach season! Get them fresh. Less processing, fewer food miles. And how about some corn on the cob instead of tins?'

Kylie shook her head.

Monica frowned and shook the tin of corn like a maraca. 'The CWA would not be happy with you,' she said.

Back in Gloria's time capsule of a kitchen, Kylie stood with her fingers on the cream laminate bench in front of the brown-tiled splashback while Monica ferried in the groceries from the car.

Gloria limped to the kitchen bench on her crutches. 'Finally you're back. I thought you'd kidnapped Monica and dyed her hair and moved to a commune interstate.'

'We bought . . . I guess you could call it food?' said Monica, arriving with bags in hand. 'The good news is, we bought it without ration tickets. The bad news, Ottolenghi it ain't.'

'Cooking of any kind is extremely overrated,' Gloria said. 'I avoid it at all costs.'

'No wonder everyone was so skinny back in the nineties.' Monica pulled the tin of corn out of one of the bags and waved it at Gloria. 'I always wondered if it was an optical illusion caused by the baggy clothes but apparently everything was borderline inedible.'

'Just you wait. I know what I'm doing,' said Kylie, unpacking things onto the counter.

'I'll show you where everything is,' Gloria said to Kylie as she hobbled towards the sink.

'I know where everything is.' Kylie spun Gloria around. 'I used to live here, remember? Out, both of you.'

Gloria sniffed. 'Come along, Monica. I can tell when I'm not wanted.'

'Can you, though?' said Kylie.

Gloria ordered Monica to set up some ice and drinks in the lounge room so Kylie wouldn't be disturbed in the kitchen when everyone arrived. 'Is there anything else I can do to help?'

Monica asked her. 'Not that I would know how to cook any of that stuff.'

'You can set the table,' Kylie said. 'Then take Mum into the lounge room and work on her Instagram.'

'Excellent suggestion,' said Gloria. She took hold of Mon's arm for balance.

Once Monica and Gloria left, Kylie closed her eyes and took a moment to centre herself. In her mother's kitchen, in the soft light of the early evening, there was a vaguely cinnamon scent in the air. Decades fell away. She listened for the sound of Nick's bike in the driveway when he arrived home from after-school football training and for Tansy being dropped off by one of the other mothers after piano – but there was no sound except a pigeon cooing on the gutter outside the window and a distant car in the next street.

Kylie had a thirty-minute head start before everyone arrived. She poured herself a mineral water, opened her eyes and began.

Chapter 32

In front of Gloria's laminate altar, Kylie slipped an apron over her head and grew another four hands and each of those hands was continually in motion. She knew the contents of every drawer and every cupboard, where every spoon and bowl and baking dish was kept. She found the flour in the green Bakelite canister, exactly where she knew it would be. She tripled everything. Her clever arms remembered how to force the cheese against Gloria's box grater with the heel of her hand and watched the creamy shreds yield to the steel and curl into a bowl. She melted butter and added flour until it clumped in small uneven balls then bubbled and melted again.

The macaroni clattered through her fingers like beads meant for a bracelet. She knew which saucepan was the right size to boil them, felt the familiar steam facial as she drained them in the colander that had long ago lost its feet. She added tiny green jewels of frozen peas, the right amount, and the golden nuggets of corn. The cheese smelled soft and cosy, the corn, toothsome and sweet. She poured it all in the large pyrex dish and covered it with more cheese, then she found the square Corningware with the flowers for the crumble. The sausages would go in the oven on a tray, below the macaroni cheese. The lettuce would be chopped and served in the woven wood bowl with a sliced tomato, grated carrot and more grated cheese.

She couldn't see the front door but Monica could make drinks for everyone when they arrived. Kylie blocked everything else out. She kept her head down and focused on her task, suspended in a trance, back in the early nineties. Tucked away in the kitchen, trying to get dinner done before anyone arrived felt so right, so natural. Why didn't Kylie cook for other people more often? She couldn't recall, but now she could see herself feeding people on a regular basis. She knew how to look after children. She'd done it before, in this very house.

Not everything was identical to her memories, but there was enough. The time machine that was her mother's kitchen had blasted off and had taken Kylie with it.

Time passed. When the doorbell rang, Kylie started. She stopped work to hear Monica answer the door to Tansy and Simon and Mia and Lachie, and then everyone was talking at once in a gaggle.

'In my defence . . .' said a loud voice, clearly Simon. This seemed to be a continuation of a conversation he'd been having with Tansy before the door opened.

'We'll discuss it when we get home,' Tansy said.

Kylie could hear them in the hall. Lachie was jumping and Mia was skipping and everyone was talking at once. Kylie had seen Tansy and Simon and the kids arrive enough times to picture it: Tansy with a box of late cherries or a styrofoam tray of baklava because she couldn't go anywhere empty-handed, and Simon, laden with enough bags to last a week because the kids couldn't get through a day without toys and Simon couldn't get through a meal with the Schnabels without wine. He was definitely better company these days. Now that his garden business was taking off and he'd hired a few younger landscapers, though, he wasn't doing as much of the actual labouring and his paunch was returning.

Through the cacophony of voices, Kylie could make out snatches of conversation.

'Where's Kylie?' Tansy said.

Kylie heard no reply. Mon was whispering something, no doubt. Something not for Kylie's ears.

'Can I help?' said Tansy.

'I'd leave her to it,' Mon said.

'Roger that,' said Simon. 'I just need a glass.'

'Nana!' yelled both kids, which heralded a stomping of small feet down the hallway and a volley of greetings, assorted hugs and kisses.

'Nana, Nana, look at my cast!' said Lachie. 'It's blue!'

'What does your ankle look like on the inside, Nana?' said Mia. 'Is it in a million little pieces?'

'Can I show Kylie my cast?' said Lachie.

'In a minute,' Tansy said. 'She's busy right now.'

'Look at my cast, Auntie Mon!' said Lachie. 'I fell over but I didn't cry.'

'He cried like a big baby,' said Mia.

'Shut up!' said Lachie.

'You shut up!' said Mia.

Then, a chorus of barking.

'See, Dad!' yelled Lachie. 'I told you Nana's got a dog! It's not fair. Can we have a dog?'

'I should think so,' said Gloria.

'Actually, no,' said Tansy.

'You adopted a dog, Gloria?' said Simon. 'You?'

'There's no other way to get one, Simon,' said Gloria, with a tone flat enough to level bitumen. 'They're a completely different species.'

'Nana's just babysitting,' said Tansy.

'Dogs only like us because they know we're bones on the inside,' said Mia.

'She's going through a morbid phase,' said Simon.

'Gruesome,' said Monica. 'I love it.'

Kylie peeked around the corner of the kitchen to see Monica making drinks in the lounge room. Then the voices faded as they all headed to the patio through the side door. She heard someone say, 'Let's give her some space.'

No sooner had the voices faded when front door opened and closed again: Nick. She heard his voice heading out the side door, following the others.

The side door led to a cement patio edged with brick planters that held camellias and azaleas and dotted with terracotta pots. On one side was a built-in barbecue that had been there as long as Kylie could remember, its surface now scaly and bubbling. The three of them had celebrated birthdays here, and practised roller-skating and ridden their trikes and bikes and drawn in chalk on the cement. Once, Nick had tripped while trying to keep up with Kylie and Tansy, split his chin open and left a stain in one corner that now, decades later, looked like rust. Kylie could picture everyone sitting on the brick seats as conversation drifted through the kitchen window: Nick asking Simon about the wine; Lachie asking Monica which was her favourite rock in the garden bed; and Mia asking Gloria if there were any pets buried in her backyard, and if so, how did they die, and were they just bones now and if so, could she dig them up?

Then the bell rang again. Were they expecting anyone else?

Tansy answered the door. Kylie couldn't hear what she said.

'Gloria invited me,' said a voice. 'I brought a bottle of red, I hope that's okay.'

'Welcome!' said Tansy. 'I'll just grab another chair.'

Kylie peeked again. It was Leo.

Tansy directed him through the house to the patio, and when he disappeared through the side door, Kylie stuck her head out of the door and beckoned Tansy over.

'What on earth is he doing here?' Kylie said. She tucked her hair behind her ears, then shook it loose again.

Tansy rolled her eyes. 'God, Kylie. For someone so bright, you're remarkably dumb,' she said. Then she picked up another two glasses and went outside.

Kylie wiped her hands on her apron. Honestly. Nick and Gloria, and now Tansy! Humans are experts at self-deception, and Tansy was prime example – just because she was stuck in suburban monogamy with Simon, she saw relationships everywhere and thought they were the answer to everything. Imagine Kylie and Leo together! I mean, just imagine it!

Seriously. Imagine it.

'Earth to Kyles? I asked if you wanted a drink,' said Monica, somehow appearing in the kitchen.

'Sorry,' Kylie said. 'I'm fine.'

Monica went back outside, and Kylie crept to the door to better hear everyone. Wines were being poured and beers were opened, and the snatches of conversation that floated to Kylie became even more disjointed. Tansy introduced Leo and made sure Gloria was comfortable and that the children weren't terrorising Caesar.

'Is it something to do with computer games?' said Simon, in response to something Leo had said.

'Dad,' said Mia, 'do you even know what computer games are?'

'Sure,' said Simon. 'I've played more Donkey Kong than you've had hot dinners.'

'Dad, you never play Minecraft,' said Lachie.

'Minecraft?' Simon waiting; a boom-tish pause. 'Is that Sherlock's older brother?'

She heard a chorus of groans followed by further chatter, the tink of glasses, a thudding noise that might have been a small boy jumping off a brick planter. Faint laughter. Her family.

Back in the kitchen, Kylie closed the window.

When everything was completed to Kylie's satisfaction, her family and Leo sat in their places around Gloria's dining table, extended to its full length by Nick flipping up the sliding panels in the centre.

Monica had set the table with Gloria's cork placemats (the ones with sailing ships on them) and flat plates (earthenware, with folk-art flowers in different shades of brown) and cutlery and water glasses and wineglasses and salt and pepper. At the far end was Gloria with her foot up on a small stool, surveying her court like Judge Judy with better hair, rapping her diamond drill-bit nails on the surface of the table in a way that would earn anyone else a death sentence. Caesar, on her lap, was fascinated by everything. Oh, to have the enthusiasm for life of a small orange dog in the presence of strangers and the anticipation of food! His tufted ears pivoted independently of each other, scoping each conversation, an incredibly useful Darwinian advantage that only highlighted how far humans had yet to evolve.

Leo was sitting next to Gloria on the far side of the table. He looked as scruffy as always in a Batman t-shirt but he was attentive, chatting and busying himself filling everyone's water glasses. Next to Leo was Mia, her knife and fork gripped in her fists like a prisoner about to riot. Next was Simon, busy topping up his pinot. On this side of the table, Lachie, arm in a sling, sat on the corner next to Gloria, mimicking Caesar's head movements and mouth positions while Tansy, next to him, tucked his napkin into his collar. Monica, across from Mia, was listening to Gloria. Nick, beside her, was looking at his phone.

And next to Nick, at the head of the table where their father used to sit, was Kylie's chair. But she couldn't relax yet.

'Do you need a hand, Kylie?' said Gloria.

Of course she didn't. She had never needed help, any time, from anyone.

All the time Kylie had been cooking though, a pressure had been building inside her. Her thoughts were uncontrollable, moving of their own volition in directions she'd never before considered. Kylie had always known who she was. She had always been certain about herself – each detail and preference, small and large, that made up her distinct character. Now it seemed that she had been mistaken about one vital thing.

Everything in her life had been leading to this point. It was the purpose of her existence, the long-held secret plan of her selfish genes.

There was no need for a list of pros and cons or imagining how her feminist heroes would act. Kylie knew what she needed to do. She could not stand it any longer.

'It's like molten lava straight out of the oven, so it's resting,' she said to her family as she covered the food with foil. 'Give me two minutes to wash my hands.'

They were each caught up in their own moments, so no one replied. It was a normal lunch to them. They were unaware of any impending extraordinary significance. How could it be that no one – not Colin or anyone from work, not even these people she loved, those she was closest to – knew the shape of Kylie's own private landscape of thoughts? Even at this seminal point in her life, they were talking about Caesar and how many followers he would have should he join Instagram.

This should not be a surprise, Kylie thought. If she were honest, often she was opaque even to herself.

She untied Gloria's apron and left it on the counter, then she started up the stairs.

Chapter 33

Afterwards, Kylie stood in the doorway, baking dish in her mittened hands.

'Yay! Lunch,' squeaked Lachie. 'I am dying of hunger.'

Kylie laid the macaroni cheese on top of a placemat of the *Cutty Sark* in the centre of the table, then went back for the sausages and the chopped iceberg lettuce salad in its wooden bowl and Gloria's salad tossers that looked like a tree's skeleton hands. The burnished, cheesy top of the macaroni shone with oil, and its crust was tawny brown and crispy. The salad, glazed in Thousand Island dressing, smelled sweet and tangy and the sausages gleamed.

Around the table, no one spoke. They all stared at the food.

Seconds passed. Kylie sat and breathed and automatically spread her napkin over her lap.

At last Simon said, 'What is that?'

'It's moussaka, or maybe pasticchio,' said Mia. 'Yay!'

'It's not either of those things,' said Tansy. 'It's macaroni cheese.'

'Macaroni cheese?' said Lachie. 'Yay! I've died and gone to kid heaven!'

'It looks delicious, Kylie,' said Leo. 'Thank you.'

'Wait.' Lachie narrowed his eyes. 'What are those green bits poking through?'

'They're peas,' said Nick.

'Peas?' said Lachie.

'Did you make it like they do on MasterChef?' said Mia. 'Boil the pasta in parmesan water and make a cream sauce?'

'Peas?' said Lachie.

'Does it have thyme in it?' said Mia. 'That's what Jamie does. Or Taleggio? Or a panko and hazelnut crust?'

'You lot don't eat like that at home, do you?' said Leo.

'*Entertaining* is different,' said Mia.

'This is old-fashioned food,' Monica whispered to Mia. 'It's what people used to eat before normal food had been invented. Try to remember the details, it might come in handy for a history assignment.'

Mia nodded.

'A wine, Kylie?' Simon said, raising the bottle of pinot.

There was a long silence. Tansy began serving the children. Everyone was fussing with their own plates and cutlery, and Gloria was preparing to cut Lachie's food for him. Even Simon, who'd asked the question, seemed only vaguely interested in her response.

'Kylie?'

She swallowed. 'Yes, please.'

Lachie stuck his fork into the salad and flipped a square piece of lettuce over. Grated carrot stuck to the tines. 'Why is the salad dressing pink?'

'Is it blood?' Mia whispered across the table to Monica.

'Blood and peas?' said Lachie.

'Kylie has cooked us all a lovely lunch,' said Simon, visibly tensing his jaw and pouring Kylie's glass of wine. 'We are not feral. We have manners, and we are going to sit here like a normal family, and eat it.'

So much for the fallacy that children these days have a short attention span. Lachie was squirming in his seat, yes, appalled by the infiltration of peas, but Mia ate like a slow-motion Zen master, stabbing each piece of macaroni with fatal deliberation as if she were trying out for the national Precision Eating team. Kylie kept her gaze on Mia as she continued the motions of cutting her own food, transporting food to mouth, chewing and swallowing. Taking a mouthful of wine. Repeat.

What did it taste like, this meal she'd slaved over? Kylie had no idea. Everyone talked around her – of school and work, of Simon's gardens and Nick's students and the short stints that made up Leo's paid employment.

'Which I don't understand, frankly. You are an extremely competent young man,' said Gloria. 'Not your fault, probably. Poor management is endemic these days.'

'Almost always my fault!' said Leo cheerfully. 'I couldn't give a rat's, that's the problem. I'd rather be surfing.'

'So would I!' said Lachie.

'No, you wouldn't,' said Simon.

'Let's talk about something else,' said Tansy.

So they moved on to Gloria's rehab exercises and Monica's attempts to grow vegetables from seed. Kylie poured herself another wine and said nothing until at last, this interminable meal was finished.

Despite the underwhelming expectations, the macaroni dish was empty. Lachie had even scraped off the crispy cheese stuck in the corners. The sausages were also gone. The salad hadn't fared so well. It was mostly untouched, though sad bits of lettuce in gloopy pink sauce bespoiled a few plates.

'Thank you so much for lunch, Kylie,' said Leo. 'I can't tell you how long it's been since someone else cooked for me.'

Nick snorted. Tansy bit her bottom lip, took her napkin from her lap and folded it into a tiny square.

'What?' said Leo.

'Come off it, Kyles,' said Nick.

'Come off what?' said Simon.

Tansy wedged the folded napkin under the edge of her plate. 'Kylie didn't make this.'

Nick folded his arms. 'Mum made it.'

Everyone swivelled to looked at Gloria at the head of the table.

Monica blinked. 'Gloria wasn't even in the kitchen. I was here the whole time.'

'Did you make this, Nana?' said Mia.

'I have no intention of stealing the credit for this,' said Gloria. 'Kylie cooked.'

'You can't lie to us, Kyles,' said Tansy. 'We know this meal off by heart.'

'Mum made this every week at least, for close to a year after Dad left.' Nick used his fork to smear the pink gloop remaining on his plate. 'This tastes exactly, exactly like it always did, right down to the frozen peas and the tinned corn.'

'I didn't cook this tonight, and I'm quite sure I've never cooked it, although the year David left is . . . a little fuzzy, to tell the truth,' Gloria said. 'I was a little overwhelmed.'

'We had peach crumble for dessert. Is that what we're having for dessert, Kyles? Tinned peaches with oats on top, and chocolate ice cream?' Nick said.

Kylie felt the skin on her face pull tight. 'Yes.'

'I really cooked this, regularly, for the three of you?' said Gloria. 'I honestly don't recall.'

'It was a traumatic year, that's for sure,' said Tansy.

She went on to talk about their childhood, hers and Nick's, and about that terrible year after David left. About the shock they'd all felt. For the first few mad days and nights, Gloria had handled it badly, even she admitted. She drank. There were pills to sleep and others to wake up. She yelled and raged and wished for imaginative calamities of every description to rain down upon David's head. She burned things. She rent her clothing and put her tennis racquet through the stairwell wall in a series of long thin divots.

'But you pulled yourself together,' said Nick.

Gloria was a single mother with no business experience and no back-up wage-earning spouse at home. It had taken time and effort for her to qualify as a coach and start her business,

Nick explained. She worked long hours after school into the evenings and on weekends. That meant she couldn't be home for her own children, but they managed just fine. Nick went to football training after school or rode his bike around the neighbourhood with friends. Tansy would wait outside to be picked up by another mother and taken to piano classes, or she'd walk to a friend's place to play.

Kylie did neither of those things. Kylie would stay home by herself.

'Didn't Kylie do any classes or have any friends?' said Monica.

'She had friends in primary school, but by the time she got to high school she was too much of a swot,' said Nick. 'She'd stay in her room and do homework or read a book.'

'Anyway,' Tansy continued, 'when Nick and I got home a couple of hours later, dinner would be on the table. This exact dinner. And the house would be tidied and the kitchen cleaned.'

'I can't remember eating this,' said Gloria. 'Far too carby for me.'

'You didn't eat with us,' said Tansy. 'You came home in between tennis classes and cooked for us, but we didn't see you. We ate by ourselves, the three of us.'

'I can't believe I cooked this either,' Gloria said. 'There was always food available. Fruit, and so forth. And there was bread. I distinctly remember arriving home and asking Kylie if you'd eaten. She always assured me you had.'

'Kylie cooked this meal today,' Monica said. 'I swear.'

Leo cleared his throat. 'You should have seen Kylie spring into action yesterday when that girl lost her tooth,' said Leo. 'She was an absolute legend.'

'No surprise there,' said Mon.

'That woman said you wanted to be a doctor once, Kylie,' Leo said. 'How did you end up as a pharmacist?'

Kylie looked down at the flowers on her plate. How indeed.

The truth was this: at primary school, young Kylie was confident and brilliant. Concentration came easily and every lesson seemed like a reminder of things she already knew. She was every teacher's pet. She topped every subject.

Then her father moved out and only a week later, she started at a new, bigger high school. Her family of five became one of four. She was the eldest child. Gloria's lieutenant. She took over every household task she could – yes, cooking meals, and cleaning – but nothing was the same. What would they do for money? Would they have to sell the house? Where would they live? And where was her father? He rang them every week but didn't say much. Was he sad? Who was looking after him? From nowhere came a fear that Gloria would stop breathing in her sleep, or Tansy would or Nick, so Kylie crept around the house in the small hours to check on them. Back in her bed, she turned the day over in her mind, and the next day, and the rest of the week to come. It was as if she had simply forgotten how to sleep.

In the morning, her limbs were leaden, and so was her brain.

Overnight, every one of Kylie's classes at her new high school seemed to be delivered in a foreign language. Things she'd been certain of just a few months ago were unrecoverable, hidden somewhere in the quagmire of her skull. Textbooks and questions on exam papers and even her own notes seemed to dance around the page. Nothing made sense anymore.

It wasn't unusual, a bright child struggling to adjust to a new school, but Kylie's problem was that no one noticed. It was as if she had silently slipped under the surface of a churning sea. Kylie herself did not say anything. She would not add to Gloria's problems, not under any circumstances. In class, she was one fresh face among many. Her teachers didn't know the grades she'd been accustomed to, so none of them were surprised by her results.

She rarely concentrated at shcool. Overcome by the nods, she would rest her head on her forearms and fall asleep at her desk. Homework went undone, assignments unfinished. Sometimes she handed in exams with barely a word written on them. Not to mention her appalling attendance record. Yes, Kylie produced notes signed by Gloria for every absence, but the grammar and handwriting of the notes themselves didn't always match the signature.

Her teachers must have had their suspicions. A couple of them did pull her aside and ask if there was anything wrong at home. No, she told them firmly. She was a little rude in her response, to be honest, with a definite mind your own business air.

Overworked, underpaid public school teachers have enough to worry about supporting children who want to learn. Somehow over that first year she acquired a reputation as an unmotivated girl with parents who didn't care enough to enforce bedtimes or show up for parent–teacher nights. It affected her teachers' expectations and the subjects she chose in the years to come, and it altered the career advice she received and the way she conceived her own future.

By the time Kylie reached Year 8 and her attendance slowly improved and her grades began, painstakingly, to return, it was too late. By year eleven, she was dux of every subject again but by then she was on a different path. Her teachers thought her improvement due to sheer grit, plus the fact that she was now in second-tier subjects among fellow solid-but-not-exemplary students. They were proud of the way she'd knuckled down but careful not to overtax her with academic challenges or difficult concepts in case she reverted.

When Year 12 was finally over, Kylie's excellent grades in less demanding subjects saw her accepted into pharmacy. Her biology teacher considered Kylie's university attendance to be one of the highlights of her career, evidence that even an average student could see the error of her ways and lift her grades. Kylie became the poster child for the superiority of character over intelligence but by then, any chance of studying medicine had evaporated.

'Kylie?' Gloria said now. 'Leo asked you why you became a pharmacist.'

Even now, all these years later, it was a difficult question to answer. What had guided her hand as she filled out the forms? And after that initial decision, why hadn't she applied for a transfer to study medicine at the end of her first year of pharmacy? She had the marks. She won the first-year Pharmacy prize, for heaven's sake.

It was partly because she had been stuck in a groove. She'd been blinkered, focused only on forward momentum. But, also, medicine would have had her studying harder, and for longer, followed by years as an intern and then as a resident. How would she have managed if Gloria needed her again? When Tansy and Nick needed her?

She'd been forced to make a decision about the rest of her life while still a teenager, and teenage Kylie wanted stability and reliability and regular hours. She'd wanted a life she could control, rather than one that controlled her.

Sitting at the dining room table, in full view of her family, Kylie felt moisture prick her eyeballs and an ominous astringency in the back of her nose. A tightening in her throat. An abrasive feeling in the centre of her chest. *This could not be happening.* Something like panic welled up in her. She looked down at her fingers, folded on her lap. They were trembling, clammy. She blinked, furiously, and tried to think about something else.

Everyone was looking at her, and this was not her. This was not her. Who was this?

She took a short, sharp inhalation and then – all at once, there was a crash. Everyone's faces swivelled away from her.

Leo had knocked over his glass. Red wine flooded across Gloria's antique table.

'Oh my god.' He stood. 'I'm so sorry, how clumsy of me.'

'Taxi!' said Nick.

'What a waste.' Simon looked at the spreading wine and shook his head.

Tansy jumped to her feet in a flurry and lifted the placemats and the napkins. Mia kneeled beside the table to examine the beading wine at eye-level, remarking how blood-like it seemed. Lachie took advantage of the kerfuffle to slip Caesar some peas using his good arm. Simon, seeing this, bolted to the other side of the table but was unable to stop Lachie putting the fork back in his own mouth. Caesar, excited by the peas, realised he was agonisingly close to a feast of unimaginable dimensions and attempted to leap up on the table, his pink tongue darting like an adder while Gloria held him back.

The table seemed unmarked and the wineglass hadn't broken. Leo, however, kept apologising.

'Don't give it another thought,' said Gloria. 'The table was a wedding present from the children's father's parents. I should have used it for axe practice years ago.'

'Anyway,' said Simon, after everything had been restored and everyone returned to their places. 'Who would like another drink?'

Leo accepted another drink from Simon, miming an exaggerated two-handed wobble when he took the glass. 'I've been meaning to ask about Caesar, who is adorable by the way,' he said. 'When does he go home?'

'Any minute now.' Gloria sniffed. 'Which is unreasonable. We're only just getting to know each other. And he's so happy here.'

'Keep him!' said Lachie.

'That would be stealing,' said Tansy.

'I'll get the crumble.' Kylie picked up the baking dish and headed back to the kitchen. Leo also stood and started clearing plates.

In the kitchen, Kylie ran her hands under the cold tap and pressed them to her eye sockets. The crumble was cooling on the counter. She rested her forehead against Gloria's fridge for a moment, then she opened the high cupboard that held the bowls.

When she turned her head, Leo was beside her, reaching for the bowls.

'It's so weird, being a kid,' Leo said to her conversationally, counting out the bowls. 'All this stuff you haven't figured out yet.'

He was talking about Lachie feeding Caesar peas, Kylie guessed.

There were a hundred easy things that Kylie could reply. *Indeed!* or *That's a bit harsh!* or *Not only kids!* Kylie dealt with the general public at work all day – she understood the unstated social rules for bland chat when serving people in the pharmacy, and in Ubers and squeezed next to a stranger on a tram. But there were no words forming in her brain.

'When I was a kid,' Leo said, firmly yet softly, leaning against the kitchen bench beside her, 'I was mad about chocolate.'

He paused. This was a conversation. It was Kylie's turn to say something yet she said nothing. First, she'd almost cried not two minutes ago – and Kylie hadn't cried since Kurt Cobain died – and now she was lost for words. What was happening to her today?

'Yep,' Leo said. He had a faraway look in his eyes now, as if remembering his younger, chocolate-loving self. 'But Mum was a health foodie. You can ask Alice! We ate tofu before anyone else. And Nuttelex! Mum didn't let me have chocolate, no way.

Whenever she took me grocery shopping, I used to look at all the bars at the checkout and I wanted one so bad. That shiny wrapping, all the colours. It was my idea of heaven.'

'Right,' Kylie said. It wasn't cold in the kitchen, but Leo radiated a warmth she wasn't expecting. She opened the window above the sink.

'But Mum told me they weren't real.'

Kylie frowned. 'Not real?'

'Yep.' He continued, 'Mum would nod at them and say, "They're not real chocolate bars. They're empty packets, just for display".'

For some reason, Kylie's breath caught in her chest. The air was sucked from her.

Leo cradled the dessert bowls against his chest. 'Then after I'd left home – I must have been twenty – I went shopping with a housemate and she grabbed one of the chocolate bars as we were going through the checkout. I don't remember what it was. A Cherry Ripe maybe, or a Violet Crumble, something like that. They're not real, I told her. They're only for display.'

Kylie could feel the blood pulsing in her ears. 'What did she say?'

'She laughed herself stupid.' Leo shook his head. 'I felt like an idiot, hey. I wasn't a super-smart kid, der, but it was so obvious, looking back. It was something that health-fanatic mums say to stop kids nagging for chocolate at the supermarket.'

'Cool story, Leo,' Kylie managed.

He smiled again. 'It's amazing, but the things you believe as kids get fixed in your brain. It's up to adults to set things straight.' He put the bowls down on the bench and turned to her. This time he looked right at Kylie, in her eyes. 'It's up to you, Kylie, to set things straight,' he said.

She could not reply.

'Almost forgot the ice cream!' Leo opened the freezer and peered inside. 'Chocolate, right? My favourite, der. Wow, there are a lot of frozen peas in here,' he said. 'For Gloria's joints, I guess. She still plays singles tennis for fun and teaches it for a living. The state of her elbows, I can't imagine.'

Leo took the ice cream and the bowls back to the dining room.

The frozen peas, the medicine cupboard filled with painkillers. Kylie dispensed anti-inflammatories every day, yet she hadn't realised that Gloria must be in pain a lot of the time. Kylie was bracing herself against the counter for a moment, the crumble still warm in her hands, when she heard the front doorbell ring.

Chapter 34

'Finally,' Tiffany said when Kylie answered the door. 'Where's my baby?'

Brian and Tiffany were out of place against the spiral box hedged suburban backdrop of Gloria's yard, and so was their white Porsche Cayenne, parked on the street. They were both bronzed like the baked crust of Kylie's macaroni – a deeper colour than five of even the sunniest days could explain. Tiffany wore a multicoloured, bejewelled caftan and gladiator sandals with straps that wound up her calves. Brian, in white linen trousers and a beige linen shirt, was revealing more of his smooth chest than Kylie had ever wanted to see.

'Mum's just organising Caesar's stuff,' she said.

'I hope he behaved himself?' Tiffany said.

'He did. He was an absolute joy.' As she spoke, Kylie realised it was the truth.

'We had the greatest trip.' Tiffany rubbed her upper arms, like an incompetent mime communicating the cold. 'I mean, why do we live here again? I mean, Brian's job, but seriously, retire already. The weather up there, you would not believe it.'

Brian looked at Tiffany. Tiffany looked at Brian.

'Kylie.' Brian cleared his throat. 'I need to get something off my chest. To be honest, I'm disappointed.'

Take a number, Kylie thought.

'Darling.' Tiffany's voice was steel. 'We agreed to wait until we had him safe in the car before discussing this.'

Brian, caring nothing for steel or agreements, continued. 'I rang Gail on the way here to ask for her observations after working with you for a week.'

'Right,' said Kylie.

'Imagine my surprise to hear that you have shown poor attendance and a bad attitude. And the mystery shopper report came in. Apparently you didn't smile at her . . . the mystery shopper. In addition, despite her obvious wealth signifiers, you made no attempt to sell her anything.'

Mystery shopper? For a moment, Kylie was confused. Then it hit her. The weird woman with the HRT scripts who talked about her designer bag and sunglasses – she had been sent by Pharmacy King. Kylie should have known that conversation was too strange to be real.

'You were spying on me?' Kylie said.

'It's standard procedure when we're evaluating an associate to determine their training needs. Her report said you didn't even know the symptoms of menopause. I find that shocking in a health professional.'

Kylie was not a perfect person, that had become apparent over the last week. Yesterday alone she'd been useless in corralling the children at Gloria's open day. She'd been in charge when Lachie had broken his arm and Rin had lost her tooth. She was lucky that Caesar hadn't been injured also.

But Kylie was good at her job. Very good. Brian's accusation was simply untrue.

The mystery shopper had been annoyed with Kylie, that was all. Of course Kylie knew the symptoms of menopause, and of perimenopause as well. Of course she knew about the insomnia and hot flushes that heralded the change of life. She knew about unpredictable periods that might disappear for months or counterintuitively become heavier and longer before stopping altogether. She knew the role that oestrogen played in the musculoskeletal aches and pains of menopause, and she knew about the early-morning hobble of perimenopausal women when their heels and arches ache and buckle as soon as they put weight on them. She was aware of the blinding anger that comes out of nowhere, and the irritability, and of the sudden weight gain around the abdomen. And that . . . what's it called, when menopausal women forget things?

There was a shift in the planet's orbit too small for anyone else to notice. Kylie moved one foot to brace herself, lest she collapse.

It had been there in plain sight all this time and now, her cover with herself had been blown. Here was the explanation she'd been looking for.

Kylie already knew she wasn't pregnant from the test with its single lonely red line, wrapped in toilet paper and stashed in the bottom of her bag. The baby she'd imagined for the last twenty-four hours – the one that would grow to be one of the football girls, or perhaps a crazy-brave hero like Rin – did not exist. Had never existed. Standing there in her mother's doorway, decades flashed past. Kylie was no longer a twelve-year-old worried about her family, cooking macaroni and cheese so her brother and sister would feel cared for by an adult. Nor was she a junior pharmacist at the beginning of her career, looking to build a life she could control.

Kylie had tried to stop the world from turning. To hold it still so that nothing changed.

But the human body cares nothing for the acrobatic denials and cognitive dissonance of the human mind. Kylie had failed, but that was not the worst of it. Stopping change had always been the most foolish of goals. She would never hold her own child in her arms. Time had run out. Kylie was not pregnant, and she never would be.

Chapter 35

'Coming through, pooch delivery.'

Nick was all at once behind her, with Caesar on his lead in one hand and the blue Ikea tote of his stuff in the other. Kylie hadn't even heard him approach. As Nick dropped the lead, Kylie kneeled and scooped up Caesar, despite her wobbly legs. He was all grinning innocence. She hid her face in his fur and held him to her chest, soft under her chin. His small pink tongue darted out, licking her neck.

'My darling!' Tiffany was bobbing up and down on the top step. 'Thanks so much, Kylie. I'll take him now.'

'Just pop him in the car, darl,' said Brian.

'Thanks, I'll take him now, I said.' Tiffany threaded her fingers through Caesar's collar, as though it were a hostage situation.

Kylie looked down. She had meant to hand him over but somehow Caesar was still in her arms, heavy and helpless, panting up at her.

'Bri, make her give him back,' Tiffany said.

Kylie wanted to keep Caesar. To not hand him over, to run, to keep going as though she could reverse all her bad decisions and change her fate if she never let him out of her arms. She should have had more fun with him. She should have thrown a ball around the backyard or sat on the floor and played tug-of-war with one of his ropes. All those cute outfits – why hadn't she dressed him up? He was precious, why hadn't she seen that?

She didn't keep him, though, of course she didn't. He didn't belong to her. She passed him to Tiffany, and, yes, he was a stranger's dog she'd had for less a week but as the weight of him passed from her arms she thought she might fall to the ground and die of grief.

'Oh my baby.' Tiffany nuzzled Caesar's face, then positioned him over her shoulder.

As she carried him to the car, Caesar looked back at Kylie. If he hadn't been a dog, Kylie would have said there was a moment of genuine connection. There was an understanding in his gaze, as though he truly saw her. Kylie raised her hand in an awkward wave. Then Tiffany strapped him in the back of their car and the moment was gone.

When Tiffany was out of hearing range, Brian cleared his throat. 'If we could have a word in private, Kylie?'

She looked at him with dead eyes. 'Just say what you want to say.'

'Don't mind me, mate,' said Nick, folding his arms.

'Fine. Well.' Brian took a deep breath. 'Your job application isn't due until tomorrow but it behoves me to make you aware that it's Gail's advice that we decline to offer you the position.'

Kylie's arms felt heavy, as if they had disconnected from her shoulders.

'What?' said Nick. 'Are you joking?'

Brian pursed his lips. 'However, you did look after Caesar in our hour of need. Never let it be said I fail to keep my word. Despite Gail's report and the secret shopper debacle, I'll pull a few strings. You can stay. On probation, mind you, until we fix some of your attitude problems.'

'Attitude problems? Kylie? Mate, you are so wildly wrong, I don't know where to start,' said Nick.

'Training, that's what you need. Perhaps a transfer to a bigger pharmacy, where someone could supervise you. I mean, there's nothing physically preventing you from smiling at a customer, is there?' said Brian. 'If you smiled, you'd be so much—'

'I'm going to stop you right there, for your own safety,' said Nick. 'My sister has a temper.'

Under normal circumstances, Nick was right. In fact, Nick didn't know the half of it. People had told Kylie to smile more frequently that any man could imagine, for a variety of reasons, and it usually made Kylie want to punch something. Construction workers she passed on the street had told her to smile, as had men in pubs, fellow students at uni, customers at the pharmacy, baristas in cafes and, once, a woman behind the counter at Vic Roads commenting on her licence photo. Each time, she'd been infuriated.

This time, though, she only blinked. She could keep her job, that's what Brian said. That was the most important thing. She had not been passed over or left behind. She'd tried so hard to fix everything this week and, on the very edge of failure, had instead succeeded against all odds. She could continue to drive the exact same route at the exact same time every morning, and do the same job in the same place and continue to buy her coffee from the bakery every day, forever. Nothing need ever change.

All at once, Kylie could breathe. She felt a rush of relief, as though passing through a sudden shower.

She had enough air in her lungs to say, 'No thanks.'

'What?' said Brian.

'What?' said Nick.

'Give the job to Emily. She's a great pharmacist. She deserves it,' said Kylie. And then she added, 'With any luck she'll have your job in a few years, you officious, mediocre little man.'

And then she gave him her broadest smile.

Later, back at the dining table, Kylie was the one sitting down while the rest of the family buzzed around her. Gloria insisted on opening her emergency bottle of champagne and they fetched her a glass topped to overflowing, and also a coffee, as though she could drink both of them at once. Mia had saved her some crumble and Lachie offered to rub her shoulders one-handed. Gloria was spreading Jatz with the fancy cheese that Tansy brought and arranging them onto Kylie's plate.

'I'm fine, seriously,' said Kylie.

'You should have seen his face, that Brian,' Nick said. 'Hilarious.'

'You can still apologise, it's not too late. Send a nice card? It's easier to get a job while you're still employed,' said Simon.

'Exactly. What are you going to do for a living?' said Tansy.

'Who cares?' said Leo. 'Life is for living, not working.'

Tansy gave him a withering look. 'She has a mortgage.'

The answer popped into her head in an instant. 'I think I'll go back to uni,' Kylie said. 'To med school.'

'What?' said Tansy.

'Extra school?' said Lachie. 'On purpose?'

'Whoa, Kylie. Med school?' said Mon. 'How long will that take?'

Nick pulled out his phone and frowned at it while typing. After a moment, he said, 'Four years apparently, because she already has a degree and a graduate diploma.' He leaned over and showed Kylie the screen.

Four years! That required some processing, from everyone. The plate in front of Kylie was now filled with Jatz. Gloria's hands could not stop moving. She had made more than Kylie could possibly eat.

'That's forever!' said Lachie. 'Ages and ages.'

'It is ages,' Kylie said. 'It means I won't graduate until I'm forty-eight.'

'True.' There was no more cheese, so Gloria began smearing bits of quince paste on top of the finished Jatz, a gritty ruby against the ivory of the cheese. 'And how old will you be in four years if you don't go back to uni?'

'Be sensible, Mum,' said Tansy. 'She's practically middle-aged.'

'Kylie will always be sensible, that much I know. She has no dependents and that means she can live however she chooses.'

'But how will she afford it?'

'How much leave do you have, Kylie? Paid, I mean. Holidays and whatnot.'

Kylie was watching the bubbles in her champagne rising inexorably up the glass. A part of her had been happy listening to everyone arguing about her predicament as though they were discussing someone she'd never met. She swallowed. 'Eight months.'

'Are you fucking joking?' said Simon. 'How does anyone have eight months leave?'

By hardly ever taking holidays, of course. By working all the time, by putting the best interests of someone else ahead of yourself.

'But how would you afford the rest of it?' said Tansy.

'She has the money she saved up to buy the pharmacy. Or she could rent out her house and move back here,' said Gloria.

Nick burst into laughter, then stopped. 'Oh. You're serious?'

Gloria moved on to hulling and slicing a bowl of strawberries, also brought by Tansy. 'Why not? Why couldn't she?'

'Because I don't have a bedroom here, for a start.' Kylie nodded to Tansy and Nick. 'Mum left your rooms exactly as they were but she got rid of all the stuff out of mine.'

'There was a good reason for that. Tansy took quite a long time to leave. And Nick always had other priorities.' Gloria reached up and cupped Nick's cheek. 'I love you, darling, but quite frankly you could be unable to pay rent any minute.'

'Harsh but fair,' said Nick.

'But you, Kylie . . .' Gloria paused in her hulling to lay her hand on Kylie's arm, then turned her attention back to the strawberries. 'I knew that you'd burst into the world like fireworks and you would never take a step back.'

That explanation had never occurred to Kylie. It was bracing to realise that even her own mother harboured thoughts and motivations unknown to Kylie. Gloria hulled the strawberries the same way her own mother had, Kylie noticed, without a cutting board, with the knife facing towards her thumb. She dropped a sliver in Kylie's champagne glass and it bubbled against the sides. Kylie sipped her champagne, minerally and ice-cold. She absentmindedly scratched her wrist. The skin was red and shiny where the band of her Fitbit used to be.

'I'm the one who cooked macaroni cheese for you both,' she said to Tansy and Nick. 'I did the dishes, and tucked you in, and looked after you every night when we were kids while Mum was working.'

'And there it is,' Leo said.

'Wow, Kyles,' said Nick.

'I don't know what to say,' said Tansy.

There was nothing to say. Tansy and Nick had sat exactly there as small children, eating macaroni cheese and sausages and crumble made from tinned peaches, swinging their legs under their seats, secure in the knowledge that grown-ups were in charge even if said grown-ups weren't always there. Tansy and Nick slept well, they did well at school, they were healthy and growing, they had friends and hobbies. Deep inside, they knew that everything would be all right. That had been more than enough for Kylie. It still was.

'Well, I know what to say,' said Gloria. 'I'm not surprised in the slightest that you stepped up for this family. I always said what an exemplary child you were.'

Simon nodded. 'The trouble with you, Kylie, is you don't know how to ask for help,' he said, in his wisest, most fatherly voice.

Kylie turned to him. 'Oh, really, Simon? And you—' she began.

Gloria cut her off. 'She can learn, though, can't you, Kylie? You're very good at learning. Consider this career change a . . .' Gloria turned to Monica. 'What do you call it, that thing you do when my computer freezes?'

'A reboot?' Mon said.

Gloria nodded. 'A reboot.'

Kylie felt the tension drain from her shoulders. She would go back to uni, that was the first thing. After that – well, in many ways, it felt like her life was just beginning. She might travel after all. She might sit on the roof of a skyscraper in Tokyo and sip sake until the ripples of light in the sky faded to black. She might float in the Mediterranean, her black hair fanning behind her like a halo. She might find room in her life for art, or films from this century, or cooking. She might learn to fish or take judo classes. She might have a dog of her own. She was good at making a living, so she might date someone who was good at making a life. Someone who was unselfconscious, who always seemed to say or do the right thing at the exact right time. Someone who would look after her for a change. And who knows? She might fall in love.

Or she might do none of these things. This week, the week of the Three Disasters, might be the very last time in her life that Kylie Schnabel would act unpredictably. Either way, she couldn't wait to find out.

'My daughter, the doctor,' Gloria said. 'That has a lovely ring to it.'

Outside, dusk was beginning to settle around Gloria's house. Through the open kitchen window, Kylie was bathed in the scent of the mock jasmine that wound around the front verandah. The Schnabel lunch had gone for longer than anyone had planned – and it still wasn't finished. Gloria opened a bottle of whiskey she had been saving for a special occasion, though Leo declined so he could drive Kylie home. Then Mon and Nick did the dishes while Lachie and Mia fell asleep on the couch. Gloria's house seemed quiet without Caesar in it.

Kylie's own home would seem quiet too, compared with this. All week she'd been longing to be in her space, but she'd have no one to make tea for, no one to grumble at. She would email Gail tonight and make her resignation effective immediately, using her holiday leave instead of notice. Tonight, she would not pack her lunch or lay out her navy suit. She had never been unemployed before. She had no idea what she would do tomorrow.

Kylie's younger self would be appalled at this directionless display – but Kylie's younger self was no longer here.

Acknowledgements

To:

Robert Stanley-Turner, Jane Novak, Rebecca Saunders, Emma Rafferty, Dianne Blacklock, Louise Stark, Beck Feiner for my perfect donut woman, Libby Turner, various pharmacists who prefer to remain nameless, Marianne Vincent, Paddy O'Reilly, the lovely woman from Maniax in Abbotsford who explained the mechanics of axe-throwing to me and whose name I carefully wrote down and then lost, Lee Falvey and Carrie Tiffany.

I live and write on the unceded lands of the Wurundjeri people of the Kulin Nation. I pay my respects to their elders, past, present and emerging.

Toni Jordan has worked as a molecular biologist, quality control chemist, TAB operator and door-to-door aluminium siding salesperson. She is the author of seven novels, including the international bestseller *Addition*, which was longlisted for the Miles Franklin Award, *Nine Days*, which was awarded Best Fiction at the 2012 Indie Awards and was named in Kirkus Review's Top 10 Historical Novels of 2013, and *Our Tiny, Useless Hearts*, which was longlisted for the International Dublin Literary Award. Her latest novel, *Dinner with the Schnabels*, was a critically acclaimed bestseller. Toni has been published widely in newspapers and magazines. She holds a Bachelor of Science in physiology and a PhD in Creative Arts. Toni lives in Melbourne.

tonijordan.com
f @authortonijordan